SIGNAL FROM
MALTA

Malcolm L Dubber
DEC 2021

Malcolm Lloyd Dubber

authorHOUSE®

AuthorHouse™ UK
1663 Liberty Drive
Bloomington, IN 47403 USA
www.authorhouse.co.uk
Phone: UK TFN: 0800 0148641 (Toll Free inside the UK)
            UK Local: 02036 956322 (+44 20 3695 6322 from outside the UK)

Published by AuthorHouse 02/16/2021

ISBN: 978-1-6655-8567-5 (sc)
ISBN: 978-1-6655-8568-2 (hc)
ISBN: 978-1-6655-8566-8 (e)

Print information available on the last page.

AUTHOR'S NOTE

The closing days of World War II in Europe saw some of the bitterest fighting, much of which was between the partisans of the newly liberated states. This was the case in the Balkan states and especially Greece, where in late 1944 Great Britain intervened to support the Greek government and nationalists and edify them against the communists. This was much criticised by the Americans, who, for some incomprehensible reason, did not want to upset Joseph Stalin's Russia.

The seat of conflict between communist partisans and others moved into Albania and the southern part of Yugoslavia. Ironically, the bulk of Yugoslavia was under the control of Marshal Tito and his communist forces, who had separated themselves from Stalin's style of communism and notably won support from Great Britain.

It was from 1944 to 1946 that the Russian security police, the feared NKVD, became very active in liberated parts of Eastern Europe and embedded their agents in the various Allied military and civil headquarters. London was no exception. The NKVD's ruthless pedigree was spawned from the Cheka, who enforced Stalin's brand of communism throughout the Union of Socialist Soviet Republics (USSR).

The first major sign that Stalin was to renege on the Allied agreements at Potsdam and Tehran was the disregard for the Polish government in exile in London. Stalin set up his own communist Polish government, thereby reestablishing the political boundary before the invasion of the USSR in 1941. The Molotov–Ribbentrop Pact of 23 August 1939 signalled the Second World War in Europe a week later, when German forces attacked Poland. This was followed, on 17 September 1939, by Russia's invasion of Poland by prior agreement with Nazi Germany. This simple historical fact seems to have been forgotten by communists and supporters of the USSR in Great Britain and elsewhere—and this includes the British Labour Party. Furthermore, there is evidence that the Russian NKVD and the SS (Gestapo) worked together up to June 1941 to supress various groups in occupied Poland. This also included the massacre of more than four thousand Polish political and military persons, on Stalin's order, in the Katyn Woods in Russian-occupied eastern Poland.

The NKVD (Narodny Kommisariat Vntrennikh), which translates as the People's Commissariat for Internal Affairs, operated throughout the Soviet Union and elsewhere between 1936 and 1946. It was feared by most people in Russia—and that included the military. Indeed, the first Russian force to relieve the besieged Leningrad was the NKVD. Their first priority was to arrest all the leaders of the Leningrad forces and, tragically, execute them. The NKVD and the KGB have earned themselves a justified reputation for ruthlessness, total disregard for political protocol, and lack of humanitarianism. Running parallel with the NKVD was the much smaller Komitet Gosvdarstvennoy Bezopasnosti (Committee of State Security), better known as the KGB. The NKVD was eventually dissolved and absorbed into the KGB, taking with it Stalin's thuggery elements of the NKVD. Both the NKVD and KGB were political organisations, whereas the Glavnoye Razvedyvatel'noy Upravleniye (GRU—main intelligence agency) was the military intelligence service.

CHAPTER 1

ARRIVALS

THE DAKOTA DC-10 circled Malta, waiting to be given permission to land at Luqa aerodrome, the main airport. The war was almost over in Europe, and Germany was fighting on to its last vestiges of sanity. Luqa, although a RAF military airport, was busy receiving flights carrying urgent supplies and service personnel either in transit to other parts of the Mediterranean region or leaving a tour of duty—or, as was Ewan Jones, taking up a new appointment. Lieutenant Commander Ewan Jones, newly promoted four weeks earlier, was returning to Malta after leaving in late 1943 to take charge of training coastal gunboats to escort invasion forces to the D-Day landing sites. His specialist experience was with motor torpedo boats (MTBs), and apart from the odd foray encounter with German E-boats, the German equivalent of British MTBs, he had seen very little action in the English Channel. Jones was now back in Malta to shape and train MTB and other special craft crews in policing the shores of Western Greece and the surrounding territory of the Southern Adriatic Sea. He relished the Dakota circling Malta, as it was a clear sunny day for the first of April—All Fool's Day, as someone remarked during the flight. The war still raged on, but stories were emerging that increasing numbers of German soldiers were surrendering. There was also still the problem with marauding U-boats, which was something he needed to keep in mind, although the Mediterranean Sea was very much controlled by the Allies.

Lieutenant Commander Jones spotted several places where he had enjoyed relaxing between operations during the hectic, war-torn days of 1942 and 1943. The plane landed with a bit of a bump; it was quite heavily laden with personnel and cargo. He emerged from the plane and was struck by a very warm breeze and blinding sunshine. Several servicemen in a variety of uniforms were waiting on the runway apron.

A sailor approached him and saluted. 'Lieutenant Commander Jones?'

'Yes. How'd you know who I am?'

'That's easy, sir. You're the only naval officer on this flight.' The sailor perked up. 'Leading Seaman Knowles, sir. I'm to take you to HQ. ACM is expecting you.'

'ACM?'

'Yes, sir, Admiral Commanding Malta. He's also the senior naval officer and sometimes is referred to as SNO,' Knowles replied with a grin.

'What's amusing?' Ewan asked as Knowles took hold of his two cases and placed them in the back of the jeep.

'We're getting lots of new names and titles to learn. Some are quite funny. Must mean the war is nearly over.'

'I do hope so, Knowles. I really do hope so,' Ewan said sorrowfully.

Leading Seaman Knowles felt a pain in Ewan's voice. 'Beggin' yer pardon, sir. Hope you don't mind me askin', but you bin 'ere before?' Knowles's Lancashire accent was evident.

'Yes. A couple or so years ago. Left in early '44. Now seems like a lifetime. Lost a lot of good shipmates in those days. Let's hope that the Far East will be over soon too.'

Knowles drove Ewan to the admiral's HQ. They spoke very little as Ewan took in the changing scenery of bomb-ravaged Malta. The road into Valetta was dusty and still full of potholes that jerked the jeep around. *Not one of the best journeys,* Ewan thought. It reminded him of the roads in 1942; no improvement there. At least most of the rubble from bombed buildings had been removed or tidied for reconstruction. As they drove into Valetta, he noticed that lots of little shops had opened and the place was looking more cosmopolitan. It was recovering, albeit slowly. His mind turned to Hazel, his wife. She was still in Wales but would be joining him in a few weeks' time. He could only guess of what impression she would have upon seeing the more relaxed atmosphere.

Ewan recognised immediately the Naval HQ as Knowles stopped the jeep outside the main entrance. It had hardly changed. The same obligatory naval guards, except they were wearing white webbing, as opposed to army khaki. Peacetime standards were slowly returning. There were also a couple of potted green palms at the entrance. 'Go straight in, sir. The admiral is expectin' you. The guard inside will direct you. I'll drop off yer cases at the officers' quarters. Admiral's secretary will phone for me to come and collect you later.'

Ewan thanked Knowles, who speedily departed—no doubt another taxi mission.

The leading seaman guard acknowledged Ewan's approach, and Ewan responded with a short salute. Once inside the building, he spotted the guard's desk, still in the same place as when he had left in late 1943, eighteen months ago.

'Lieutenant Commander Jones to see Admiral Kelly.'

'Oh, yes, sir. No need to sign in. Go straight up. You'll find the admiral's office directly in front of you,' the guard said, pointing to the staircase.

Same office as before, Ewan thought. He guessed rightly that it would be Admiral Forbes's former office; it now had a different title on the door: SNO-ACM. To his surprise, he was greeted by Kate Davies, the admiral's secretary.

'Good to have you back, Commander,' she said with a grin.

'And good to see you.' He spotted the blue stripe on her epaulettes. 'I see you've been promoted. Third officer, isn't it?'

'And you, sir. Go straight in. The admiral is expecting you,' she said, still grinning.

'We'll chat later.' He gave a brief knock of courtesy before opening the door to Admiral Kelly's office.

Ewan entered, and to his second surprise he found some old acquaintances present. Admiral Kelly got up from his desk and walked round to greet Ewan. 'I'm Admiral Kelly, if you hadn't already worked that out, and these, er, gentlemen'—the admiral raised his hand to the others—'I think you already know.'

Commander Alec Gratton, and MI6 officers John Cross and Henry Blackwell, stood in turn and shook hands with Ewan. 'Glad to have you on board,' Gratton said.

'Have I volunteered for something dodgy?' Ewan asked, looking to Henry Blackwell.

'How are you keeping?' Gratton asked.

'Fine—or, rather, I was OK,' Ewan said, looking at each of them in turn again, 'until now, that is. So what are you cooking up this time?' He directed his words to Blackwell.

Henry Blackwell grinned. 'I think we should leave Ewan with the admiral and find a bar.'

'Good idea,' said John Cross.

'Ewan, I'll meet up with you later and then have a chat when you've had a chance to settle in at the officers' club. I think you'll find it a lot more tasteful than before,' Gratton said.

The three left.

'The war is all but finished here,' said the admiral. 'However, we have another problem which those, um, er, gentlemen will brief you on later. For the moment, I have you all to myself, before they get their grubby hands on you.'

Ewan detected that the admiral was uncomfortable with intelligence, spies, and spying. 'Is this to do with Greece and Italy?'

'No, not at all, but you will be setting up the special patrol group as you were told in London. Commander Gratton couldn't tell you much before, mainly because of security issues not strictly linked to the main reason you're here. Although you are under my command, you will, of course, report to Commander Gratton also.'

Ewan was puzzled. What on earth had he allowed himself to be caught up in?

The admiral sensed Ewan's unease.

'Don't worry. Your being posted here has coincided with another little problem, which I believe will kill two birds with one stone, so to speak. It should also provide you with a good cover story, should you need it, and take the pressure off me.'

'I don't follow.' Ewan was puzzled. 'Cover story?'

'We have a little secret or a big one—depends on your point of view— which is known only to five people at present. You will make six. And that's how I want it played.'

Ewan rubbed his chin as he always did when he felt that he was being landed with something difficult or unusual.

'We're getting a visit from a VIP in the next couple of weeks or so—no date yet—and you setting up this special patrol group will work very well for security. Eventually, it will obviously be made public, by which time your special patrol group will have the right credentials, if you know what I mean,' the admiral said.

'So the formation of the special patrol group will be noticed, but when the VIP arrives, it will be thought that it is for the VIP and not for our real reason,' Ewan said.

'You got it.'

'Who's the VIP?' Ewan said.

'Can't tell you just yet, but our so-called allies in Eastern Europe are already interested.'

'You mean the Russians?'

'Yes, and all their evil entourage,' said the admiral. 'They have agents here!'

'I've heard rumours that Stalin's NKVD are snooping around back home.'

'More than snooping. Damned evil. Downright nasty. Even more dangerous than the Nazi Gestapo and the Japanese Kempeitai rolled into one! They're here in Malta also. Our intelligence characters will brief you on them later,' the admiral said.

'So, Admiral, what do you want me to do?' Ewan guessed that a direct question to an admiral was always a good move. It was.

'Put together a guard of honour party, properly drilled, that would knock the spots off the Grenadier Guards and the like. There are some characters back home who don't think we're up to it and that we've been sitting on our hands for too long, having it easy out here.'

'Sounds like a challenge,' Ewan noted. He visualised staff officers making disparaging remarks in the Admiralty.

'It is. And you're just the man for the job. You've been in the ranks, so you know how our lads think and will respond.'

'Thank you, Admiral. I'll do my best.'

Admiral Kelly put on a wry smile. 'Thank me later, after your chosen detachment hate you and curse you during their drills. Or, I should say, I'll thank you. This might be a bit different from what you've been used to, but judging by your record, I think you'll acquit us quite well. Any questions?'

'Yes, sir. Two questions. When do I start, and how will the honour guard be selected?'

'Day after tomorrow. You need to settle in, and you will have an experienced CPO to select your volunteers. CPO Gordon Miles. I've scrounged him from the *Nelson* before she sets off for the Far East.'

'HMS *Nelson*. Hmm. I've been on the receiving end of her big guns when she bombarded Tobruk and we finally pushed back Rommel.'

'Yes. I heard that you got up to some tricks with our lads behind the lines.'

Ewan grinned.

'One more thing, Commander. There's an unsubstantiated report that a German Army group is still fighting in the Albania. It complicates the rivalry between the communist and nationalist partisans, and for good measure it affects Greece and Yugoslavia.'

'Do you mean no one knows who's fighting whom?'

The admiral chuckled. 'I suspect you're right. But to make matters worse, the German Army group includes a fully equipped SS Panzer division. It's possible that they might evacuate by sea. Only a rumour. But they're thought to be hidden on a coast road. Aerial recon hasn't turned up anything yet. They're trying to avoid running into Tito's partisans in the north. Could be they're trying to block our Eighth Army breaking out of Italy into Trieste. Seems there are a lot of equations.'

'And that's one of my tasks?' asked Ewan. There was a distinct moan in his voice.

'It is. You are going to have to stop them or at least find them,' said the admiral. 'It won't be easy. We can only guess at their plans, but they're a dangerous addition to this whole mess. Gratton will fill you in later.'

CHAPTER 2

THE DECEPTION

Ewan stopped to chat with Kate Davies while he waited for Knowles, his driver. She said that little had changed for her. The opportunity to return to Malta had arisen after Admiral Forbes was put in charge of the reconstruction of the port of Antwerp. Although Admiral Forbes had asked her to join him, she thought it would not help her personal future plans. She had passed several exams in administration and was promoted to WRNS third officer. In addition, her knowledge of Malta was considered valuable, especially for the closing stage of the war. This was something she had in common with Ewan. After speaking of this, their conversation switched to Hazel.

'I understand that Admiral Kelly is responsible for Hazel's redeployment, or should I say that it is you?' Ewan said.

'It's part of my job. I can't wait to meet up with her again,' Kate said.

'She'll be over the moon to meet you.'

'Should be here in three weeks, by which time your quarters should be ready. You're having one of the new apartments with the latest gadgets, including a refrigerator.'

Ewan chuckled. 'Now that will be a novelty.'

'You must have a welcome-home party,' said Kate. She grinned as Knowles appeared.

Ewan found the officers' club very different from when he last had visited in 1943. He noticed that the windows were now free of the masking tape that would hopefully reduce the effects of flying glass from explosions. There were also more green plants adorning the entrance and the foyer. It looked every bit as colonial as before the war had started. He found the reception desk and a young naval rating sat behind it. It was the rating's age that took him aback. *Couldn't be more nineteen,* he thought. For a brief moment, he shuddered at the thought of how young many of the servicemen and servicewomen were.

The rating stood up and greeted Ewan. 'Sir. You must be Lieutenant Commander Jones. I was informed that you were on your way from HQ.'

'Yes, that's right,' said Ewan. Then he wondered what else the club had been told about his arrival. He was about to find out.

'Your cases 'ave bin put in yer room, sir. You're in Room 40, on the first floor, overlookin' the 'arbour,' said the rating. 'There's also another officer waitin' to see you in the bar. It's just to yer right, sir,' said the rating, with an unmistakable London accent, nodding to the bar entrance.

Ewan thanked the rating and made for the bar. It was certainly different. It seemed as though it had been completely redecorated, although the gleaming polished bar with brass fittings was the same. He looked around and didn't see anyone he recognised. He was expecting Gratton. He turned to leave, when from behind a potted palm near the door to the veranda, a low voice said, 'Ewan. Glad to have you back.'

It was Captain Mark Williams, Royal Artillery, Malta garrison.

'Mark! It's great to see you. How did you know that I would be here and, for that matter, back in Malta?

'Good question. Not much goes unnoticed around here. I thought I would get in to see you socially before your friends grab you. Got you a cold beer, if that's OK.'

'Certainly is,' replied Ewan, who sat in a vacant armchair opposite Mark. 'So, Mark, how are you keeping? Not much of a risk of invasion now, thank God.'

'Right, but the general defences still need to be maintained. I'm more of a policeman these days. Got most of the redcaps under my small command. There's enough going on to keep me busy,' said Mark, grinning.

Ewan guessed that there was more to Mark Williams's military police role than simple policing and keeping all servicemen on Malta from causing too much mayhem. The two men reminisced and soon got on to the topic of Ewan's married life with Hazel; Ewan mentioned that she would be joining him. Half an hour passed, when Mark spotted Gratton enter the bar.

Gratton smiled. 'I see the army have gotten to you first.'

'Yes, Commander,' said Mark. He turned to Ewan. 'Meet here tomorrow evening for drinks and dinner. About seven-thirty suit you?'

'Good idea. See you then,' replied Ewan, who stood up to let Mark leave as Gratton took his place.

'I thought Mark Williams would get to you. He's got a tough job here and will give you all the support you might need once your jaunt for the admiral is over.'

'Is Mark in on this operation too?' Ewan asked.

'Not directly, but he's good at his job and is making my life much easier. But I'll explain that later. For now, I guess you want to freshen up before dinner. I have a small errand to do. See you back here in about an hour. Oh, and one more thing: Kate Davies will be joining us. So will John Cross.'

'No Henry Blackwell?'

Gratton sniggered. 'Er, no. He's up to something tonight but sends his regards.'

Or is it his regrets? thought Ewan. Anything to do with Blackwell always spelled trouble.

Ewan went to his room. On the way, he wondered if Kate Davies was involved in his mission as Admiral Kelly's secretary. He had a quick shower, which was much welcomed after the travelling and the warm dusty air of the Malta streets. His memories of Malta in 1942 began to reemerge. Somehow, he felt at home and wondered whether Hazel would feel the same. His case containing his uniform had been unpacked and the various garments hung in a spacious wardrobe. His other case contained personal clothing and a small photo of Hazel taken on the evening of their wedding day, two years earlier, overlooking the straits to Gozo. He was already missing her as he propped the photo up on the small sideboard next to a table lamp. It would be three weeks or more before she joined him, although Kate had indicated that it could be less.

Ewan dressed in clean casual navy whites, except for his white cap cover, which seemed to have attracted some dust. He shook it vigorously, lightly banging it on the sideboard; he would get a spare later.

Ewan entered the bar and found Gratton with Kate Davies sitting near large open windows. It was early evening. The warm atmosphere filtered uncomfortably into his throat. A cool beer would be the remedy. Gratton had anticipated this. On a small low table before him was a large glass of beer with condensation clinging to the outside of the glass.

Ewan sat down as John Cross poked his head around the door. 'Ah, there you are,' he said, looking at Gratton.

'What's up?' Gratton was a little surprised.

'Admiral wants you urgently. Didn't say what for,' said Cross, who then shot a glance to Ewan. 'Might want you to be in on this also.'

'OK, bang goes our evening. Sorry, Ewan,' said Gratton with some feeling of dejection.

'Oh well, I guess I should go with you. Kate, see you later,' Ewan said.

'Shouldn't take too long. I'll keep Kate company until you return.' Cross smirked.

'Keep your hands off,' Gratton said.

Ewan and Gratton walked towards the Naval HQ. 'I wonder what it's about?' Ewan queried.

'I have an idea. You might get more deeply involved before we planned,' Gratton said.

'Talking about getting involved, are you and Kate seeing each other?'

'Perceptive of you. We'll make a spy out of you yet.' Gratton grinned.

Ewan was pleasantly surprised. He recalled that Kate Davies generally kept herself to herself, although sometimes took up a date, but this with Gratton seemed more than casual.

CHAPTER 3

BRIEFING

THE WORLD OF espionage was new to Ewan. Murders in dark alleys, late-night liaisons, and bomb-damaged derelict warehouses were a far cry from being shot at by an enemy in a uniform and in broad daylight.

Ewan and Gratton entered the admiral's office.

'Come on in, you two. Park your bums. Won't take up much of your valuable drinking time. Ewan, thanks for coming also. Will save some time, this,' said Admiral Kelly.

'Alec, I've had a message from Henry Blackwell. That little jaunt he was overseeing this evening has turned up something disturbing.'

Ewan screwed up his lips. *What jaunt was this?* he wondered.

'Alec, you know that Blackwell has had a couple of harbour workers under surveillance. He suspects that they've been passing information on our shipping to the Russians.'

'Is it important?' asked Ewan.

'Was just general stuff at first, but then we got a tip-off that an NKVD agent was involved. Tonight Blackwell found a body behind some old crates of aircraft parts in a derelict warehouse,' said Admiral Kelly, who then tapped his pencil on his desk. 'I don't like this one bit.'

Alec Gratton was worried; Ewan could see he was. Admiral Kelly explained what Blackwell had thought had happened. Ewan had difficulty following the plot and, at first, thought that the body was that of an NKVD agent. 'I'm sorry, Admiral, can you run it by me again?'

'The essential point is that the body is believed to be one of the characters whom Blackwell had under surveillance. He was killed by a single shot to the back of the head, the hallmark of the NKVD. That leaves the other man, who also worked on the harbour front. The question is, if these men were working for the Russians, why was one of them shot?'

'If it was the NKVD as opposed to a criminal gang, why leave the body in a place where it could be found?' said Ewan.

'The body wasn't found that quickly. Blackwell reckons the man was murdered three days ago,' said Admiral Kelly.

'And also, the NKVD don't care. They're a bunch of ruthless thugs. They could give respectability to the Mafia!' chipped in Gratton.

The admiral continued his briefing. 'Ewan, I want you to carry on with your guard of honour duty, but at the same time start pulling together a crack team, commando trained, to work from our MTBs. It means you won't get much rest and you'll have no spare time. I'll see you tomorrow afternoon for a thorough briefing. Now I suggest you both get back to your evening dinner party,' said the admiral, turning to Gratton, 'and my lovely secretary.'

The dinner at the officers' club was not quite as formal as Ewan had expected; it was a relaxed atmosphere, which suited him. He ordered a rabbit dish as his main course. It was a Maltese traditional dish and something of a favourite. As the dinner companions chatted about their menu, Cross enquired of Ewan. 'So, Ewan, you like rabbit. Throwback to your time here before?'

'Not really. Often had rabbit in South Wales. We used to catch rabbits on the railway embankments,' said Ewan, taking a swallow of cool beer.

'Oh yes. You used to work on the railways before you joined the navy,' noted Cross.

Ewan grinned. *Not quite Oxford, Eton, or Harrow,* he thought.

'Do you miss it?' Cross asked.

'Sometimes. Maybe when this war is finally over, I'll return and complete my engineering degree.'

'Do I detect a hint of doubt?'

Ewan smiled. 'Depends on Hazel. We both love Malta. Might even settle here. No serious plans yet.'

Up to this point, Kate Davies and Gratton had been talking between themselves. Now they joined the conversation.

'Thought about a family?' enquired Kate in a soft tone.

'Discussed it, but not until the war is well and truly over. Not right to bring children into this broken world of ours,' Ewan said.

Gratton shot a glance at Kate and then at Cross. 'Pretty strong thoughts, Ewan.'

Ewan sported a wry smile. 'More drinks, anyone?'

The evening wore on; conversations eventually dried up. The group parted, with Ewan aiming to retire to his room, while Gratton walked Kate to her quarters nearby. Cross remained in the lounge but moved himself to sit at the bar. Ewan wondered why he was drinking alone. He had learned over the past years not to interfere with a man who wanted to drink alone; there were often personal issues that needed their own space and time. However, unbeknown to Ewan, Cross wasn't exactly drinking alone; he was waiting for Gratton to return. They had more business to discuss and did not want to reveal their investigation to eliminate the security leak from Malta. It was not a matter of trust but simply one of keeping the knowledge limited to a few so that they could ascertain more easily who could be the traitor or spy.

The next morning, Ewan awoke early. After showering and changing back into his formal no. 2 navy whites, he sauntered into the restaurant, where breakfast was being served. He was surprised to find that there appeared to be no rationing as there was back in Britain. He took advantage of the varied menu and attacked a large plate of bacon, eggs, sausages, toast, and marmalade. He was surprised yet again to find freshly ground coffee. Needing no prompting, he found an orderly preparing several pots of hot coffee. He ordered one.

The remainder of the morning was basically free for him—at least that is what he thought when he grabbed his cap and was about to leave the officers' club. Commander Gratton met him outside. 'Ewan. You must have read my mind.'

'Did I? You want me?' asked Ewan, feeling that something had come up and that his planned stroll around Valetta had now been shelved.

Gratton grinned. 'We've brought our briefing forward. Blackwell wants to discuss a few points with you.'

'Hmm, that bothers me. What's he up to?' Ewan was cautious from his past experiences with Blackwell.

'Not as bad as you think. Admiral Kelly's meeting is still on for this afternoon. Come on, I'll give you a lift.'

'Where are we going?' Ewan asked, still apprehensive.

'You'll see,' replied Gratton, appearing secretive. Ewan did not like this.

The driver, Leading Seaman Knowles, drove slowly through several side streets and out onto a dust-ridden road. It appeared to Ewan that Knowles was taking a roundabout route, crossing back on himself twice. He was.

'Why are we driving around streets that aren't really on our route?' asked Ewan. 'I know my way around here, but this is odd.'

Gratton laughed. 'Don't want to worry you, but we're dodging being followed.'

'We've had a tail ever since we picked you up, sir,' said Knowles.

'Really! Did they follow you to the club?'

'Er, no,' said Gratton. 'They were parked over the road opposite the officers' club. A reasonable deduction is that they have you under surveillance.'

'Me! Why me?'

'Good question. I don't know, but I can tell you that both the characters watching you are NKVD.'

'Why?' asked Ewan naively.

'It's possible that your mission here has been leaked,' Gratton said.

'Hu!' Ewan was surprised and so was driver Knowles.

'I'll explain later,' Gratton said.

More secrecy, thought Ewan.

When Knowles was satisfied that they were no longer being followed, he headed them north to the village of St Julians. After negotiating the narrow streets of St Julians, he took a battered rough road off the village that led to the end of Paceville inlet and harbour, where the MTBs assigned to Ewan's patrol group were assembled. Ewan remembered the berths from 1942. They were dispersed from the main harbours as a precaution to minimise aerial attack. The area, however, showed signs of bomb damage and dereliction and was generally unkempt. This added to the secrecy of their special patrol group. They passed by a large warehouse with rusted sheet metal doors, showing signs of battering from vehicles.

'Is that the warehouse where the body was found?' Ewan asked.

'No. That was in an old warehouse in one of the harbour inlets off of Grand Harbour.'

'So can we assume that these NKVD agents don't know about this place?'

'Hope so. We moved in here two weeks ago and have taken every precaution we can to avoid any attention. That includes moving stores at night in nonstandard trucks. But eventually they'll find out,' said Gratton in a matter-of-fact, relaxed tone.

Ewan thought for a moment. 'Is this because of a leak in security?'

'Yes. And for good measure, Knowles here is our eyes and ears at HQ in case the leak is there,' Gratton said.

Ewan looked to Knowles. 'I've found nothing so far. I don't think the problem is here.'

'Here in Malta?' queried Ewan.

'Right, sir.'

'I agree with Knowles. Blackwell thinks the leak is in London.'

'Oh, that's bloody marvellous. So, has our special patrol group been compromised?'

'Don't think so,' said Gratton, 'at least not yet. But there is interest in your being here.'

Knowles turned the jeep into a narrow stone-walled entrance and stopped near a sad-looking crane next to the short quayside. Two motor torpedo boats were tied up along the jetty, with another two abreast of them. Ewan spotted two more MTBs moored further out and a larger motor gunboat near an outcrop of rocks. He climbed out of the jeep and looked again back to the small fleet that he was to command. Gratton led the way to a small house. Two naval guards were eyeing them and guessed that one might be their new commanding officer. One ducked back into their small guard lodge and phoned to one of the moored MTBs connected by a shoreline telephone. He was alerting the duty chief petty officer.

Ewan and Gratton entered a ground-floor room tucked into the back of the small house. The only window in the room was curtained off, although it had a closed view of a rocky cliff and overhanging olive tree.

Blackwell was poring over a chart of the Southern Adriatic Sea. He looked up as they entered the room. 'Ewan, thanks for coming.'

'Did I have a choice?' Ewan chuckled.

'Quite. Anyway, grab a drink and take a look at this.'

Gratton sat away from the large desk and let Blackwell explain a problem. Communist partisans were holding most of the Albanian coast, but initial reports indicated that the Germans were about to break through. It was the SS Panzer division that Admiral Kelly had told Ewan about. It was now confirmed.

A lot of the naval forces in the Mediterranean had been deployed to the North Sea and the Far East. It was planned that Ewan's special patrol group would prevent the SS Panzer division from escaping and would support or evacuate the partisans, if necessary.

'Any questions?' asked Blackwell.

'No. It's almost clear to me—this is very dodgy indeed,' commented Ewan with a sigh.

Cross joined them. He placed another chart on top of the main chart. It showed in more detail the Strait of Otranto and the Italian Salento peninsula.

The briefing was finished except for tidying up a few finer points that really didn't involve Ewan. However, he had learned that any information from Blackwell and Cross was always useful as they had a habit of leaving out an odd fact that might be useful later. He remained with them, listening attentively to their conversation.

'As I have said before, the political situation in the Eastern Mediterranean, and particularly Greece and the Adriatic area, is unstable to say the least,' Blackwell said.

'The communists, nationalists, ex-Nazis probably?' commented Ewan, who decided to join the conversation.

'And just to muck things up, the Americans want us to keep out of it. They're so narrow-sighted at times,' Cross said.

'The big issue. Are the Russians stirring it up? We have information that guns, ammunition, and Red Army mercenaries, NKVD or KGB if you like, are being run in from the Black Sea and Balkan states. The main route appears to be by sea, direct from Odessa and the Crimea via Turkish waters into the Aegean, then Albania and the Adriatic. Italy could also be a target,' Blackwell said.

'The question is, what will the Russians do next in Albania? Are they to be Stalin's vanguard or satellite to expand the Soviet sphere of influence in the region?' Cross said.

The conversation drew to a close. Cross suggested they retire to the officers' club for a drink before lunch. Ewan respectfully declined as he needed to set up the next day's drills for one of his crews; he might as well get started in earnest. In addition, and more importantly for him, he needed to write to Hazel. He agreed to join them for dinner later, after Admiral Kelly's meeting.

Gratton arranged for another transport to take them back to the officers' club, leaving Leading Seaman Knowles to wait for Ewan.

Ewan wanted to take the opportunity to make a cursory visit to the nearest moored MTB. He was greeted by CPO John Davy, who had already been alerted earlier by the naval guard.

CPO Davy saluted Ewan.

Ewan returned the salute. 'Just saying hello, Chief. I'll come by tomorrow morning at oh-eight-hundred hours. No formalities, but I want to see all the boat skippers and POs.'

'Very good, sir,' replied CPO Davy.

Ewan was about to turn away, then stopped. 'Oh, Chief. One more thing. Add that I want to meet with all the senior engine room ratings of each boat.'

CPO Davy acknowledged and saluted as Ewan turned to stroll back to Knowles and his jeep.

A petty officer from the other moored MTB, abreast, approached CPO Davy. 'What gives, Chief? What's the new CO like?'

'I think we have a CO who knows where he's at. Tell all POs I want to see them in the shack immediately. I'll inform the skippers. We need to tidy up around here.'

The shack was the near-wrecked assembly room attached to the small house where Ewan had met with Blackwell. It was their main briefing room and occasionally doubled as a bar and restroom. CPO Davy briefed the skippers, other officers, and senior ratings of the special patrol group.

It was a strong group of three lieutenants, five sub lieutenants, five chief petty officers, six petty officers, and six leading engine room ratings. The senior officer was Lieutenant James Callendar, who was skipper of MGB 650.

Lieutenant James Callendar put a direct question to CPO Davy: 'OK, Chief, no formalities. And to squash any misgivings, what do you think of our new CO?'

It was an unusual question, but Callendar knew that most of the crew had had a hard time around the Italian coast for over two years, and some beforehand.

CPO Davy knew that he could only answer positively, but he had no difficulty with this. 'Sir, I think that Lieutenant Commander Jones knows where he's at. I think we need to be on our toes tomorrow.'

'You're right,' said Callendar. 'I've been told that he commanded one of our boats here in '43 and, before that, had a boat shot out from underneath him.'

CPO Davy gave an approving nod.

'One more thing about our new CO. He's come up through the ranks. He came here as PO and had an interesting time in the desert. I'm guessing that he knows all the tricks—he's a proper sailor,' Callendar said.

The gathering dispersed back to their respective crafts. There seemed to be satisfaction but also some apprehension. They all knew that they were being assembled for special duty.

Knowles dropped Ewan off at the officers' club. Ewan strolled to his quarters and thought for a moment about what the intelligence officers had said. It struck him that perhaps they were pointing to the presence of Russian agents in Malta and maybe Italy. He was right.

He passed the lounge bar and had the brief thought of getting a beer. But, deciding not to, he went to his room.

Ewan was not good at writing letters and didn't know where to start, but he did know how to end the letter with an 'I love you'. He wrote about his uneventful flight and a little detail about the job that Admiral

Kelly had for him. In itself, it was quite innocuous, but if the letter were intercepted, it would give a greater degree of authenticity to the guard of honour duty and its apparent confidentiality. Letters were still censored; this one could take days, if not weeks, to be delivered. Given this, Ewan reckoned that Hazel would be with him before she received most of his letters. Hazel had also realised this before Ewan departed for Malta and had arranged with his mother and father for them to open any letters to her that arrived after she left.

CHAPTER 4

LOVELY DAUGHTER-IN-LAW

THE FIRST WEEK of April 1945 was dismal in Neath, South Wales—cloudy grey skies with the odd flurry of rain and a light breeze coming off Swansea Bay. Hazel was just about to sign off duty when the matron called her into her office. Hazel got on well with the matron, who described Hazel as one of the most reliable nurses that she had encountered. The matron was sorry to see her leave. This was what the meeting was about. Hazel guessed that they were aiming to sort out a date. She had agreed to stay on for as long as she could as there were mounting casualties being flown in from Germany. Although the war was almost finished, there were die-hard groups of German soldiers, mostly SS, who were continuing to put up resistance. The hospital was receiving not only soldiers convalescing from injuries but also others requiring postoperative care. It was in this aspect that Hazel proved her valuable worth, particularly from her experiences in Malta more than two years earlier. The matron knew this.

'Hazel, I think you know why I want to see you. You have a couple of days' leave owing to you, and I thought that the good news might help you make arrangements to join your Ewan in Malta.'

'They have my travel date?' Hazel asked, trying to supress her excitement, although she was also tired. She had finished eight days' duty with very little time off since Ewan had left.

'Yes. In less than three weeks. The navy have you a placement. You will fly out to Gibraltar then onward to Malta,' said the matron, who was pleased for Hazel.

'Three weeks. That's earlier than I thought, but great.'

'I've been well informed that Malta and the entire region is short of qualified nurses, especially with prisoners of war being released and what appears to be fighting between different factions in Greece and Albania. Seems very messy to me. I know you'll do a good job. And, of course, you will be with Ewan.'

'Thank you, Matron. It will please Ewan's mum and dad, although they really want me to stay. They've been so good to me.'

'They're good, hard-working people just like you. Now take care,' said the matron.

Hazel turned to leave, when the matron added, 'Oh, one more thing. The girls want to lay on a leaving party for you. I'll let them know your last working day. Should be quite a shindig. I'll also sort out the off-duty rota.' The matron smiled and was actually envious; it was almost a miracle that any married couple could stay together in wartime when both were serving in the forces.

The next two days off duty allowed Hazel to sort her clothes and pack a suitcase and a large travel trunk with her own personal effects and some of Ewan's. Ewan's mother, Helena, helped Hazel pack the trunk, which they completed by midday of her second day. 'Done,' said Hazel.

'Yes. Now, how about you relax for the rest of the day? We can arrange shipment of the trunk tomorrow,' said Helena.

'Relax? Hmm. I've an idea,' said Hazel. 'Mama, how about we both have the afternoon off and go to that little cafe that overlooks the station? We can meet Papa when he comes off his shift at four o'clock.'

Hazel always referred to Helena as Mama in Italian when they were alone, and rarely the formal Italian *Madre* for 'mother'. This pleased Helena, especially when, as she occasionally did, Hazel referred to Albert, Ewan's father, in Italian as Papa, although he preferred to be called Bert.

Helena and Hazel wrapped up in warm outerwear before walking down the valley road to Junction Café, opposite Neath railway station. Although April and spring, it was cold and grey on this day. They met a couple of their neighbours, whose husbands also worked on the railway. Helena was so proud to be with her daughter-in-law, and Hazel was relaxed in Helena's company. They ordered tea and Welsh drop cakes, a sort of flat scone, popular in the Welsh valleys. Their conversation was mainly centred on Ewan. They both missed him, especially Hazel. She yearned for the day when she would join him. The good news was that it would be only three weeks at most, much earlier than they first had envisaged. Hazel realised that Helena would miss her. Helena had gotten used to Ewan's being away, as so many men and women were serving in the military and navy. She also realised that both Ewan and Hazel had been through a tough and quite dangerous time in Malta and North Africa. Hazel did not speak of her experiences in any detail, particularly of those when she was a prisoner of the Gestapo. She didn't need to; Helena seemed to feel her pain. There was a powerful bond between mother-in-law and daughter-in-law, only to be equalled with Bert and, of course, Hazel and Ewan.

However, Helena had been disturbed by an event that had taken place two days earlier. She had said nothing to Hazel. It was her intuition that struck home. Now was the right time to ask a question of Hazel as she ordered second cups of tea.

'Hazel, my love. I understand that when you were captured by the Germans and taken to Tobruk, you thought at the time it was to be Tripoli. Why was that?'

'Yes, that's right. Why do you ask?' queried Hazel. It was a question that came with no warning and not as part of their earlier conversation.

'Oh, nothing really, except that a soldier enquired about you. They thought you had been in Tripoli before the Eighth Army captured it. It was strange. The soldier wasn't local, but I think he was on leave. He didn't say who he was, but I guess he may have known you. He was with another soldier whom I think was in the Free Polish Army. He had "Poland" on his shoulder.'

'I've no idea who they could be. I did come into contact with soldiers, but mainly navy and, of course, POWs. Did the soldier leave a name?'

Helena thought for a moment. 'No, neither of them did. This was about two weeks ago, just after Ewan left. It was in the Railway Club. Bert will remember.'

Hazel did not think any more about it. The two women switched to talking about where Hazel and Ewan would be living. The couple had been told that Ewan's posting would initially be for two years, so there was the opportunity to move out of the married quarters to rent a house or private apartment. Hazel joked with Helena about whether they could find anywhere that was not damaged. The good news was that they would be able to return to Wales about every four months or thereabouts. With the war coming to a close, Ewan's patrol group would take on routine coastal policing with little or no danger. Helena realised that Ewan's past operations were always fraught with danger, and she dreaded the day when he might be injured or worse. She was also aware that Hazel, although robust, was deeply in love with Ewan. If the worst were to happen, how would Hazel cope? Selfishly, Helena wondered when one day she might become a grandmother, but never once did she mention this to Hazel. Privately she had discussed this with Bert. His attitude was that it was entirely a matter for Ewan and Hazel, but he felt that one day it would occur.

The two women's time in the cafe seemed to melt away. They cleared two cups of tea each and the Welsh drop cakes. The cafe door opened, not only letting in a draught of cold air but also allowing the shrill steam engine whistles to pierce the otherwise quiet atmosphere.

'Must be nearly Bert's end of shift,' said Helena.

'Let's go down to the engine shed and meet him,' said Hazel.

They rewrapped up warm from the cold breeze that seemed to penetrate every part of their lightly clad bodies and marched off, arm in arm, down the street towards the station. The cool air bit at Hazel's legs; her skirt was much shorter than Helena's, which was ankle length as befitting a mature woman. They gripped each other a little tighter as they swung into the entrance to the engine yard a few yards beyond the station building. There were already men in dirty overalls and caps, clutching their gas masks and tea flasks, strolling towards them. They did not seem in any hurry. Any work in the engine yard and shed was gruelling, dirty, and physically tiring. One or two of the men were hurrying, interspersed with several young women who did most of the cleaning of the steam locomotives, especially the clearing of ash and soot from the front boiler boxes. They looked grubby and dishevelled but were smiling through the grime of their day's work.

In the distance, emerging from the main engine shed was Bert. He was ambling along chatting with Ron Davies, his fireman.

'I think that's your wife and lovely daughter-in-law up ahead,' chirped Ron.

'Sure is,' said Bert, grinning to Ron.

'I envy you. Wish I had a daughter like that,' said Ron. There was a hurt in his voice. He had lost his daughter in an air raid on Swansea docks in 1941.

Bert knew how much this still hurt Ron from four years earlier. He did not respond immediately but cast a glance to Ron. 'See you in the club later, maybe?'

'Good idea. But make sure you bring that lovely girl with you. She seems to glow happiness. We all still need that,' said Ron.

Ron broke away and continued his lonely walk home.

'What's this? An escort home by two lovely ladies?' said Bert.

'We've had the afternoon off. Gallivanting, of course.' Hazel chuckled.

'She means the Junction Café,' said Helena.

'I guess you've finished packing then?'

They walked slowly up the hill towards home with Helena in the middle, flanked by Bert and Hazel.

That evening all three went to the Railway Club. It was to be Hazel's last foray out with Helena and Bert before she would fly out to Malta.

CHAPTER 5

THE DINNER

THE NKVD WERE already taking an interest in Ewan's presence in Malta. Ewan did not know this, but Blackwell and Cross did; they kept this morsel of information to themselves, except it was already known by Admiral Kelly, who by chance came up with the idea that the training of the guard of honour might just throw the NKVD off balance. It had, but they were still suspicious. Such was the NKVD's web of spying operations in Britain. They had gone as far as checking on Ewan's background. This was why two agents disguised as soldiers had been sent to Neath in South Wales to investigate Ewan's background. The NKVD had been passed information about a special patrol group that might be being assembled in Malta and that Lieutenant Commander Ewan Jones was to lead it.

To complicate matters, several MI5 officers, of the Security Service in London, believed that they had at least one communist sympathiser or traitor, depending on the point of view, within their organisation and maybe several in MI6, the Secret Intelligence Service. There was also mounting suspicion that the British Special Operations Executive (SOE) had NKVD agents in their headquarters in Bari, Italy, and elsewhere. Information was being passed to Moscow. The British intelligence had their own agents in Moscow, but too few to be effective. It was also dangerous for them; several were missing. They had no choice but to play out their plans in the Mediterranean, which might expose the traitors and spies. It was a dangerous game, and as with all spying and intelligence operations, the least number of people knowing the plot would provide a measure of protection. Hence, Blackwell and Cross did not want to reveal the NKVD threat to Ewan.

The smell and the bluish haze of tobacco smoke emanated from the lounge bar. It was not something that Ewan liked, but he had learned to put up with it while using the officers' club. Most of the bars in Malta, like elsewhere, also had this atmosphere; it was why he liked being out at sea in the fresh air.

Ewan entered the lounge and found Captain Mark Williams sitting at the bar, nursing a large glass of beer. He appeared to be looking into the near-empty glass.

'Mark, are you OK?' asked Ewan, sensing that something was on Mark's mind.

'Oh God! Completely lost in my thoughts,' said Mark, who summoned the barman. 'Two more pints, Bob.'

'Right away, sir,' said Bob the barman.

'Am I late?'

'Heavens no. I'm early. Needed to clear my mind and relax over dinner with you this evening. I'm pleased you're back and that Hazel will be joining you in a couple of weeks.'

'You sound harassed. What's up?'

Mark gave a long sigh. 'Oh, the drudgery of policing, I suppose. What should be a straightforward assignment is turning into a bit of nightmare. And it involves our friends Blackwell and Cross.'

'Oh, now that is trouble. What's happened?'

The barman placed two pint glasses of cool beer before them and returned to the other end of the bar.

Mark waited until the barman was out of earshot. He explained that the military police, which he ostensibly was in command of, were assisting the Maltese police with a number of incidents in the harbour areas, mainly involving black market trafficking and now the murder of a dock worker. It appeared to involve espionage and foreign secret services, notably the Russians. To complicate matters, local workers' unions were involved and now Italian communists.

'I know about the murder. I understand that Blackwell is concerned,' said Ewan.

Before Mark could continue, he spotted Blackwell and Cross entering the lounge. 'Talk of the devil, here they are.'

'Are they joining us?' asked Ewan.

'Er, yes. Although this was supposed to be a welcome dinner for you … Well, I'll let these two characters explain.'

'Characters, eh?'

'I can't bring myself to call them gentlemen, but then this is a change of the times,' said Mark, stroking his glass of beer. He summoned the barman and ordered beers for Blackwell and Cross.

'Sorry to interrupt—or should I say upset—your evening, but something urgent has arisen. Has Mark explained?' said Blackwell.

'No. He's left that to you,' replied Ewan, taking a large mouthful of his beer.

'I've arranged a table over in the far corner, away from everyone else,' said Cross.

'Hmm. Do I need a cloak and dagger?' mused Ewan.

'Nice one,' retorted Cross.

'You might,' added Mark with a wry smile.

They took their drinks to the table reserved for them. The club steward came to the table to enquire what they wanted from the menu.

'There's someone else joining us soon, so we'll order then,' said Cross.

'Alec Gratton?' asked Ewan.

'Yes. He'll be along in a moment,' said Blackwell, glancing at his watch. 'I'll wait for Alec and explain then. Anyway, changing the subject to you, Ewan. Are you settling in?'

'Just about. I suppose any trips around Malta are off for the time being,' said Ewan. There was a distinct tone of disappointment in his voice.

''Fraid so,' said Blackwell.

'I see you visited your little fleet earlier. What do you think of them?' Cross asked.

'Not had a chance to look them over yet, but will in the morning. First impression? They're on the ball. The CPO, Chief John Davy, seems to have everything worked out. I couldn't help but notice that he has a tight rein on the security. He's got the guards well trained. They knew who I was before I introduced myself.'

'Just like in the army, the sergeants and petty officers run the show,' chipped in Mark.

Alec Gratton joined them. He had overheard Mark's comment. 'You're right, and your crews are some of the best we could put together,' said Gratton.

'They'll need to be,' added Cross. There was an ominous tone in his voice.

'Priorities first,' said Blackwell. 'Dinner, then I'll explain.'

They were partway through their main course—they all had ordered roast beef—when Blackwell explained that they needed to get a look at the eastern shore of Sicily and especially Catania. Gratton suggested to Ewan that he take two boats to explore the coast, saying that it needed to be done immediately—and by this he meant the next day.

'Ewan, I've taken the opportunity to brief CPO Davy and Lieutenant Callendar. He's your number two and skipper's MGB 650. I'm sorry I've had to do this above your head, but these, er, two gentlemen have impressed the urgency of this,' said Gratton.

'So, what's the urgency?'

'We need you to make a quick survey of all the craft along that coastline. It's connected with the murder,' said Blackwell.

'Won't this blow the cover of the whole special patrol group?' Ewan asked, showing his concern for his overall operation.

'Hopefully not. Firstly, we only need involve two boats. Callendar will stay behind and take charge of the rest of your squadron or fleet, whatever you want to call it. And if you run into trouble, he'll come to your aid. You will also have half a dozen soldiers split between each boat. They'll be Mark's lads,' said Gratton.

'And I'll be with you,' interjected Mark.

Gratton continued. 'It will make it look as though it's a policing operation looking out for black marketeering and running illicit goods. For good measure, you will also have two Maltese police officers with you, one on each boat.'

'Right, I think. Seems straightforward enough. How long will we be away?'

'Twenty-four hours tops,' said Cross.

'And you two?' Ewan asked, directing his gaze to Cross then Blackwell.

'We'll make our presence obvious here to lend more support to the cover and to show that it doesn't involve our, er, business,' said Blackwell.

'Ewan, any questions?' asked Gratton.

'No. I don't think so. Except, what time do we slip?'

'Immediately after your quick, very quick, inspection tomorrow morning,' said Gratton.

'Oh-eight-thirty hours then?' said Ewan.

'My party will be with you at eight,' added Mark.

Gratton looked around the table. 'More drinks, I think.'

'I think I need one,' muttered Ewan, almost grumbling. 'At least I'll be back for the first honour guard drill practice on Friday.'

They all grinned.

Their drinks arrived. Just as Ewan was about to take a large gulp,

Gratton piped up, 'Oh, I nearly forgot. Ewan, I—or rather we—have a surprise for you tomorrow. And then there's another surprise on your return.'

'Oh, really? I hope it's a pleasant one! Or is it two? So, what's the surprise?'

'It wouldn't be a surprise if I told you, and it will be,' said Blackwell.

Their evening broke up. Ewan returned to his room. He was left wondering what the surprise would be. It couldn't be Hazel's arrival as he had received a telegram to say that she would be with him in ten days, which was much earlier than he had anticipated.

CHAPTER 6

FIRST MISSION

THE EARLY MORNING air was cool, but the residual stored heat from the surrounding buildings was still prevalent. This was typical for the weather in Malta in late April. The sun was already making its presence felt as Knowles drove Ewan to his base hidden near St Julians. They arrived at ten minutes to eight. Ewan spotted Mark Williams's party, congregated on the quay in front of MTB 700; MTB 701 was stationed abreast of MTB 700. The crews from the other boats were congregated in small groups with a party formally paraded in front of MTB 708, which was not putting to sea. Ewan hopped out of the jeep, clutching a briefcase. Chief Petty Officer John Davy greeted him. 'All present and correct, sir. I know there's been a change of plan, but will you be carrying out your inspection and briefing before we slip?'

'Not bloody likely, Chief. I'm all in favour of a good turn out and the usual stuff, but we need to get this show moving. I'll see you and Lieutenant Callendar first though.'

'I'll get him, sir,' replied CPO Davy, who was pleased. He had been right about their new CO; he was direct to the point and would park normal protocols to get the job done.

Ewan went to Captain Mark Williams. 'Good morning, Mark. Everything set?'

'Yes. Thanks, Commander,' said Mark, respecting the formal courtesies.

'I'm dividing my party as we suggested last night. I understand that you are taking the 700 boat, so I'll ensconce myself on the 701 if that's OK?'

'Good idea. Who's your senior?'

'Sergeant Cropper,' replied Mark, who called the sergeant to join them.

Lieutenant Tolley joined them. 'Good morning, sir. I haven't had a chance to brief you about our boat, but I'm skippering the 700 boat for you, and we're ready to slip.'

'Right, no problem. Just one small change. Whose your coxswain?'

'CPO Hammond, sir,' replied Lieutenant Tolley, who was an experienced MTB skipper and had a good knowledge of the Italian coast.

'OK. You and CPO Hammond are in charge of the boat. You are its skipper, not me. CPO Davy will be staying behind. I have a special job for him. My job is to get this operation completed without any undue attention from shore.'

'Very good, sir,' said Tolley, who saluted. 'Chief, let's get the engines warmed up.'

Ewan saw Mark, his soldiers, and a police officer clamber across MTB 700 and onto MTB 701. A youngish-looking sub lieutenant crossed over from MTB 701 and MTB 700. He saluted Ewan. 'Sub Lieutenant Stanford, sir, skipper of the 701 boat. Engines warmed up and ready to go.'

Ewan returned the salute and could see that Stanford was a little nervous. 'Right. You are Stanford. Slip when you want to and wait out in the bay for us to join you. We'll sort where to station you once we're out at sea. Radio use as normal except for the observations. Is that clear?'

Stanford was puzzled but had a feeling that his new CO knew what he was doing, just as CPO Davy had alluded to.

MTB 701 slipped her mooring to MTB 700 and slowly motored away from the inlet and towards the open sea.

MTB 700 was ready to slip and was only waiting for Ewan to climb aboard.

Ewan had a few words with Lieutenant Callendar and CPO Davy. 'I guess both of you wish you were going on this bit of a cruise, but I need to have a heavyweight command left behind to cover my arse, and that's you two. One other thing, Chief. While I'm away, I want you to do two things: firstly, continue with the honour guard drill—that should keep any prowling eyes from suspecting what we're up to—and secondly, make list of all battle-experienced crew members, especially gunners.' He glanced to Callendar. 'I think you can guess what we're up to. We need to be ready within two weeks—not six!'

'I understand,' said Callendar. He added, 'And good luck, sir.'

Ewan grinned and had a final few words with Callendar. 'James, it might be a good idea that you get all the other boats ready for sea, just in case something untoward crops up. I somehow get the feeling that this is not a simple surveillance job.'

'Very good, sir,' said Callendar. He paused. 'You know, sir, the war isn't over yet, and there's been a couple of reports of a marauding U-boat off Taranto and possibly in the Adriatic. I'll make sure everyone is on their toes.'

'Good. One more thing. If we do get into trouble, it will be sent as an open signal. There'll be no messing about. Also, the RAF will be shadowing us. See you tomorrow evening.'

'Yes, sir. I'll make sure the bar is stocked,' replied Callendar.

Ewan stepped aboard MTB 700, and Tolley gave the order to slip.

MTB 700 slowed to an idle pace to join MTB 701 outside the entrance to the inlet. Tolley signalled MTB 701 to follow at twenty knots a few hundred yards to their starboard aft quarter. He then joined Ewan in the boat's small compact ward room, where Ewan had opened a chart of the eastern coast of Sicily.

'How close to the coastline will we need to get?' asked Tolley.

'Close enough to get some pictures and have a good nose around Catania. Same for the Taranto coast. Then back to base.'

'Are we on the lookout for anything particular, sir?'

Ewan smiled. 'Yes we are. Any freighters, any small cargo ships sailing to uninhabited parts of the coast, and anything that we might think is out of place in any of the harbours.'

'So it's an intelligence-gathering mission,' said Tolley.

Ewan nodded.

A sailor appeared. 'Coffee, sir?' Ewan did not take much notice, but he did nod.

'Do you want to see our guests now, sir?'

'Guests! You mean the army and police?' said Ewan, looking up from the charts to the sailor.

'Oh, sorry, sir. Clean forgot,' apologised Tolley. 'We have a surprise for you.'

'Blackwell said I would have a surprise. It's not my birthday. So, what is it?'

Two sailors dressed in dark navy-blue boiler suits emerged from next to the galley.

Ewan was stunned, near speechless. He recognised them.

'Good morning, sir. Good to see you,' said the petty officer.

'God almighty! Tom. Tom Reynolds and Dan Perry. Where the hell did you two spring from?' Ewan was delighted. Tolley had been told that Ewan would know of them.

Ewan explained to Tolley who they were. Tom Reynolds and Dan Perry had been with Ewan in North Africa in October 1942, just as the Battle of El Alamein culminated in the destruction of the Afrika Korps.

'So, Tom, I see you've made PO; and you, Dan, a kellick. So, what's your part in this operation?' Ewan used the traditional Royal Navy term kellick for a leading seaman.

'We're part of your naval commando unit. We're here to help train the crews,' said Petty Officer Tom Reynolds.

'And, sir, my main job is to take photographs,' added Leading Seaman Dan Perry.

'I guess you two lads know this part of the Med quite well?' queried Tolley.

'We certainly do, sir,' replied Reynolds.

The two MTBs motored north to Sicily. Ewan leaned on the edge of the open bridge and looked out to sea; Malta and the island of Gozo were fading into the distance. He thought for a moment. There were two surprises. Having Tom and Dan along was one surprise—or was it that the two of them were the two surprises? But then Blackwell had said that the second surprise would be on Ewan's return. He concluded that it must be someone else from his past desert experience.

CHAPTER 7

OF INTEREST

THE FLIGHT FROM Britain to Gibraltar was comfortable and relatively quick, taking four hours. This was mainly owing to the safe airspace over France. During the occupation of France, the Gibraltar run meant flying farther out into the Atlantic to avoid the German Luftwaffe nearshore fighters and the long-range Condor bombers. However, the journey from Gibraltar to Malta was very different. Instead of a pleasant Dakota, as from Britain, the plane was a converted old Wellington bomber, used mainly as a small troop carrier and for mail. Nursing Sister Hazel Jones sat on a metal chair bolted to the floor and hastily kitted with thin cushions and a blanket; there was no headrest. At least it was not the side benches, which looked decidedly more like a torture, thought Hazel. Air turbulence buffeted the plane; almost everyone on board was feeling airsick, including Hazel. Their relief was near when the copilot emerged from the cockpit cabin and announced that they were in sight of Malta and would be landing in fifteen minutes.

'Sorry about the bumpy ride. Is everyone OK?' said the copilot, who grinned.

Among the passengers were four soldiers, including a sergeant.

'Do you really want me to answer that?' The sergeant scowled.

Hazel tried to hide a smile of relief. Her bottom was sore, and she had a pins-and-needles sensation in both legs. She was told, along with the other passengers, to tighten her seat belt. She had a foreboding feeling that the landing was also going to be uncomfortable. It was, although not as bad as she had thought it might be. The numbness in her bottom seemed to dull any pain.

'At last we're on the ground!' said one of the soldiers. There was a distinct feeling of relief in his voice.

Several other passengers, who had heard his utterance, muttered something similar.

The Wellington taxied slowly towards a nearby building. The engines began to wind down, and their rattling noise diminished as the cabin door was opened by the flight attendant, a tired-looking RAF airman, who yawned. A set of steps was attached to the plane and the passengers began filing out, carefully climbing down the steps facing backwards in case they slipped. Hazel was guided down the steps, first by the airman flight attendant, and then by the ground staff at the foot of the ladder.

Another RAF airman greeted them and asked them to wait for their cases and bags, which were being unloaded by the ground staff. Hazel spotted her case, a slightly battered leather case with the initials 'HA' neatly painted above the handle on the side of the lid. She looked at the letters. She had not changed them to 'HJ' after she married Ewan. Maybe it was time to change it, or even buy a new case.

She picked up her case and followed the other passengers to the nearby building, a rough pockmarked concrete structure still showing the signs of bomb and machine-gun damage from earlier years. An RAF military police corporal signalled the stream of passengers to a large double door. This led into a reception room, with a line of tables along the wall opposite the double door. There were three more RAF personnel in the room who directed the passengers in groups to the tables. After an inspection of travel and identification documents, the passengers filed through another door into a much larger foyer. There were many more people milling around, waiting for flights and looking to greet some of the passengers.

Hazel looked around for her escort. She had been told on her departure from Gibraltar that she would be met by a sailor. There was no sailor to be seen, at least not in uniform. She sauntered to a group of chairs that were vacant, opposite the entrance, so that she could see anyone in a naval uniform arrive. It was infinitely more comfortable than the flight.

She continued to look around, but still there was no sailor in sight. What Hazel did not know was that Leading Seaman Knowles had been delayed by a road accident on the main road from Valetta to Luqa airfield.

She became aware that someone was watching her; it was one of those uncanny feelings. She was indeed being observed by a man in a dark grey suit. She glanced to the man, who seemed to be immersed in a newspaper. She had an uneasy feeling about him but then put it down to her feeling the anxiety from the flight, which had left her a little distraught. The minutes passed by. It had been twenty minutes from the time she had landed and cleared the inspection, according to the clock above the reception desk.

During this time, she became more aware of the man whom she thought was watching her. He was. He did not appear to be waiting for anyone and was not in the departure queue to the reception desk. She also observed that he had not changed pages of the newspaper. This made her feel even more uneasy. What could she do? She picked up her case and moved nearer to the entrance of the foyer. A quick glance back and she saw the man move from where he was reading his newspaper to get nearer to her. Her heart began to pound. Was she feeling silly? *It can't be anything sinister,* she thought, *not now that I am in Malta.*

Her anxious thoughts and her dilemma was suddenly interrupted by the sergeant, who had been a passenger on the plane. 'Are you OK, miss?' he asked.

'Oh, what?' she stuttered. 'I'm afraid my escort hasn't arrived. Supposed to be navy. A sailor.'

'Not like the navy to be late,' he replied. There was none of the usual interservice banter.

'I'm not sure what to do. I could get the bus into Valetta.'

'You know Malta, miss?' asked the sergeant.

'Er, yes I do. I'm to report to Naval HQ.'

'Fort St Angelo. OK, we'll drop you off there. Our transport has just arrived.'

One of the soldiers in the party had heard Hazel. He grabbed her case. 'Come on, miss. We'll give you a lift.'

Before she had time to think, the sergeant directed her to an open Austin 10 Tilly utility truck.

'Take the passenger seat up front. Far more comfortable than that flight,' said the sergeant, nodding approval to the driver.

'Oh, Sergeant, should I tell reception that you've picked me up?'

'Good idea. I'll do that. Don't want to worry the navy that the army have grabbed you,' replied the sergeant, chuckling. The driver laughed.

They drove to Valetta. On the way, the driver remarked to the sergeant, who was sitting in the back, 'Hey, Sarge. You see that old beaten-up black car following us?'

The sergeant looked back. 'Yes. I see it. What about it?'

'It's been following us from the airfield,' said the driver.

'Maybe just the same route?' said one of the soldiers, who looked back to the car.

'No. I've taken a shortcut and it's kept close on our tail.'

'Well, we can't be of any interest,' said the sergeant.

'And it's not the coppers,' said one of the other soldiers, who also looked back.

Hazel looked back also. She was sure that the passenger in the car was the man who had been watching her at the airfield. 'Sergeant, I thought I was being paranoid earlier, but now I'm not so sure. I thought I was being watched by a man at the airfield, and I think he's the passenger in that car.'

'Miss, what are you?' asked the sergeant. Hazel was in civilian clothes.

'Just a nurse. I'm joining my husband here.'

'That can't be it. But I think we need to see you right into Naval HQ,' said the sergeant.

'You'll be OK with us,' reassured one of the soldiers seated in the back. Hazel felt safe.

They arrived at Fort St Angelo, Naval HQ. The driver stopped directly in front of the main entrance. The sergeant beckoned a naval guard and explained the issue with the tailing car. The naval guard, a leading seaman, looked towards where the car was parked, a hundred yards away across the road leading to the Naval HQ entrance. 'I see it,' said the guard. He summoned one of his other guards. 'Charley, look after the lady.'

The guard took Hazel's case to the guardroom.

Hazel turned to the sergeant and the other soldiers. 'Sergeant, thanks for looking after me. Where are you based?'

'Pembroke barracks. I'm Bill Hampton. Maybe we'll meet up again.' He grinned.

'Anyway, lads, thanks,' said Hazel, giving a short wave goodbye.

The leading seaman naval guard approached the car that had followed them. Two men were in the car, which suddenly revved its engine and sped off down a side street.

The naval guard, Charley, guided Hazel to the reception desk and put her case to one side.

'Frank,' said Charley, 'this lady has been told to report here. I think she was followed by some dodgy characters. We'll follow it up, but I think you should report it.' He turned to Hazel. 'You're in good hands now, miss.' He turned away, back to his post at the entrance.

Hazel thanked him.

Frank, the naval attendant, eyed Hazel and smiled, as sailors usually do when confronted with an attractive woman. 'Can I see your ID card, miss?'

Hazel handed over her ID card and a letter that she had been given when she left Britain. She was not in any uniform, so the naval rating went through the motions of checking. His face suddenly lit up. 'Oh yes, it's Mrs Jones—or I should say Nursing Sister Jones. We've been expecting you. I believe Admiral Kelly would like to see you. I'll get someone to escort you to his office.'

'That's OK. Is the admiral's office the same as the one Admiral Forbes used? If so, I know the way,' said Hazel, producing a wide grin.

'Right, miss. I mean Mrs Jones,' said the naval rating. 'Leave your case here. I'll look after it until you leave.'

Hazel dragged herself up the stairs—she was tired—and found herself outside the admiral's office. She opened the door, to be greeted by Kate Davies.

'Hazel!'

'Kate! What a surprise.'

'Admiral's on the phone. Will see you as soon as he's free. Sit yourself down. Would you like a drink after that journey?'

'A glass of water would be good.' Hazel felt parched; her throat had become dry from the apprehension of being followed.

The two women chatted like long-lost friends, which is what they were. Kate had made all the arrangements for Hazel's journey and had been looking forward to meeting her again.

Meanwhile, the naval rating at the reception desk had phoned the duty Naval Intelligence officer to inform him of Hazel's possible encounter. The naval guard had already alerted the intelligence office. Their standing order was to report any strange events, however trivial they might seem.

The admiral's office door opened, and out stepped a short, almost podgy man dressed in naval whites sporting a rear admiral's shoulder epaulettes. 'Hazel, come on in. May I call you Hazel? Kate, can you arrange tea for us, including yourself?'

'Er, yes, please do, Admiral,' said Hazel, acknowledging his request to call her Hazel.

Hazel entered the office. Admiral Kelly showed her to a comfortable chair. She made a quick glance around the office. It had not changed since late 1943, except now there were a couple of plants on the windowsill and a battered, dirty-looking naval ensign flag hanging on the wall next to a map of Malta.

'Hazel. Kate will take you over to the married officers' quarters later. I'm afraid that Ewan, Commander Jones, is not here but will be returning tomorrow afternoon. He's out on a patrol. Routine stuff. If there's anything you need, let Kate know or, of course, the matron at RNH Bighi. The matron is looking forward to meeting you,' said Admiral Kelly.

'Thank you, Admiral. I'm very grateful for how well this has all been arranged.'

'Kate's really done all this. As Ewan is away, I thought it would be appropriate that I take you out to dinner this evening, so I arranged a bit of a soirée at the officers' club. The restaurant there is much improved since you were here last.'

'Thank you again, Admiral. I don't know what to say.'

'Say nothing. It's my pleasure—or I should say our pleasure.'

'Our pleasure'? What is all that about? thought Hazel.

They talked about Hazel's journey. The admiral enquired about the mood back in Britain as the war in Europe seemed to be in its last weeks.

They were interrupted by Kate Davies, entering with a tray of biscuits, a teapot, and three cups and saucers. Admiral Kelly insisted on pouring the tea.

'Hazel, I've asked Kate to be present as I have something important to say to you.' There was now a tone of seriousness in his voice. Hazel realised that something was up.

'Before you came in, I had a phone call from Naval Intelligence. They told me about your problem of being followed from the airfield and mentioned that you suspected you were being watched at the airfield.'

'Yes, Admiral. A bit unnerving. And if it hadn't been for those soldiers, I would have dismissed it as my overreacting a little and being excited, if that is what it is, about being back here in Malta and being back with Ewan,' said Hazel.

'Firstly, I'm glad those soldiers looked after you. I'll make sure their CO is made aware of their service to you. Secondly, I'm glad they also spotted your undesirable admirers, if that's what they are. You see, from their description, we believe they're foreign agents. NKVD, to be precise.'

Hazel did not understand. 'NKVD? What's that?'

'Narodny Kommisariat Vntrennikh, known as the NKVD,' interjected Kate.

'Excellent pronunciation,' remarked Admiral Kelly.

'Russian?' mused Hazel.

'Oh yes. The People's Commissariat for Internal Affairs to you and me,' said Kate.

'So what's this all about? Aren't they our allies?' Hazel's naivety was exposed.

The admiral smirked. 'Good point. But you wouldn't think so by what they've been up to. What bothers me is why the NKVD should be interested in you.'

'Admiral, you're speaking as though the Russians are also our enemy. Back home, a lot of people would find this unbelievable,' said Hazel.

'I know. But they've quickly forgotten that the Russians were actually against us in 1939. They attacked Poland. Anyway, the Russians are expanding their communism and sphere of influence in this whole area, especially the Balkans. Well, that's it. Our people will find out why you were put under NKVD surveillance. Don't worry,' said the admiral reassuringly.

Hazel gave Kate a searching look.

The admiral could see that Hazel was concerned.

'Right, Kate. Off you go. And take Hazel to her newfound home. I'll see you both later at seven-thirty in the officers' club lounge.'

Kate gave a warm smile to Hazel.

CHAPTER 8

LEAVING PARTY

THE NEW MARRIED quarters for officers was located within the grounds of the Naval HQ. Kate showed Hazel the way. To Hazel's surprise, her case had already been taken to her new home. Kate left Hazel to unpack and find her way around the apartment. Hazel was pleasantly surprised once more to find that Ewan had already made himself at home. She found his shaving kit in the bathroom and several items of uniform hanging up in a closet in the bedroom. She unpacked and went for a bath to soak away the dusty humid atmosphere. This brought back her memories of two years ago. She lay on the bed with only a towel partly covering her body. She dropped off into a light sleep but reawakened, thinking about how quickly everything had happened in the last few days. The speed with which she had been whisked away from Neath startled her.

Hazel's two days' leave had been curtailed the next morning at eight. She received a message from the matron to return to the hospital as soon as possible. It was a direct order. Hazel was startled by the hand-delivered message, and so was Helena; Bert had already gone to his engine shed. Something serious had occurred. *It must be a large influx of casualties,* she thought. It had happened before, especially when the Allies had crossed the Rhine in February.

She went directly to the matron's office and was met by one of her nurses, who was leaving the office. They looked at each other. The nurse glowered a big grin. *What was all that about?* wondered Hazel. She knocked on the matron's door before entering.

'Hazel, come in. Sit down. You will need to!' said the matron.

'What the ...' Hazel was cut short as she began to sit down.

'Your transport to Malta has been brought forward. There's space on a flight out of RAF Lineham tomorrow morning, if I can let you go. And I have agreed.'

The news was earth-shattering for Hazel. She was speechless.

The matron continued.

Hazel was still stunned by the sudden turn of events. Although she was listening to the arrangements being made by the matron, none of it was registering. Less than twenty-four hours before, she had been packing her cases. Helena had suggested that they pack Hazel's bags as soon as possible as, 'You never know,' she had said. Was it a premonition? The meeting with Bert at the end of his shift, and their evening together at the Neath Railwayman's Club, seemed to reinforce this.

The matron had been contacted the previous evening about releasing Hazel earlier. Much earlier. She had agreed even before the priority request had been explained. It had originated from the Admiralty, Naval Intelligence. It was felt that Hazel should be placed with Ewan as a matter of priority and for her own safety. The matron had been told about the two men dressed as soldiers who had been enquiring about Hazel. 'Is this anything to do with her husband?' she enquired with Naval Intelligence. They couldn't say, was the reply. The matron guessed that it was.

The matron had marshalled what available nursing staff she had from the end of the evening shift to put together a leaving party for Hazel. It would be only a small affair. By the time Hazel had reported to the matron in the morning, everything was in place. Four medical officers from the Royal Army Medical Corps arranged for wine, beer, and other drinks. The matron decided not to ask how they'd done it; 'Better not to know,' they had said. Hazel's popularity was evident by the number of nursing, medical, and support staff who either attended or popped in during the party, which started at seven-thirty to coincide with shift changeover.

Hazel had only one main concern, and that was Helena and Bert. But this was solved by the matron, who used her connections with the railway stationmaster to get a message to Bert, whose locomotive, by good fortune, was on freight standby. The stationmaster was able to get a relief engine driver to take his place. No one noticed that Bert turned up in the nurses' restroom, where the party was held, dressed in his almost grubby-looking driver's overalls; however, he did remove his cap. One of the nurses arranged a car to collect Helena, who first of all was shocked, thinking that Hazel had had an accident. At least Helena had had time to dress in one of her best frocks.

Hazel was overwhelmed by the party and particularly by the number of people who came to see her off. The party broke up at nine. After Hazel said her goodbyes to the last of her colleagues, the matron had a quick word. 'Hazel, take care of yourself. As you now know, this has been arranged quickly for your own safety.' Hazel had been told as much earlier by the senior medical officer. 'There's something sinister in all this. But you will be in good hands. They must think a lot about you, and that's good.'

Sinister. Good hands. These words brought home the realisation that Ewan must be involved in something very serious and probably dangerous. Hazel's thoughts and anxiety for Ewan came to the fore, but then Bert and Helena were with her. This made her feel good. With Bert on one side of Helena, and Hazel on the other, they strolled out of the hospital and towards a waiting army staff car. Hazel had no idea that she was being shadowed by a middle-aged man who earlier had introduced himself to the matron and the senior medical officer as a military intelligence officer, MI5. His presence and his interest in watching over Hazel gave the matron and the medical officer a feeling of reassurance for Hazel, but on the other hand, they prayed that nothing untoward was in store for her. They both guessed that Hazel was the subject of interest because of her relationship with Ewan.

The medical officer commented to the matron, 'You don't have to be a genius to know that this has got to be something to do with the Russians or some other undesirable buggers. This damned war is far from coming to a clean end.'

'Yes. I've heard the stories coming out from the Eastern Front. And Poland. Stalin is certainly putting his boot down hard there,' said the matron. 'I do hope Hazel will be all right.' The medical officer nodded.

Unbeknown to Hazel or Bert and Helena, two MI5 officers were sitting in a parked car near the end of the road to their house. They would be there all night, keeping an eye on Hazel, until the time she would be picked up by a special car in the morning. The Security Service were taking no chances; the operation put in place by Blackwell and his associates seemed to be working.

CHAPTER 9

DINNER WITH THE ADMIRAL

HAZEL WAS AWAKENED by someone knocking on the apartment door. She slipped off the bed, clutching the bath towel to cover the essential parts of her body, and opened the door.

'Oh, Kate. I must have dropped off.'

'We've plenty of time. I thought we would get a drink first. Anyway, you had better get some clothes on. You might shock some of the younger matelots.' Kate chuckled.

'Oh, right.'

'There's a little bar nearby. Used by locals. Some of us go there to avoid some of the attentions we might get in the officers' club,' said Kate. 'The officers' club is only a short walk away.'

Once in the Lorenzo Bar, they settled in a quiet corner with a couple of gin and tonics. They talked about their respective lives since Hazel had left more than a year earlier. Eventually, Hazel asked about Ewan and his new command. Kate did not reveal anything sensitive to Hazel and made out that the patrol group was basically policing the waters around Malta, Sicily, Southern Italy, and the Adriatic. Hazel detected that Kate was holding back on some of Ewan's duties except for the guard of honour, which surprised her; she could not see Ewan in charge of a parade, let alone an honour guard. She decided not to ask anything further of Kate and put her to any embarrassment by her declining to answer.

Kate grinned.

'What's so funny?' asked Hazel.

'Nothing funny. In fact, quite the opposite.' Kate chuckled. 'Glad you're not in uniform, and that dress suits you. It's good to see people in civvies these days.'

'Are you sure it's OK? It's a bit tired. Got it on my last clothing coupons at Christmas. The rationing at home is biting hard.'

'It's great. Truly.'

Kate glanced at her watch. It was time to meet Admiral Kelly at the officers' club.

The officers' club was a throng of uniformed officers mostly in naval whites with a smattering of light army khaki and air force light blue. Hazel and Kate strolled into the lounge. Both felt the piercing eyes of nearly all the men. There were a few uniformed women who gave passing glances, but it was the younger naval officers, mainly sub lieutenants, whose attentions were grabbed. The two women negotiated their way around several tables to the veranda, where they were met by an army captain.

Hazel recognised him and beamed a smile.

'Captain Williams! What a pleasant surprise.'

Captain Mark Williams shot up to his feet. 'Hazel. It's good to see you again,' he said. 'Less of the captain—it's Mark.'

'Right, Hazel, I'll leave you in Mark's capable hands while I dig out the admiral.'

'Mark, are you joining us for dinner?' Hazel asked excitedly. She always enjoyed his company after she had married Ewan and settled into routine naval patrols in late 1943.

'Hazel, I've already met with Ewan—sort of working together, which I can explain later. So, how is married life treating you? Are you glad to be back?'

'Wonderful. And yes, I am glad to be back, especially with Ewan. Silly, but I miss him.'

'It's not silly. He's a pretty wonderful guy. He did sterling work for D-Day, and that's why Their Lordships in the Admiralty want him here. But then you know that.'

'Know what?' queried Hazel.

'D-Day, of course. I thought you knew,' said Williams, who suddenly realised that Ewan had not revealed the actions he was involved with during the D-Day landings.

'He hasn't spoken much about it, except that I believe he was involved in some fights with the Germans.'

'Ah, yes. Maybe he wants to put it behind him. This whole war has crept up on us, but at least it's nearly over—at least here anyway,' said Williams.

'Do you know what happened? With Ewan, I mean?'

'All I know is that he encountered several German E-boats and had a pretty rough scrap with them. They lost, of course. The story is that he was directly responsible for sinking four E-boats and damaging a U-boat. I guess it was the destruction of the E-boats that got to him.'

'You mean it brought back memories of here, when I first met him,' noted Hazel.

'Exactly that. He's been through a lot. You both have,' said Williams in a low tone. But then he perked up. 'Let's change the subject. Drink?'

'Not until you tell me something of yourself,' said Hazel, 'When we left, you were seeing a delightful young woman. Seemed to be getting serious.'

'Serious. Now there's an understatement. If you had still been here, I would have wanted you as Natalie's maid of honour and Ewan as best man,' chirped Williams.

'You've gotten married!'

'Sure have. And we're very happy together. I'm thinking of settling down here in Malta once this lousy war is over.'

'She's Maltese, isn't she?'

'Yes. And I've a great mother-in-law and father-in-law. Treat me like a son. Spoil me, in fact. You and Ewan must meet them. Thinking of inviting you to dinner next week, once your marauding husband has returned.'

'On that subject, Mark, what exactly is Ewan up to, if you're allowed to tell me?'

'That's better coming from the admiral than me, but I can reveal that his job is more a policing action than enemy engagement.'

Before Hazel could interrogate Mark Williams further, Kate reappeared with Admiral Kelly. His face shone as he set eyes on Hazel.

'Hazel, my dear, you look every part a naval officer's wife, but more importantly it makes me envious of Ewan. Now let's go to our table that Kate has reserved at the end of the veranda.'

They moved to the table that was marked 'Reserved for Admiral Kelly'.

Admiral Kelly shot a quiet question to Mark Williams: 'Any news?'

Although the men were speaking in soft voices, Hazel could not help but overhear.

Kate Davies spotted Hazel's concern. Was Ewan in difficulty?

'Hazel, don't worry. It's not Ewan,' she whispered.

'Something wrong?' said Hazel.

This time Admiral Kelly overheard Hazel.

'Yes, my dear. Someone whom Ewan and I believe you know has got a problem,' said Admiral Kelly.

Hazel looked puzzled.

'You remember Blackwell and Cross?' said Williams. 'They have a bit of a problem.'

Hazel's heart sank. Blackwell and Cross—what were they up to? Their spying operations almost caused Ewan and her to nearly end in tragedy.

Was Ewan involved with them again? Her mind began to tumble with apprehension.

'Admiral, is Ewan involved with Blackwell and Cross again?' It was a direct question.

The admiral thought for a moment before answering. She deserved a direct reply. 'Yes he is. We will tell you as much as we can. We don't think he is in any more danger than any of us out here, except for a complicating factor: the NKVD!'

'But that's who you thought was following me,' said Hazel.

The others were silent for a few seconds.

'Hazel, Ewan's mission here was secret, but somehow we think the mission has been compromised,' said Admiral Kelly.

'Betrayed more like,' interrupted Williams.

Kate stayed quiet. She was concerned about Hazel's experience at the airfield earlier and was tasked to keep a close eye on her.

'Let's order dinner and enjoy the evening,' said Admiral Kelly. It was more of an order than a suggestion. 'Incidentally, Hazel, rationing is no longer a problem here, so enjoy this newfound freedom with Ewan.'

The evening drew to a close. They parted ways, leaving Kate to escort Hazel back to her quarters. Hazel wanted to ask Kate more about what Ewan was doing, and Kate sensed it. 'Hazel, I know it's easy to say not to worry, especially given what you have been through in this damned war up to now, but I really believe Ewan will be safe. If I have a concern, it's you.'

'Me?'

'Yes. These Russian agents apparently try to coerce people into providing them with intelligence information by threatening their families, in this case, you. What Cross is trying to find out is why they think that getting at you will make Ewan susceptible to—.'

'Blackmail?'

'Sort of. Can't say much more. There is one thing for certain from what I've been able to glean so far: it's that the Russians and the Germans are worried about the group that Ewan is to lead. No one knows why so far. It's all confusing.'

'And you, Kate, are more involved in this spy stuff than simply as a secretary to the admiral—yes?'

Kate nodded and clutched Hazel's arm affectionately as they turned into the officers' quarters. Kate was about to say goodnight, when she remembered something. 'Oh, Hazel, nearly forgot. You report for duty day after tomorrow at RNH Bighi?'

'Yes, that's right.'

'You are in for a pleasant surprise. Guess who the matron is?'

'Who?'

'Margaret Stanton. She can't wait to meet with you again. She's moved from the British Red Cross directly into Queen Alexandra's Royal Naval Nursing Service. They desperately wanted a senior nurse to take charge of nursing here as there are so many injured and many needing long-term care.'

'That's great. Maybe everything will work out fine after all,' Hazel said, feeling much better in her mind than earlier. Then she thought of what the matron in Neath had said to her before she left: 'Your nursing skills will be put to a great test; you will be tending not only to Allied wounded but also to Germans, Italians, and thousands of civilians—quite a challenge.'

CHAPTER 10

TARANTO

THE TWO MTBs sailed into Sicilian waters. They completed their passage by passing in the shadow of Mount Etna, which continued to spill lava from the great eruptions of 1943, albeit now a much reduced amount. The patrol found nothing of any interest, even though they lingered around the port of Catania for over an hour. They moved on farther north into the Gulf of Taranto off the Italian mainland. The hours passed by, and the two MTBs edged closer inshore, cruising slowly along the coast at about ten knots. They exchanged radio messages from patrolling RAF reconnaissance planes. There was no sign of any U-boats. Several fishing boats were observed, but they did not intercept any of them. However, Leading Seaman Dan Perry took photos of each, noting their positions and the times.

In the early hours of the morning as the sun was rising, they closed on the Italian naval base and the port of Taranto.

Ewan joined Tolley on the bridge, clutching a hot mug of tea. 'Anything?'

'Nothing. Not even a fishing boat. Here we are twenty-seventh April, with a shooting war still going on in the north, and we're patrolling a quiet shore,' said Tolley, feeling left out of the war.

Ewan thought that Tolley might change his mind later if they ever got involved in a major firefight. War was not kind and Tolley had probably not experienced much of it, *lucky bugger* thought Ewan. In fact Tolley had seen enough but did not let it show.

Apart from the odd U-boat to hunt, there had been very little action since December, even when the civil war in Greece had all but come to an end. There were several German garrisons holding out in the area, notably western Crete, but Allied High Command had decided to leave them alone until the war was effectively over in Germany itself, unless these garrisons caused any trouble. There seemed to be little reason to expend lives and be diverted from the inevitable end of the Nazis. Ewan was of two minds about this philosophy. The British Channel Islands were still under Nazi German occupation, the local commander having no intention of surrendering.

'Will we be going into the Straits of Otranto?' asked Tolley.

'Not until we get the whole squadron here. But we'll return to Malta first,' said Ewan.

The inactivity was beginning to concern Ewan. He had a growing feeling that this was not normal; there should be at least the odd boat or ship heading from Italy to Greece or, further still, to Palestine. There was nothing. In fact, one of the veteran petty officers made the same comment as Ewan. It was unusually quiet. Why?

A couple of hours passed. Tolley noticed Ewan looking at his watch. 'Thinking of turning for home, sir?' he said.

'Yes. Let's give another turn of the bay then make home. No sense in hanging around here. We can heave to off Catania for the night. Let the 701 know, but also keep an eye out for anything, and I mean anything,' said Ewan. He had a strange feeling of foreboding; it was a sense that had served him well in the past.

The MTBs were well on their way to returning to Malta, just about leaving the Bay of Taranto at midday, when MTB 701 flashed MTB 700 by Aldis lamp.

'It's 701 signalling, sir,' shouted Able Seaman Weaver, the MTB 700 signaller.

Ewan, Tolley, and PO Tom Reynolds looked to MTB 701.

Leading Seaman Dan Perry read out the Morse message as it was transmitted. 'ASDIC contact three thousand yards on our port beam.'

'Reply: "Hold your station. Advise if direction changes,"' instructed Ewan.

'You're wondering why I don't want to take any action?' said Ewan to Tolley. 'We maintain radio silence and keep on course because, if it is a U-boat, we need to know what it is up to.'

'Is this something to do with that Blackwell fellow I saw you talking to at our base?' said Tolley inquisitively, almost whispering.

Ewan grinned. 'Something like that. You know Blackwell?'

'I only know that he's probably behind our operation and that he doesn't wear a uniform, and that makes everyone nervous.'

'Enough said. Better you don't know too much at present,' retorted Ewan, grinning.

Tolley was about to acknowledge Ewan's advice, when their radar operator shouted, 'Surface contact, eight miles. Green 0-4-5.'

'What!' responded Ewan, surprised.

'Course, direction,' boomed Tolley.

'Due south 1-80 at about ten knots,' replied the radar operator.

Ewan thought for a moment and looked to Tolley and PO Reynolds. 'I'm guessing, but I think that U-boat isn't lining up to sink whatever the surface contact is.'

'Meeting up with it?' queried PO Reynolds.

'That's my guess,' agreed Ewan. 'But we can't take any chances. Steer south-south-east and go to fifteen knots. Tell 701 to do the same and follow abreast of us. That should confuse the U-boat. Then wait for my order to break away.'

'Do you think the U-boat has made us?' asked Tolley.

Ewan chuckled. 'If that U-boat captain is worth anything, he should have spotted us by now and at least picked up our ASDIC signal. But as we are line-abreast, he won't know that we are two boats—hopefully.'

The minutes passed. The radar operator reported, 'Surface contact should be visible now.'

The lookouts trained their binoculars in the direction of the surface contact. The low profile of the MTB to the surface did not allow for clear distance vision until they were about five or six miles away, at best. To confound their visibility, the hot glaring sunshine distorted the horizon.

'Got the contact, sir. Looks like an old freighter,' reported one of the lookouts.

'Close at full speed,' ordered Ewan.

'Action stations. All gun crews close up,' yelled Tolley. The alarm klaxon was sounded.

Everyone on board MTB 700 held on tightly as the MTB racked up her speed to forty knots.

MTB 701 spotted the sudden change of speed of MTB 700. Her skipper sounded action stations. The order from MTB 700 was flashed immediately—'Engage U-boat.'

MTB 700 closed on the rusty old freighter. Within five minutes they saw the violent eruptions of the sea from the depth charges dropped by MTB 701 onto the U-boat.

CHAPTER 11

SHELL SPLINTERS

ROYAL NAVAL HOSPITAL Bighi seemed quiet as Nursing Sister Hazel Jones made her way to the matron's office. Dressed in her white naval nursing uniform and still supporting her Voluntary Aid Detachment badge and fob watch, she attracted the attention of several servicemen, both orderlies and patients. She looked attractive and she knew it. The thought that such young men, and some older, were gazing at her put a spring in her step. She arrived at the matron's office at a few minutes before eight o'clock, the time she had been told to report. She was about to knock on the door, when almost by magic it opened. Out stepped a nurse who looked a little dejected. She stepped aside for Hazel to enter.

Once Matron Margaret Stanton spotted Hazel, her face lit up. 'Hazel! Great to see you. Come on in and sit yourself down.'

Hazel moved towards a chair and gave a glance back at the nurse, who left, closing the door behind her.

Margaret Stanton noticed Hazel's gaze at the nurse. 'Oh, I've just given her a telling-off. More of a dressing-down, if that's the right way to put it.'

Hazel's expression was one of questioning.

'That's Nurse Grayling. She's a very good nurse, but her off-duty antics are another matter. She came into the nurses' home late last night, which is not unusual, except she was carrying her bra in one hand and a glass of wine in the other. Alcohol is not allowed in the nurses' home. As for the other—well, I have it on good authority that a young naval sub lieutenant received an education! If you know what I mean?'

'So, nothing's changed then?' quipped Hazel.

'Too right. Anyway, I'm glad you're here. There will be plenty to do,' said Margaret Stanton, who then went on to explain what they were expecting. 'Hazel, the majority of casualties up to now have been servicemen from Italy, as you know. The high command have advised that we shall be getting prisoners of war, civilians—mainly refugees from the Balkans. We're getting some horrendous stories that take some believing, but then given your experience with the Gestapo three years ago—well, you know what I mean. Oh, sorry, shouldn't have brought that memory back.'

Hazel crumpled her lips and then smiled. 'No apology necessary. I'm over that now, thanks to Ewan. What about the POWs?'

'Not so much German and Italian; they're taken care of by the army. We are getting Allied POWs who have been badly treated in camps in Northern Italy. Also some escapees. They mainly need nourishing and convalescence before shipping home,' said Margaret.

'Home. Hmm. Where's home these days?'

'Some New Zealanders, Aussies, and Americans, and of course our lads.'

'OK, Margaret, or should I say Matron?'

'Oh, stick to Margaret—maybe Matron when you think we should be formal,' said Margaret. 'Right. Well, I'll get on, and you can familiarise yourself with the ward.'

Hazel began to leave, when Margaret added, 'How about meeting for lunch at one?'

Hazel sauntered around her ward. She noted that there seemed to be more equipment and a plentiful supply of bed linen and dressings. She acknowledged a nurse changing a patient's dressing. Eventually she entered the nursing sisters' office that doubled as the nurses' duty station;

it had a clear window across the entire ward. Sitting at the desk was Nurse Grayling. She was thumbing through several folders of patient notes and writing a few notes. She didn't hear Hazel or see her enter the office.

Hazel spoke, 'Nurse Grayling? Busy updating notes?'

Nurse Helen Grayling looked up suddenly. 'You must be Sister Jones!'

'Yes I am, and I am a stickler for good nursing practice, but informally you can call me Hazel. And your first name?'

'Oh, Helen. Helen Grayling, state registered nurse. Pleased to meet you,' she replied, and went on to give a status report of the ward. There were two other registered nurses and two auxiliaries, all taking a midmorning break. She went on to give an update on the patients under their care. There was no one demanding any special care except for a British soldier who was recovering from shell splinters in his legs.

'Shell splinters. I hate them. Always a high risk of infection. Is the patient stable?'

'Yes, Sister. His temperature is still elevated but not getting any worse.'

'Let me see,' said Hazel, knowing only too well that if the patient's temperature has not returned to normal quickly, it could mean that an infection is still present.

Helen Grayling led Hazel to Corporal Meaks's bed at the far end of the ward. The soldier, partly propped up in bed, eyed the two nurses approaching. He smiled. Helen picked up the temperature chart from the clipboard hanging on the foot of the bed and showed it to Hazel.

The temperature chart showed a steady temperature of 100°F. Hazel was concerned; the patient's temperature had been unchanged for five days.

'When was the last time Corporal Meaks was examined by the medical officer?'

Helen looked quizzically towards Hazel. 'Er, yesterday morning. He wasn't unduly concerned.'

Hazel was not impressed and knew otherwise. 'Who is the MO?'

'Second Lieutenant Crosby, RAMC.'

'The Royal Army Medical Corps must be getting desperate to put newly qualified doctors into the field,' said Hazel. 'I'll bet he's been here for less than a month and is just out of medical school?'

Helen Grayling gave a wry smile. 'How did you know? He's been here two weeks.'

'Seen it before. It's not in the normal training for doctors, or nurses for that matter; you pick it up from experience. I'll have a quiet word with our MO. For the time being, make sure that all wounds are cleaned with Lugol's iodine, and remove any fragments that might surface naturally. There's also some new antibacterial drugs available.'

'You certainly have been around,' said Helen. 'I mean, you know your stuff.'

'I'll take that as a compliment. So how about a cup of tea and then you take me through the other patients.'

The morning passed quickly. Helen introduced Hazel to the other staff when they returned from their break.

Matron Margaret Stanton entered the ward as Hazel was assisting one of the nurses to change a patient's dressings.

'I see you're getting involved,' said Matron Stanton.

'No other way of understanding how this ward is run,' said Hazel, grinning.

Matron beamed an approving grin. 'Time for lunch?'

Hazel checked the ward clock. 'Good God, where's the time gone?' She left the nurse to finish the patient's dressings and washed her hands at the sink at the entrance to the ward.

Hazel and Margaret strolled through the grounds of the hospital towards the cafeteria, near the hospital entrance. The blazing sunshine cast sharp beams through the olive trees. It was very warm at a few minutes to one o'clock. Hazel suddenly felt a shiver as a bead of sweat trickled down her spine.

'Are you OK, Hazel?' asked Margaret, seeing Hazel suddenly take in a deep breath.

'Oh yes, just had an uneasy feeling about a patient's shell splinters. Reminded me of my first encounter with Ewan. He was lucky—no splinters, just a few aggressive bruises and a slight burn. I just felt he might be in trouble. Silly of me really.'

'Not silly. Just intuition. Anyway, isn't he here?'

'No. He's out on a special patrol, but that's all I know. Apparently returning tomorrow afternoon,' said Hazel.

Margaret knew how close Hazel was to Ewan. 'Look, Hazel, things are rather quiet for the next few days. Why don't you take yourself off early tomorrow afternoon to his berthing quay? Kate Davies will know where it is.'

MTB 700 closed in on the freighter until she was less than three hundred yards away. The crew were all closed up at their action stations, the two 40 mm Oerlikon guns trained on the ship.

'Can only see some figures on the bridge,' said Tolley. He lowered his binoculars momentarily. 'Not much activity, if anything at all.'

'Sorry-looking rust bucket,' someone muttered.

'PO, hail them to heave to and be prepared to be boarded,' ordered Ewan.

He turned to Tolley. 'I don't like this. Throttle back. Reduce speed and come up on her stern.'

MTB 700 began to fall back on the ship's stern.

'It's the *San Agnes*, registered in Rimini,' said a gunner, who could just make out her markings through the aged paint, grime, and rust.

'She's a bit out of her way. Rimini is North Adriatic, captured by our lads several weeks ago,' said PO Reynolds.

'I wonder what she's doing down here?' mumbled Tolley.

'Break away,' bellowed Ewan.

The helmsman swung the MTB hard over to port before restraightening her. Suddenly there was a puff of smoke from the rear superstructure of the ship. A rocket tore past them, crashing into the sea fifty yards from their stern.

'That was a Panzerfaust!' said Ewan with a sick feeling.

The gun crews already had their fingers on their weapon triggers when Ewan shouted, 'Open fire!'

MTB 700 increased speed and circled the ship. Her main armament of 40 mm Oerlikon automatic guns pounded away at the upper structure of the ship, while four Vickers 303 heavy machine guns racked the decks. MTB 700 slowed back onto the port side of the ship. PO Reynolds repeated the order for her to heave to and stop engines.

'Tolley, get a boarding party together. Five men and me. We'll use the rubber dinghy. Don't want to get too close. I don't trust these bastards,' commanded Ewan to Tolley.

'Is that wise, sir? You're the flotilla commander. This is my job,' questioned Lieutenant Tolley.

'Eh? Oh, I suppose you're right. OK, but be careful. Take PO Reynolds with you; he can certainly handle himself,' replied Ewan, feeling a little dejected. He knew Tolley was correct.

The shipmaster ordered the Jacob's ladder to be slung over the side in readiness for the boarding party. There was not much buffeting from waves as the sea was relatively calm—a small blessing for a boarding party in a small rubber dinghy.

Ewan watched as the boarding party clambered up the swaying ladder. He looked around him and saw Leading Seaman Dan Perry clutching his rifle. Dan Perry was a marksman with a Lee–Enfield rifle, his favourite weapon, apart from being a good signaller. Dan Perry had guessed that the 'boss', Ewan, wanted him to cover the boarding party. They had served together in late 1942 when loaned to the Long Range Desert Group prior to the Battle of El Alamein. This was also the case with Petty Officer Tom Reynolds.

Tolley split the boarding party into three groups of two. He and a rating went to the bridge, while PO Reynolds and a rating examined the cargo holds. The remaining two ratings stayed on the main deck, observing and guarding the crew who had gathered. These two ratings, armed with Thompson sub-machine guns, could easily handle the crew if needed.

The captain of the *San Agnes* appeared nervous, thought Tolley.

'Do you speak English?' asked Tolley.

'A little. I am Italian,' replied the captain. 'I am Captain Messimo, and—'

Tolley interrupted. 'Before you protest about being boarded, you must realise that you are in hostile waters and—*and* you fired on my boat!'

Captain Messimo shrugged his shoulders and looked at the other members of his crew on the bridge and then towards the main deck below. The naval rating raised his Thompson sub-machine gun slightly; he sensed some tension on the bridge.

'Would you like to explain why you fired on us?' said Tolley impatiently.

'My crew are nervous. They thought you were Germans,' said Captain Messimo.

'Really?' retorted Tolley. 'So how did you acquire the German Panzerfaust?'

'I don't understand,' bleated Captain Messimo.

'Show me your log and papers,' demanded Tolley.

Tolley half expected the ship's log and carriage papers to be worn and tattered, but he was surprised to find that they were in a clean and neat condition. Suspicious, he thumbed through the papers and log.

After a few minutes, with a little uneasy shuffling by the ship's crew, PO Reynolds appeared on the bridge. Tolley looked up. 'Looks like crates of machine parts. Several weapons, all German, which we've secured. Anything here, sir?' reported PO Reynolds.

'Nothing that I can make heads or tails of. It's all in Italian,' said Tolley.

There was some whispering among the crew on the bridge and Captain

Messimo. PO Reynolds nodded his head to Tolley to go out onto the wing of the bridge.

'Sir, don't let on that I can understand Italian. I'm picking up from the crew that they're very nervous. Haven't found who fired on us though,' said PO Reynolds.

'Didn't know you speak Italian,' said Tolley.

'Learned a bit while with the boss in the North African desert and with the LRDG.'

'The boss speaks Italian?'

'Oh yes, fluently, and some German.'

'I think it's safe to bring the 700 boat alongside,' said Tolley. He was bemused by the revelations about Ewan and PO Reynolds. 'Somehow I think our commander will want to look at these papers and talk to the captain.'

MTB 700 came alongside the SS *San Agnes*. Three more ratings clambered aboard to strengthen the guard. Ewan made his way up to the bridge. Tolley showed Ewan the freight manifest and ship's log. He also noted, as Tolley had done, that the documents were in a clean and tidy condition, unlike the rest of the ship. After studying the documents, Ewan spoke with Captain Messimo.

'Captain. I am not satisfied with these papers or your log, so we are going to escort you into Catania,' said Ewan.

Captain Messimo shrugged his shoulders and cast a sickly grin to his crew of three on the bridge. They muttered some words in Italian about their escorting U-boat.

'Your U-boat has been sunk,' said Ewan in perfect Italian.

The surprised look on Captain Messimo's and his crew's faces was also one of disbelief.

Ewan turned to Tolley. 'The 701 got it and are picking up survivors. They'll follow us.'

'Bit of a catch today. And I thought this was going to be a quiet run,' said Tolley.

'I have a strange feeling that this is only the beginning,' said Ewan. 'I'll explain later,' he whispered and then turned to PO Reynolds. 'Keep a close eye on the crew. I think there are some cuckoos in the nest.'

PO Reynolds acknowledged Ewan's order. There were indeed some German Nazis among the crew.

Later that day, the MTBs entered Catania and turned over the ship to the naval commander for the port. The crew were taken away by the military police, along with the survivors of the sunk U-boat. Ewan advised the senior military police officer that he suspected there were hard-line Nazis among the crew who probably had fired on them. The two MTBs rode out at anchor a mile off Catania harbour and near to a destroyer. It was a comfort to have a large neighbour for the night.

CHAPTER 12

JONES'S EMPIRE

THE SHARP SHADOWS of the late afternoon sunshine began to succumb to the soft and blurred grey and amber of the early evening. Hazel strolled to the small harbour and quay where the special patrol group was stationed. The naval guards at the entrance recognised her from the previous day, when she was taken to 'Jones's Empire', a phrase coined by Captain Mark Williams, who, along with Kate, took Hazel to see what Ewan was up to. She had been introduced to Chief Petty Officer John Davy, who made it abundantly clear that she was welcome at all times and that if there was anything she needed, he and Jones's Empire would sort it.

'Mrs Jones, the boss should be here in about an hour,' said one of the guards. 'Would you like us to get you a cuppa?'

Hazel smiled approvingly. 'That would be great. I'll wander down to the first boat.'

'Right. I'll let them know,' said the guard, who ducked into the guard hut to phone the nearest boat, MTB 702.

Hazel turned momentarily back to the other guard. 'Who's the boss?'

'Oh, sorry, marm. It's Lieutenant Commander Jones. We've nicknamed him "the boss". Hope you don't mind.' The guard smiled, guessing it met with her approval.

'Boss, eh? What makes you think that I'm not the boss!' She chuckled.

'Oh, that's a good one. Thanks for the correction,' replied the guard, grinning.

Hazel gave a small flirtatious turn and made off for MTB 702.

The other naval guard emerged from the guardroom. 'Bob, what was all that about?'

'I think we've got a real special boss and not just a good senior officer.'

Hazel was met by a young-looking sailor holding a large mug of tea. He couldn't be more than eighteen years old, she thought. *Oh so young these days.*

'Tea, Mrs Jones?' said the rating, offering the mug.

Hazel took hold of the mug. 'Thanks. This is very welcome. Been a warm afternoon.'

'Is there anything else I can get you?'

'No, this is fine,' she replied, taking a sip of the tea. Somehow it tasted better than that on her hospital ward. She looked over the rating's shoulder to a young officer appearing on the small gangway. It was Sub Lieutenant John Marsden, skipper of MTB 702.

'Hello, Mrs Jones. Is Richards looking after you?' said Marsden, shooting a glance to Ordinary Seaman Richards.

'Yes,' said Hazel, raising her mug of tea. 'Tea is just fine.'

'Sorry, we don't have cups and saucers,' said Marsden.

'Sir, would you like a cuppa?' asked Richards.

'Good idea,' said Marsden. Richards scurried back on board MTB 702.

Hazel looked at a pile of crates and moved herself to sit on the one nearest.

'Things are a little spartan here. Not really geared up for visitors.'

'Same in the hospital. I've got a few hours off, so I have come down to greet the "boss", as you call my husband.'

'Oh, you've discovered our little secret.'

'You mean he doesn't know?'

'Er, that's right,' said Marsden hesitatingly. 'At least we don't think so.'

'Not a problem. I'll keep the secret, but I fancy he will approve,' said Hazel, smiling.

They continued to chat idly after Richards returned with Sub Lieutenant Marsden's tea.

The time seemed to melt away. They were joined by CPO Davy.

'Anything up, Chief?' asked Marsden.

'No, sir. They're due in about half an hour. Spotted off of Comino,' said CPO Davy.

'Right. I'll get the berthing hands to get ready. Maybe you will look after Mrs Jones?'

'My pleasure, sir.'

Marsden marched off back onto MTB 702.

'Is this just a routine patrol?' asked Hazel.

'Yes, ma'am, sort of. I can say that it was a bit of surveillance. Nothing dramatic.'

Hazel revealed a slight grin. Maybe she should not have asked.

'Am I OK here when the boats come alongside?'

'As good a place as any,' replied CPO Davy. 'Don't worry, if you were in the way, we would tell you.'

Hazel smiled. CPO Davy took her empty mug. He marched off onto MTB 702.

The sound of a whistle blowing could be heard from beyond the moored MTBs. It was from MGB 650. The shrill sound seemed to wake up all the boat's crew. Some one shouted over to Hazel, 'They're on their way in!'

CHAPTER 13

VALETTA

THE SHORT PARADE called by Ewan was to appraise the rest of the flotilla's crews of what the patrol had encountered. The only crew members not present were those on watch on their respective boats. Ewan had already seen Hazel waiting on the quayside and had given her a short wave. She knew that he needed to debrief his crews and put the others in the picture. It all took less than ten minutes. The parade was dismissed by CPO Davy, then Ewan strode off to greet Hazel. Without any care for who might be watching, Ewan hugged Hazel and gave her a big kiss.

'I guess you missed me?' she said softly.

'Now what makes you think that?'

'I can see you've got some new toys,' she said, nodding to the moored MTBs.

'Yes. Although I can play with them, playing with you is far better.'

'So that's what you want to do, play with me?' She giggled.

'What else is there?'

'I think Chief Davy wants you,' Hazel said, looking over Ewan's shoulder.

'Er, what? Oh, er, yes. I need him to sort out a duty rota and things,' he replied, but then, thinking aloud, he quizzed her. 'You know CPO Davy?'

'Yes. I popped down here yesterday. That's when I found out that you were out playing with a couple of your boats. Chief Davy introduced me to some of the crew and skippers and showed me around. And they gave me tea,' she replied, followed by a big grin.

He turned away. 'Back in a couple of minutes.'

Hazel could not take her eyes off of him. She wanted him so badly but had to hide her desire. She fidgeted her feet and slowly strolled in a circle around a large crate.

Ewan spoke with CPO Davy and asked him to arrange the off-duty for all crews, telling him to clear it with the individual skippers but make a note of where everyone was going just in case they were summoned to put to sea at short notice.

'You've got a feeling that something is afoot?' CPO Davy asked.

'Yes. I've given Lieutenant Callendar my report to go to the admiral. I shouldn't wonder if something happens after he reads it.'

'Yes, sir, I agree. PO Reynolds and Leading Seaman Perry said you've been blessed with a sixth sense that is usually right,' replied CPO Davy.

'Er, yes. And that reminds me. Can you call them over to me and my wife? It will be a surprise for her.'

'Certainly will, sir,' said CPO Davy. 'Of course, they were in the desert with you.'

Ewan rejoined Hazel and returned a salute to Lieutenant Callendar, who was marching off to take Ewan's patrol report to Admiral Kelly. Callendar shot Hazel a warm smile.

'I think Jimmy Callendar likes you,' said Ewan.

'He is rather good-looking,' noted Hazel. She turned away from the MTBs and looked towards the entrance to the quay.

Ewan took her by the arm, ready to walk off. 'Got a surprise for you.'

'Surprise?' she said, instinctively looking back to see two sailors marching at the double towards them.

'Good God! Tom Reynolds and Dan Perry.'

They closed quickly. Putting protocol aside, they shook her hand.

'This is one of the best surprises I've ever had. So you two are covering Ewan's back.'

'Something like that, Mrs Jones. It's good to see you. And are we allowed to say,' said Tom Reynolds, looking to Ewan, 'that you're looking great?'

'Steady on, lads. You'll make me jealous,' replied Ewan, grinning.

'Anyway, sir, see you tomorrow,' said PO Tom Reynolds. He saluted.

'Yes, but it won't be too early. Now get off with you both and have a night out on the town. You deserve it.'

They parted. Hazel hooked her arm into Ewan's arm. They strolled to the guardroom, outside of which was a jeep.

A naval guard approached them and told Ewan that the jeep had been arranged for him by HQ to take them to the officers' club. Ewan thanked the guard and saw Hazel safely into the passenger seat.

'Not exactly a carriage to the ball, my dear, but at least we will be alone.'

'This is just fine. Are we going to our quarters first to get washed and changed before you take me out?' she said.

Ewan did not need to answer, but beamed a big grin.

He drove the jeep slowly over the short dusty road connecting his flotilla's harbour at Dragonara with the main road in St Julians that led to Valetta. Their new quarters were in Sliema, overlooking Manoel Island and Marsamxett Harbour, which was on the near side of Valetta and the Grand Harbour, with Fort St Angelo, Naval HQ, on the southern side of the Grand Harbour.

Ewan parked the jeep next to another jeep and a line of shabby, dust-shrouded old sedans that had seen better days. Hazel did not need any help alighting from the jeep; she thought that the passenger seat was as comfortable as the Austin truck ride from the airfield when she arrived in Malta. Fortunately, Ewan drove fairly slowly, even though he exhibited an urgent desire to get to their quarters when on clear and flat stretches of road. The journey took about ten minutes.

The door to their quarters slammed shut as Ewan kicked it to close. Hazel was barely able to slip off her shoes when Ewan grabbed her about the waist and pulled her onto him in a tight grip. They kissed and entwined their bodies with such passion that no words were spoken until after a few minutes, when Ewan opened the front of her nurse's uniform.

'I need to take a breath,' Hazel mumbled. Feeling her hands wending their way into his shirt, he continued to undo her uniform buttons.

Within seconds she had removed his shirt and was working on the belt to his naval white shorts. She was completely void of any clothing except for her panties. She felt a trickle of sweat dribble down her spine. Then Ewan's impulsive desire slowed as he gently pulled down her panties.

There was no ceremony; they simply lay on top of the bed and made love.

He eventually slipped off her, and she turned on her side to hold him, which he welcomed. There was a silence and a contentment joining them together.

Hazel ran her finger across Ewan's chest. 'You've hardly said a word to me.'

'I'm just so glad that you are here with me. I love you very much. Hate it when we have to be parted. That whole D-Day affair drove me to distraction. It was the thought of you that kept me going. Hopefully we will only have a couple of days apart when we're on patrol.'

'You've never mentioned much about D-Day. Yet from what I've heard, you had a bad time of it but didn't lose a boat. Surely that was good,' she said gently and softly.

He turned, looked deeply into her eyes, and put on a guarded grin.

'Jerry had a bad time.'

'Huh,' she croaked, wondering what he meant.

'The German E-boats were good and damned dangerous, but we

were able to fend them off and sink several. They took a lot of casualties. Then the weather turned to a storm. Caused chaos.' He chuckled. 'Biggest problem we had was seasickness.'

Hazel felt there was a hurt in his voice as he continued. 'The German E-boat crews were good, but somehow we were better. We fished several Germans out of the water. Many were just youngsters. Reminded me of my days here in Malta in '42. I'll be glad when this lousy war is over. I think we all will.'

'I didn't know you felt like this. It's gotten to you, hasn't it?'

'Yes it has, and now our bloody allies the Russians are playing silly buggers. What's it all about? I really don't understand it. Why can't we all get on with working for peace?'

'Yes, I think I know what you mean. The Russians, I mean,' said Hazel, running her hand across his shoulder as though soothing away a hurt.

Ewan propped himself up on his elbows and looked furtively at her. 'What do you know about the Russians?'

'Oh, nothing really, except I had a strange encounter when I arrived.'

Ewan slid his hand across her breasts, caressing them gently. 'Tell me.'

She went on to explain what had happened, how the British soldiers rescued her, and how Admiral Kelly had taken an interest.

'So, Admiral Kelly mentioned the NKVD to you?'

Hazel pursed her lips and nodded.

'The question is, why should they be interested in you?' said Ewan.

'Yes. That's what the admiral wondered too,' said Hazel.

For a moment Ewan felt helpless and forgot that he was handling her breasts.

She suddenly flinched as he pinched one of her nipples. 'Ooh!'

'Oh, sorry, my mind was elsewhere,' he said, and then began sucking her pinched nipple.

She writhed under his amorous attention.

'Make love to me again,' she murmured.

An hour later they had showered and changed into fresh uniforms.

Ewan led Hazel down the stairs of their quarters to the road outside, where he was able to hail a taxi to take them into Valetta. Although Valetta was only a mile across the harbour, the roadway was nearly three miles into the centre of the city.

It was still relatively early at seven, when they arrived at the Schooner Restaurant. It was a popular place to eat out among all services and especially the navy; the clientele was a sea of white navy uniforms with a smattering of RAF light blue and British Army light khaki. It was already busy, but a waiter was able to find them a table. Ewan hoped that they would not meet anyone he knew as he wanted the evening alone with Hazel. She felt the same.

As they were being guided to a table, Ewan spotted Captain Ross of the cruiser HMS *Bermuda*. They exchanged glances and smiles. He also saw in the shadows near the stairs, which led to private apartments, Henry Blackwell and John Cross. They made no recognition of Ewan, even though they had seen him enter the restaurant with Hazel. Ewan, guessing they did not want show any outward association, transferred his vision back to Hazel and the waiter who had shown them to a vacant table.

The waiter provided a small wine list and menu. Hazel began to study the menu.

'This menu is certainly substantial compared to back home,' said Hazel, who then looked to Ewan. 'I see two characters from our past are here?'

'Er, yes. Don't look round to them as I think they don't want to be acknowledged.'

'So are they up to their usual tricks?'

Ewan smirked. 'Something like that. I can explain later.'

'You're not involved with them, are you?' Hazel asked with a reluctant tone.

'Sort of. Don't worry. It's pretty well a routine operation,' said Ewan in a low voice.

'I've heard that one before.'

Ewan put his arm across the table and met her hand on the menu. He squeezed her hand gently. 'Truly, nothing to worry about. I'll explain later. For now, let's get a bottle of local Maltese white. And how about a fish main—or would you prefer rabbit?'

The bottle of Maltese white wine was delivered and served by a waiter, who quickly said that it was by courtesy of two gentlemen, nodding in the direction of Blackwell and Cross. Ewan turned to them. They both grinned and raised their glasses to him and Hazel.

The evening passed by quietly. The restaurant began to slowly empty, leaving three couples, including Ewan and Hazel. A naval rating entered the restaurant. Ewan raised his hand, attracting his attention. 'Hazel, my dear, our carriage awaits.'

The rating nodded to Ewan, and left. Ewan summoned the waiter and paid the bill.

Ewan and Hazel approached the rating, who stood beside a Naval HQ staff car.

'Staff car. How did you arrange that?' asked Hazel.

'Courtesy of Third Officer Kate Davies. An amazingly resourceful woman.'

'I do believe you fancy her,' said Hazel as she stepped inside the car, the rating holding the door open for her.

Ewan sat beside her on the rear seat. The rating shut the door.

'I think Alec Gratton would have something to say about that,' said Ewan.

'Do you mean they are together?'

'That's my understanding,' said Ewan. 'She is attractive though.'

His comment beckoned a small dig into his ribs.

The driver drove carefully, avoiding ruts in some roads and the odd cat and stray dog.

Ewan and Hazel exchanged very few words on the journey, Hazel taking the opportunity to snuggle up to Ewan, not caring what the driver could observe in his rear-view car mirror.

They left the car outside the entrance to their quarters. Hazel hooked her arm into Ewan's and looked passionately at him. It was a warm smile; Ewan felt it.

'Is there something on your mind?' he said.

'Blackwell and Cross. Where do you fit in with them?' she spoke softly.

'I can tell you that I'm leading a special patrol group tasked with surveillance and interception in a wider intelligence operation. What concerns me is your being followed by Russian spies. That is, unless they are targeting me through you! Why, is the question. It doesn't make sense, but John Cross will be briefing me tomorrow.'

'Does this include me?' Hazel asked, gripping Ewan's arm more tightly as they approached their quarters.

'Yes. Was going to tell you earlier but needed to think it through. Stupid me. Should have told you earlier.'

They went to bed immediately with Hazel cuddling closely up to Ewan, which made her feel safe. She had an uncomfortable sense that something unusual was afoot.

CHAPTER 14

NURSE GRAYLING

THE MORNING SUN shone relentlessly into their apartment within the naval officers' quarters. The only part of their quarters that was free from the searing sun was the small kitchen. It was here that Hazel hid while boiling a kettle to make a pot of Taylor's Earl Grey tea. Ewan was in the bathroom taking advantage of the cooling shower. He emerged in the lounge with only a large white bath towel wrapped around him. He opened the French windows and let in the sun. Flinching to protect himself from the blinding sunshine, he sat on one of two wooden canvas loungers. Hazel joined him with the pot of tea and two mugs; she had already put milk into each of the mugs. As she placed the pot of tea and mugs down on a small low table between the loungers, she greeted Ewan with a cheeky smile. 'I'll just get the sugar.'

'You might want to get at least a towel on. It's not that private on this balcony.'

Hazel swung her body to face him fully, placing her hands on her hips. 'But you don't object.'

'Nope—but what about the balcony opposite? I think some young lieutenant is in residence. He might be spying on you,' said Ewan, grinning.

Hazel returned with a small bowl of sugar. 'I don't think he's interested in me; he's got other things on his mind.'

'How d'ya know?'

'I spotted him yesterday morning when he opened his window. He has a friend. She has a better body than me and is younger. Makes me feel a bit inferior. He's nice-looking though.'

Ewan puckered his lips. 'Ooh! I like the bit of inferiority—at least it's only a bit. So, you've got your eyes on young officers?'

'That's a bit wild of you,' she said. 'I do believe you're jealous.'

'I certainly am. Now what are you going to do about it?' challenged Ewan.

Hazel spun around, tugged his towel off, and sat astride him. She lowered her upper body onto his chest.

'Just a tiny bit inferior, eh?'

'Not much,' he said softly, wrapping his arms around her.

Forty minutes later they were getting ready to leave for their individual duties. Ewan remarked about the young lieutenant and his friend. Hazel said she recognised him as a lieutenant when she was in the officers' club, then added, 'Funny thing though. I'm sure I recognise his friend. Seen her recently, but with her clothes on.'

Ewan laughed.

Hazel changed the subject. 'When will we be seeing Blackwell?'

'Not sure. Kate will let you know,' Ewan answered.

They parted as Hazel recognised the small bus that was waiting to take her to RNH Bighi. Ewan was picked up by a jeep from his harbour base.

The small bus, part of the naval motor pool, stopped en route to pick up other nurses, before arriving at RNH Bighi twenty minutes later. Hazel recognised another nurse. The two of them walked together to Ward 5, Hazel's ward. The other nurse, Marjory Shaw, pointed to Nurse Helen Grayling, who was emerging from the nursing sisters' office and seemed to be in a rush.

'What's the hurry?' Nurse Marjory Shaw asked.

'Hope I haven't missed the bus! Got a date in Valetta,' she replied, agitated.

'Oh! Right.' Marjory giggled. She threw a grin to Hazel, who laughed.

They entered the office to find, to their surprise, Matron Margaret Stanton seated at the desk. She looked up. 'Hazel. Nurse Shaw.'

'Yes, Matron,' said Hazel. 'Nurse Grayling in trouble again?'

'No, not this time,' Margaret replied. 'I've accidentally kept her over her shift time. That's why she's in a hurry. Got a date, I suspect.'

'Is there a problem?' Hazel asked, suspecting there was.

'Yes. I'm afraid so. Sister Till is off sick. Flu. I covered for her last night for the night shift, but to make matters worse, two of the auxiliary nurses have gone down with it also, so you'll be short-handed today. Anyway, let's get the handover done, and then I'll be in my office for an hour before going off for a rest,' said Margaret.

With the handover completed, Hazel worked with Marjory to attend to the patients whom they had on the ward. It was just as well that they had only a few and were far short of the full capacity. Nevertheless, it took them more than two hours to complete the basic nursing needs of each patient and administer the various drugs and medicines. At twelve o'clock, a couple of nurses from another ward came to relieve them for a break so they could get something to eat and drink.

They finished their break and returned to the ward. Marjory went into the ward to make a cursory check on the patients, while Hazel started on some paperwork that bedevilled such nursing managers. She preferred the direct patient contact but also accepted that the administration of patient records was just as vital.

Hazel's concentration on a patient's notes was interrupted by a phone call.

'Hello, Sister Jones, Ward 5,' she said.

'Good afternoon, Sister Jones. Third Officer Pickering, admissions, here. Just to update you, we have no new admissions for you today or tonight. You can take it easy. Matron will sort out your auxiliary nurses later this afternoon.'

'Oh, that's good. Does that mean that Nurse Shaw and I will be signing off at eight?'

'At present, certainly. Enjoy the rest of the day,' replied Third Officer Pickering.

Hazel replaced the handset on the cradle.

Marjory Shaw appeared. 'An admission?'

'No. Quite the opposite. I think we're off the hook for new admissions, at least until tomorrow. We should get away on time tonight as long as Matron can get us a night shift.'

'You know, Sister Jones, I do believe that you are bringing us good luck,' said Marjory.

Hazel simply smiled.

The afternoon drifted on towards early evening. It gave both Hazel and Marjory a chance to engage in conversation with their patients. They were both cognisant that this helped the healing process by not leaving patients alone to possibly wallow in their worries and concerns and, of course, self-pity.

It was a few minutes to seven when the phone rang; it had been silent for most of the afternoon. 'Hello, Sister Jones, Ward 5.'

'Hazel. Margaret here. We have a full nursing shift for this evening, so you and Nurse Shaw can make whatever arrangements you want to for this evening. Staff Nurse Lemmings will be with you shortly; she'll be in charge for tonight.'

'Thank you, Matron. I'll give the good news to Nurse Shaw now,' said Hazel.

'Hazel, don't thank me just yet. Tomorrow you will be very busy. We're expecting a large intake from Venice and Brindisi, Italy—both our lads and some Italian soldiers fighting with us. Your Italian will be much in demand. Have a good evening. You'll need it. Oh, one more thing: I'm giving Nurse Grayling the evening off also as she'll be working with you tomorrow.'

Hazel and Marjory completed the handover to the night shift. They met the waiting bus at the main entrance. 'Have you anything planned for this evening?' Marjory asked.

'No, nothing. Not sure what Ewan will be doing. He hasn't contacted me, so I guess he is busy. Why? Do you fancy meeting up for a drink?'

'We might need it if tomorrow is going to be a heavy day.'

'Right. After dinner, meet at the officers' club, say, about nine. Ewan might join us.'

The bus tumbled along the dusty, potholed road to their respective naval quarters, with Marjory staying in a special wing reserved for nurses.

As Hazel approached the main entrance to her quarters, she got her pass ready to show to the naval guard, but she didn't need it.

'Ah, Nurse Jones. Lieutenant Commander Jones sends his apologies. He is likely to be late this evening and suggests you meet with him in the officers' club if you want,' said the naval guard.

'Oh, right. Thanks. I was planning on that anyway,' Hazel replied.

Hazel made her way through the small garden to her block of flats. She passed an adjacent block for single men. To her surprise, she saw Nurse Helen Grayling leaving the foyer door.

Helen Grayling recognised Hazel. 'Oh, good evening, Sister Jones. I understand I'm with you tomorrow.'

'Yes, er, you are,' said Hazel, taken a little by surprise. 'Are you off out?'

'Yes, but only to the nurses' home; my partner for this evening has been recalled to duty,' said Helen.

'Oh yes, that nice young naval lieutenant I saw you with,' said Hazel without thinking, remembering the image she had seen from her balcony that morning.

'Yes. It was at the officers' club, wasn't it?'

'Er, yes,' squeaked Hazel, almost gagging on her breath. 'I'm off to the officers' club at nine with Marjory Shaw. Why don't you join us?'

'That's a good idea. OK. See you later,' said Helen, which seemed to put a spring in her step as she walked towards the nurses' home.

Hazel thought for a moment. What had Helen been doing all day? Had she rested from her night duty, or had she been with the young naval lieutenant? So what? They were young and should enjoy themselves when they can. The war wasn't over yet, and no one knew what the future held in store.

Hazel met Marjory and Helen at the main entrance to the nurses' home. She noticed that both were chatting to two naval guards, who seemed to be enjoying their company. Hazel could only guess what was on their minds; it certainly wasn't their guard duty. A jeep arrived with an army lance corporal driving. 'Your transport, ladies,' said one of the naval guards.

'Who arranged this?' Hazel asked.

'I did,' said Helen, putting on a big grin.

'I forget. You have all sorts of connections!' perked Marjory.

Hazel chuckled and realised that Helen Grayling might be an asset even if her reputation was somewhat suspect.

The lance corporal dropped them off at the officers' club. It wasn't every day he had three attractive women, and nurses at that, to chauffer around. It made him feel good. He only wished he could spend the evening with them, and possibly the night with at least one. Hazel could detect the lance corporal's attention.

The three women entered the club lounge, causing several heads to turn. Hazel spoke first: 'OK, we're a gang of three and can fend off any of these marauding girl-hungry matelots.'

'Speak for yourself,' said Helen. 'There's an army captain I fancy at the bar. You can have the sailors.'

'So much for looking out for each other. Ah well, drinks,' said Marjory.

The club steward directed them to a vacant table near to the veranda and took their bar order: three G and Ts. The warm late evening Malta air drifted through the lounge from the veranda. Eventually, the army captain came to their table as their drinks arrived.

'Well, Nurse Helen Grayling, we meet again,' he said.

'Yes. Let me introduce my colleagues,' said Helen. There was a formality to her tone.

With the introductions over, the army captain, Edward Simms, asked what plans they had.

Hazel jumped in, saying, 'I'm not sure about these two, but my husband may be joining us later. But don't let me spoil the evening.'

'How about I simply keep an eye on all three of you. Would that help? Sort of an escort,' he replied.

'That'll be a good idea. That's if you don't mind. We've got a pretty heavy day ahead of us tomorrow,' said Helen, to both Hazel's and Marjory's surprise.

'I quite understand, but I will make sure you get the steward's attention,' he replied, then left for the bar.

'Now there's a surprise, Helen. You sure you want to be with just us?' asked Hazel.

Helen's reply was another pleasant surprise. 'Hazel, I know I've gotten myself a bit of a reputation. I like a good time, but I do take my nursing duties seriously.'

Hazel and Marjory exchanged nods and grins of approval.

The evening changed into early night-time. At eleven, the three women decided to leave. It was not any surprise that Helen had arranged transport back to the naval officers' quarters and nurses' home. The driver was the same lance corporal. He dropped them off at the main entrance to their quarters, where the naval guards were quite visible. They alighted from the jeep and began to make their way to their respective blocks. Hazel turned and saw the lance corporal jump out of the jeep and speak with the naval guards. She and others did not know that the lance corporal had suspected that they had been followed and reported it to the naval guards. The guards reported the driver's concern to their HQ.

CHAPTER 15

THE MALTESE CONNECTION

IT WAS ONE o'clock in the morning when Ewan arrived home. He tried not to disturb Hazel, but she was a light sleeper. This was nearly always her sleep pattern when Ewan was not with her. She found him in the kitchenette drinking a glass of water.

'Wouldn't you like tea?' she said sleepily.

'Good idea. It's been a long day, and tomorrow isn't going to be any easier. I've also heard that you are going to be busy too,' said Ewan wearily.

'You get into bed and I'll bring you a cuppa,' she said.

A few minutes later, Hazel brought Ewan a cup of tea, but he was asleep, dog-tired and half undressed. She covered him lightly with a single sheet and got back into bed beside him, following him into a deep sleep.

Hazel awoke at seven with the gleaming sunshine heralding a new day. Ewan was in the position she had left him in six hours earlier. The cup of tea was still on the small bedside table, now cold. The room was very warm; the evening had not cooled it. She crept, sliding stealthily from the bed and to the bathroom, and closed the door, hoping not to wake him. She ran the shower, relying on the unheated water to cool her. It did. It was invigorating. She felt clean and refreshed.

Hazel dried herself with a large white naval-issue bath towel but allowed herself to remain a little damp for comfort. She opened the bathroom door to be confronted by Ewan rubbing his eyes. She stood before him naked but still clutching the towel.

'Now that's a welcome sight,' he said feebly, still tired.

'Steady, tiger. I don't think you're up to anything, more's the pity.' She chuckled.

He wrapped his arms around her. 'I can try.'

'I don't have time. And somehow I'll bet you haven't either.'

He glanced at his wristwatch and struggled to focus on the clock face, showing ten past seven. 'Hell! You're right,' he mumbled. 'I've to be back in HQ at eight.'

'You shower. I'll make tea and some toast.'

Fifteen minutes later, the two of them were sitting opposite each other in the lounge, drinking tea and munching on the last slices of toast, each with a dollop of marmalade. Hazel had bought some provisions once she had found their quarters.

They both agreed that the next few days were likely to be intensive and hard work, realising that although together, they might not have much time with each other. However, Ewan had not told Hazel in any detail what he was doing or that he had an urgent meeting with John Cross and Henry Blackwell; she assumed his immediate meeting was with his commanding officer and Admiral Kelly. Ewan knew that Hazel had not really forgiven the two MI6 officers for their past escapades, which nearly cost her her life and that of Ewan.

The hospital transport took Hazel and other nurses from the nurses' home to RNH Bighi and other hospitals and clinics as usual.

Ewan paced slowly at the main entrance to their quarters, waiting for his jeep. One of the new duty naval guards spoke with Ewan and informed him of the lance corporal's suspicion that Hazel had been followed the previous night. Ewan was concerned. What was this all about? Why did it involve Hazel—or did it?

Ewan arrived at Admiral Kelly's office exactly at eight, the scheduled time for their meeting. Also present was John Cross, Commander Alec Gratton, and Captain Mark Williams. Admiral Kelly was in a gruff mood, having spent a late night discussing the problem they were about to tackle with his American counterpart in Rome, and getting nowhere.

'Ah, Commander, come in. Bang on time, not like some. Any idea where Blackwell is?' the admiral said, looking to Cross for an answer.

'Not sure, Admiral. I know he stopped off at the signals office,' Cross replied sheepishly.

'Hmm. Well, let's get on with it. We have a busy day ahead. Gratton, give us an update,' ordered Admiral Kelly.

Commander Gratton gave a concerned look to the admiral. 'Our latest intelligence suggests that things are moving faster than we first thought. There is also a considerable level of confusion, which I will explain in a moment. Ewan, that ship you intercepted'—he looked at Ewan—'revealed something we had not considered. It was carrying what seemed to be machine parts, in fact described in the manifest as "agricultural machinery", and was bound for Brazil. Here's the first bit of confusion. Our agents in Brazil and the Brazilian government have no knowledge of this. Their thought is that it was bound for Argentina. That's one issue. The next is really odd. Nationalist partisans in Albania have reported seeing SS Panzer officers talking to communist partisans, which is most unlikely. However, this has been sort of confirmed by Tito's partisans in Yugoslavia. They loathe the SS and the Germans for that matter. Also, although Tito is a communist, he doesn't trust the Russians, and there's every indication he's wary of the NKVD.'

'What's the bottom line?' said Admiral Kelly, searching to understand the puzzle.

'We thought that the SS Panzer division, which we have been following, was trying to get back to Germany. General Alexander's Eighth Army is moving on to Austria, so that cuts off that route. The bottom line, or should I say the top line, Admiral, is that we need to find out what that Nazi SS Panzer division is up to and exactly where it is.'

The admiral glanced to Ewan. 'And, Commander, this is where you come in, I guess.'

'Yes it is,' added Gratton.

John Cross now added his requirement: 'We want you to take your flotilla or fleet, or whatever you call it, with some commandos in case you get into trouble, and make a sweep of the Albanian coast—recce the area. We have some aerial recon photos which show that the Panzers are held up in a valley on the main coastal road from Tirana, but we don't have the exact location. We haven't got much idea of its strengths, but by all accounts it is well provisioned with fuel, ammunition, and other supplies.'

'Commander Jones, this isn't going to be an easy ride, which Blackwell has suggested,' said Admiral Kelly, looking deeply to Cross. 'And where is he?'

John Cross did not answer, but his body language indicated that he agreed with the admiral. Ewan was about to ask a question, when in walked Henry Blackwell.

'At last! Are you gracing us with your presence?' jibed Admiral Kelly. He certainly disliked intelligence spies, particularly when they seemed to hold themselves aloof from everyone else, but he accepted that they were an essential part of any military operation.

'Apologies, Admiral, but I received an important coded signal. We have some important news,' said Blackwell. He looked at every person in turn before continuing. 'Hitler is dead.'

'What!' someone exclaimed.

'Does that mean the war here is over?' asked Ewan, rather naively.

'It won't be long now, but now the real fun begins. The Russians are playing silly buggers. They're already demanding that we withdraw behind agreed lines. Montgomery, in the north, has reached the Baltic and has dug deep towards the Polish border. And by all accounts, Patton has done the same in the south. He should be meeting up with Alexander coming up from Italy. However, there's a lot of isolated German Army groups scattered across Central Europe. The news may not have reached them yet, but there are stories that large numbers of German forces are surrendering.'

'Gentlemen, we need to be on our guard, especially at sea,' said Admiral Kelly, shooting a glance to Ewan. 'U-boats are still active. I was told last night that the Americans captured, or should I say took the surrender of, two U-boats in Genoa. By all accounts, that leaves at least another four lurking around here and particularly in the Adriatic.' Admiral Kelly looked more intensely at Ewan. 'Take no chances. If in any doubt, sink the sods!'

'When do we set off?' asked Ewan.

Admiral Kelly turned to Henry Blackwell. 'It's your show. When?'

'Tomorrow morning, just before daybreak,' replied Blackwell. Looking towards Ewan, he asked, 'Will you be ready?'

'We're ready,' Ewan responded.

Commander Gratton chipped in, 'Ewan, I'm arranging for a small detachment of naval commandos to meet with you at Brindisi. They will be your insurance, and they are well versed in reconnoitring hostile territory. I will also be with them. I'm flying to Brindisi tomorrow. We'll see you when you put in. Should be day after tomorrow.'

'Right.'

'One more thing,' said Admiral Kelly. 'Gratton will have your sealed orders.' Admiral Kelly looked around the room. 'Any questions?'

Captain Mark Williams coughed slightly.

'You've been remarkably quiet, Captain Williams. You have a question?'

'An observation, Admiral. My military police lads have been monitoring suspected NKVD agents. They seem to be taking an interest in you, Ewan.' He stared at Ewan. 'And your wife!'

'Yes, I understand Hazel has been followed, but why?'

Admiral Kelly gestured to Cross.

'We think they're trying to get you to reveal details, especially dates, times, and the areas of patrol of your mission, not by threatening you but by threatening your wife!' said Cross.

'They're mad,' retorted Ewan.

'They're bloody dangerous and not to be underestimated,' shot in Blackwell.

'We're on to it, so no need to worry. Any approach you get, let us know, preferably quietly so they will not fully understand that we have them tagged,' said Cross.

'Ewan, you also take care. I'm also keeping an eye this,' added Admiral Kelly, dropping the formalities of rank.

The meeting broke up with Ewan scurrying off to his flotilla of MTBs. The others went their own ways, but John Cross remained to talk with Admiral Kelly.

'Admiral, for yours ears only. Henry Blackwell is off on a jaunt to sort out this situation. In fact, he's flying off now. I can't tell you where,' said Cross.

'Cross, I know that the NKVD get up to all manner of nefarious acts and that this with Ewan's wife is one of their usual ploys. Ewan Jones can look after himself, but his wife, Hazel?'

'We have her under surveillance. Haven't told her anything, but we think that the NKVD are desperate to find out as much as they can of this operation. Admiral, what makes this whole affair important is that we believe we have at least one mole, a Russian spy, in our operations department in London—maybe more than one.'

'So that's why the Admiralty are using Naval Intelligence as well,' said Admiral Kelly.

'Also, MI5, the Security Service, are taking an active interest back home,' added Cross. 'The war with Germany may be over, but another with Stalin is looming.'

'Christ's sake, where is all this leading?'

'Don't know, Admiral. But if we can neutralise that SS Panzer group, it will put a big dent in Uncle Joe Stalin's Balkan plans.'

'You know, Cross, it still doesn't make sense, the Russians in cahoots with the Nazis.'

John Cross puckered his lips. 'Admiral, that's the bit that I don't like. Somehow I get the feeling that we're not getting the whole picture.'

'And Ewan hopefully will be able to shed some light on it,' muttered the admiral, half under his breath. 'I think we need to get a little insurance in case he runs into trouble.'

John Cross looked quizzically to Admiral Kelly. *Insurance.* He thought for a moment. *Now what does the admiral mean by that?*

CHAPTER 16

BRINDISI

ROYAL NAVAL HOSPITAL Bighi, Ward 5, was buzzing with activity, as were several of the other wards, with auxiliary nurses making up beds with fresh linen in readiness for the expected large intake of injured servicemen. Although the war in Europe was coming to a close, the endgame was attracting more casualties among the Allied forces as die-hard Nazi troops fought on. These were mainly fanatical SS. The fighting was remorseless, almost suicidal, as the Allied commanders pressed on. On the other hand, the Wehrmacht, German Army, were surrendering in droves, including senior officers. They recognised the futility of carrying on a war where their fate effectively had been sealed ten months earlier on D-Day, 6 June 1944. This now posed an additional and greater burden for the management of prisoners of war (POWs). There was also the associated catastrophe of thousands of displaced people of several nationalities. Indeed, this was exacerbated by the deluge of refugees who were not sure of their national status; they were effectively stateless. However, the immediate issue was the large number of Allied injured servicemen, which was causing a strain on the military medical services. Thankfully, the number of injured naval personnel had diminished greatly, but this was offset by the increase in army casualties. Therefore, it was inevitable that the Royal Naval Hospitals would take on this important role and relieve the pressure on the Royal Army Medical Corps' hospitals.

By midmorning, Ward 5 had settled into a routine. The 'organised mayhem' that had been described by a nurse earlier was now calming. A break was needed. At ten-thirty Hazel sent off half her nurses for a tea break, while the others, including her, began to wind down their work, switching generally to administration. Hazel had put Nurse Helen Grayling in charge of replenishing the linen stores. The last beds were made up for receiving patients; a nurse provided jugs of water at each bedside locker, covered to keep out dust. The windows to the ward were open as it was already approaching another hot day. The air-circulating fans were working but did not seem to make any difference; the place was getting stifling.

At eleven the relieved nurses returned and Hazel released the others, which included her and Helen. As they were leaving Ward 5 to go to the canteen, Nursing Sister Chaloner from Ward 4 stopped them.

'Hazel, Matron would like to see you both when you return from break.'

'Do you know what it's about?' asked Hazel, guessing it was an update on arrivals.

'Not sure, Hazel. Might have something to do with me releasing one of my staff nurses to work with you,' said Nursing Sister Chaloner, who then disappeared to her ward.

'More work, I suppose,' grumbled Helen.

'Can't see how we can. We've squeezed in six more beds, which puts us way over capacity. Well, let's get a cuppa and find out later,' said Hazel.

Hazel and Helen finished their tea within twenty minutes and strode off to the matron's office, sensing that they should be back at Ward 5 as soon as possible for the intake.

Hazel knocked on the matron's door, which was ajar.

'Come in,' said Matron Margaret Stanton.

They entered the office expecting the worst, namely greater numbers than expected.

'Hazel, Helen, you are both being reassigned as a matter of urgency. Come back here at six, when I will have your orders ready. In the meantime, expect your first patients at noon and also a couple of senior nurses from the Malta General Hospital who will be taking over from you. Sister Chaloner will take on the management of both your ward and her own. I'm sorry about this—just when we desperately need you both here,' said the matron.

'Er, Matron, can you tell us what it's about?' asked Hazel, somewhat stunned.

'I'm afraid not, but you've both been selected by our principal medical officer, along with three other nurses. I don't know where you're going or for how long exactly, but it has been indicated that it will only be for a few weeks at most,' said the matron. She added, 'Hazel, as the senior nurse, you will be in charge of your party. See you back here at six.'

Hazel and Helen left the matron's office and walked slowly across the quadrangle and lawn to Ward 5. It had not gone unnoticed by them that Matron Margaret Stanton had referred to Nurse Helen Grayling by her first name.

'This must be serious or something very special if Matron called me by my Christian name. She's never done that before.'

Hazel turned to Helen. 'And I suspect that she fought to keep us. All sounds a bit dodgy to me. And the PMO is involved!'

It was four in the afternoon when they had received all their patients, thirty-six in total. There wasn't time for an official afternoon break; Hazel arranged for the canteen staff to bring tea and coffee to the ward. It was most welcome. It arrived in time for the two Maltese nurses to meet all the nursing staff of Ward 5. Hazel introduced them and showed them around the ward and its facilities. The nursing staff buzzed with the news that Hazel and Helen were being relieved to be sent somewhere else. Some tried to get information from Helen, who politely said that she hadn't a clue. This added to the intrigue.

Six o'clock arrived. Hazel and Helen said their goodbyes. Hazel thanked her team for a 'magnificent' effort and added that she and Helen hoped to be back in a couple of weeks.

The matron's office door was open. Matron Margaret Stanton beckoned them in. Standing just out of view behind the door was Royal Navy surgeon Commodore Beresford, principal medical officer (PMO) for Malta, and three other nurses, whom Hazel and Helen recognised. The matron made the introductions and then handed over to the PMO.

'Ladies,' said the PMO, 'I am to blame for this uprooting, so moan at me later. I believe we owe you all an explanation, which I will come to in a moment. Firstly, Matron Stanton has objected to your being redeployed, especially at this time, but even I cannot go against an order from the General Officer Commanding Mediterranean, GOC General Alexander. This mission is not secret, but we don't want it in the news just yet. So, we would appreciate it if what I am about to tell you is kept to yourselves.

'We are facing an unprecedented humanitarian problem that's looking like a disaster. We have a large number of our troops as casualties who cannot be looked after in Northern Italy, and we cannot evacuate them quickly enough back to Britain. And, as you are aware, we are very stretched here and in Egypt. We need to set up general receiving hospitals along the Adriatic coast to include primary convalescence.' The PMO spotted that Hazel had a question.

'Why the Adriatic?' asked Hazel.

'That's a very good question. Quite simply, we have a complicating factor—refugees from the Balkans, particularly Albania and Montenegro. They're crossing the Adriatic to get away from the fighting between communist and nationalist partisans. Frankly speaking, it's a bloody mess, and the Americans aren't interested in getting involved. Your main job will be to train local nurses, mainly Italians, and some of our auxiliaries to a higher standard.'

'Does that mean once we have done the job, we can come back?' quipped Helen.

'Yes, Nurse Grayling, it does,' said the PMO.

'But, sir, that could take months,' chipped in QARNNS Nurse Lesley Grant.

'Humph!' grunted the PMO. 'I am assured that the Italian nurses are good and don't need much training. Some are even ex–Italian Army.' He sounded unconvincing. 'Matron Stanton has your individual orders. You will all be picked up tomorrow afternoon and taken to Luqa airfield, from where you will be flown to Brindisi. I suggest that you make any personal arrangements and have a few drinks this evening—maybe more than a few.' The PMO bit his lips together and grinned.

The PMO turned and was about to leave the matron's office when he turned back to Hazel. 'Sister Jones, I understand that your husband is Lieutenant Commander Jones in charge of the patrol group that will be working out of Brindisi. Maybe you will have a chance to meet with him. You never know.'

'We've been apart for several months off and on. I think I'm getting used to it. Bit of a blow though. I arrived here a few days ago and we've only had a couple of days together. Still, at least we'll both be away at the same time.'

'Yes. This damned war has intruded into all our personal lives. Take care. See you on your return,' replied the PMO in a warm tone of sincerity.

Matron Stanton handed Hazel her envelope of orders as the others left the office. She whispered to Hazel, 'Take that husband of yours to bed before having a drink tonight.'

Hazel grinned. 'You can bank on that!'

They congregated at the entrance to the hospital. A car had been provided to take them to the nurses' home and Hazel's quarters.

'What was that the matron said to you?' asked Helen.

'Oh, nothing. Just a bit of advice,' said Hazel.

Helen chuckled. 'Like get your man into bed ASAP!'

'Christ's sake! You've got good hearing,' choked Hazel.

'Not really. That's what I would have said and would do,' said Helen.

'And you?' Nurse Marjory Shaw asked Helen.

'I'll find that nice sub lieutenant and get his pants off!' Helen smirked.

'Is that before or after we meet up for a few drinks?' someone said.

They were all infected with a fit of giggles like schoolgirls.

CHAPTER 17

BRIEF ENCOUNTER

C HIEF PETTY OFFICER John Davy finished discussing their operational arrangements, for the embarkation the next morning, with Lieutenant James Callendar. The skippers of the other MTBs had left earlier. CPO Davy spotted Ewan coming along the quay with Petty Officer Tom Reynolds and Leading Seaman Dan Perry. 'Sir, here comes the boss with our two commandos,' said PO Davy with a hint of envy.

Callendar looked up from the chart table. 'Yes. I guess they'll tell us what they're up to. Reynolds and Perry are good for our group. I hope we can keep them after this little escapade. Which reminds me, I would like to assign PO Reynolds as your right-hand man when the boss doesn't need him.'

'That'll be good. He should be a chief PO,' said CPO Davy.

'I agree. He would certainly look after our other boats along with you.'

'Sir, what about Perry? He's a damned good signaller.'

Callendar chuckled. 'His future is in his own hands. If he stays in the service, I'll bet he ends up as an instructor in signals.' He shuffled passed the chart table to the boat's bridge. 'Better greet the boss and his two minders!'

So that is what they are, thought CPO Davy; it made sense.

As was tradition, two seaman manned the gangway to MGB 650 and piped the flotilla commander aboard. The shrill sound of the boatswain's pipe had barely subsided as Lieutenant Callendar saluted Lieutenant Commander Jones aboard. Reynolds and Perry followed, each saluting the white ensign aft, which for a moment fluttered in the light breeze.

'Welcome aboard, sir. Everything is ready as ordered,' said Callendar. 'Only the boat skippers, officers, and POs know roughly where we're going. No one else.'

'Good. That means that those lads not on duty can have the evening off but must stay together and report back by midnight. That's if you're happy with this?'

'Sir. Isn't that a bit risky on security?'

'Would certainly attract attention to us if we kept everyone on base,' said Ewan. The serious tone could be felt in his voice.

'I get your reasoning, sir. Will you be returning ashore?'

'Yes. But I'll be back at midnight.'

CPO Davy, with the other petty officers, worked out who should be off duty. There were a few grumbles, as normal, but on the whole the crews settled on visiting the bars in St Julians. Only two of the skippers, Sub Lieutenant Ron Stackley of MTB 701 and Sub Lieutenant John Marsden of MTB 702, decided to go ashore.

Callendar stayed aboard his MGB and planned to go over their operation again. He asked if Reynolds and Perry would join him. They willingly did so, sharing Callendar's sense of misgiving about the operation. All three agreed that they were not being given the full picture, but Reynolds added, 'Sir, one thing is for sure: the boss won't take any undue risks.'

'If he has the full picture!' added Callendar.

Perry looked at Reynolds. 'Just like before when we ended up in the desert. And that was damned dodgy.'

Reynolds nodded.

Ewan arrived at his quarters at seven after having phoned the hospital, only to find that Hazel had come off duty early. He found her finishing packing a small valise. 'You off somewhere?'

'Er, yes. I'm sorry. Been temporarily posted. I suppose we guessed this could happen, but not so soon.' She sighed. 'I will miss you. Are we going out tonight?'

'Oh yes. Anyway, I have similar news. I'm off tomorrow. It's a short operation—should be back in a week or so. Can't say where I'm going.'

Hazel turned and folded her arms affectionately around him. 'Brindisi.'

'What? How the hell did you know that?' Ewan was gobsmacked.

'The principal medical officer told me.' Hazel smirked.

'How'd he know …,' mumbled Ewan.

'That's where I'm off to also.'

'What are you doing there?' Ewan was regaining his composure.

'Not supposed to say, but I'm leading a group of nurses to train others because of the increase in Allied casualties and especially refugees from the Balkans.'

'So why are you going to Brindisi?'

'Er, that's the rub. I cannot say. Let's just say it's a routine patrol,' Ewan lied.

'I've heard that before. You know I don't like all this secrecy; it's worse now, more than when we first met!'

Hazel let go of Ewan and lightly held his hands.

'Shower, get changed, and make the most of tonight?' said Hazel.

'Hmm. "Make the most of tonight"? Well, that's got to be an order as I will be reporting at midnight, so we had better really do something special,' said Ewan.

'Oh, and I'm not flying until tomorrow,' said Hazel disappointedly, thinking that they would have had more time together.

Ewan started to undo Hazel's uniform. 'Bed first, then shower.'

They rampantly attacked each other, barely allowing the buttons on her uniform and his shirt to come free. He grabbed her naked body and flung her down onto their bed. The metal-framed bedsprings creaked in protest as he straddled her body. They made love and began to fall into a sleep.

They were startled by a knock on their apartment door.

Hazel made it to the door before Ewan. She wrapped a large towel around herself and then opened the door as it was knocked on again.

Marjory Shaw, standing before her, grinned. 'I guess you took Margaret's advice,' she said.

Hazel blushed a little and smirked.

Ewan popped his head around the corner of the hallway to the front door, also wearing a large towel.

'Are you still meeting with us later at Mount's Bay bar?' asked Marjory. It was a superfluous question as she guessed that Hazel wanted to have the evening with Ewan.

However, Ewan answered. 'We'll be joining you,' he said, chuckling to Hazel. 'Gives us another half hour.'

'Go on, embarrass me,' said Hazel.

'I'm full of envy for you both,' said Marjory, chuckling. 'See you later.'

Hazel closed the door and turned to find Ewan readying himself to grab her again.

'You know, Ewan, sometimes you're just an animal.'

'I know. Good, isn't it?'

He grabbed at her towel and flung it away. Within seconds he was grappling with her body and carrying her back into the bedroom. The bed creaked again.

Mount's Bay bar was heaving with sailors, mostly from Ewan's flotilla. Ewan and Hazel found Marjory Shaw, Lesley Grant, and Jo Mitchell sitting near a large door that led to a courtyard behind the pub. The courtyard, too, was filled with sailors holding pints of beer, laughing, joking, and generally enjoying themselves.

Several sailors spotted Ewan, their CO, with Hazel. Most had met

Hazel before and would have loved to engage in conversation with her, but they maintained the formality of being in the presence of their CO. When they saw Hazel settle in with the three nurses, they commented among each other that the boss, Ewan, was well in with the three women— lucky him!

Ewan, able only to guess at their thoughts, decided to approach them, but not before ordering drinks for Hazel and her three nurses.

He approached the first group, which also included a petty officer, whose name Ewan was not sure of.

'Sir,' said the petty officer, acknowledging Ewan.

'Lads, I see you're enjoying yourselves,' said Ewan, not being too formal.

'We would ask you to join us, if that's OK, but we can see you are with your wife and three nurses,' said the petty officer.

'I would certainly love to join you, but as you can see, I'm otherwise engaged. And, yes, it is OK. I think the days of officers and other rates not mixing are numbered. Maybe it will change one way or the other when this damned war is over,' said Ewan.

The group of sailors were relaxed and began to turn away, when he heard one of them say, 'Now who's this?'

Ewan followed their gazes towards the main door of the bar to see a sub lieutenant and a nurse enter. He recalled having seen the sub lieutenant with Captain Mark Williams the day before.

The nurse was Helen Grayling. She immediately steered her escorting sub lieutenant towards Hazel and the other three nurses. Ewan followed.

'Helen! Good to see you. Are you joining us?' said Marjory.

'If we are welcome,' said Helen. 'And this is Sub Lieutenant Andrew Starling.'

Ewan was within earshot. 'Lieutenant. You're welcome to join us.'

'Thank you, sir. We will,' replied the sub lieutenant confidentially.

There was something about this young officer that Ewan liked, yet he thought he was relaxed. He wasn't part of Ewan's flotilla, but Ewan knew he had something to do with HQ.

As they began to settle into a drinking group, Nurse Jo Mitchell remarked to Helen, 'So, this is your secret lover?'

'Oh yes! But not a secret any more. Now keep your hands off him,' said Helen.

Ewan took the opportunity to drag Sub Lieutenant Starling away from the women. 'Lieutenant, fancy giving me a hand to get some drinks from the bar?'

'Oh yes, sir. These nurses can be a bit of a handful, don't you think?'

'You have no idea!' chortled Ewan.

As the barman was assembling their order of drinks on to a tray, Ewan made a searching question. 'Tell me, are you attached to Admiral Kelly's staff?'

'Sort of, Commander. I actually report to Commander Gratton, if you know what I mean?'

'Yes I do. So, is this a meeting by design or just chance?'

'I was told that you were sharp. I would like to say by chance, but I steered Helen to join you all tonight.'

'You're on duty then?'

'Never off duty, sir.' The sub lieutenant grinned.

'Quite so. But this won't stop you having a few drinks, will it?'

They rejoined the group, each carrying a tray of drinks.

The evening wore on. Soon the bar was closing. Most of the sailors from Ewan's flotilla had already gone, leaving a few die-hards who could handle their liquor and themselves if anything rough were to occur. They were the traditional tough-looking sailors whom Ewan had become accustomed to; they were also the best allies to have in a scrap.

Ewan started the closing conversation. 'So, ladies, I won't be seeing you for a few weeks. Maybe we should arrange a party on your return,' said Ewan.

'Now that's a good idea,' someone said in reply.

'I think the bar's closing,' said Sub Lieutenant Starling.

'Time to go,' said Hazel.

They all stood and made their way to the main door.

Sub Lieutenant Starling nudged Ewan. 'Sir, a quick word.'

Hazel overheard. 'I'll catch up with you in a minute. I'll trail along with the others.'

'What's the matter?' Ewan asked Andrew.

'I'm being a bit cautious, but we have been under observation for most of the evening. That fellow near the bar has been slowly drinking all night. He's not local but appears to be.'

'I did wonder,' said Ewan. 'You are certainly good at your job. So, what do we do with him?'

'Nothing. I'll take care of him later. If I had to put money on it, I would say he's NKVD.'

Without turning to look at the man, Ewan said, 'Is he interested in Hazel or in me?'

'Both.'

'But why?'

'Good question. I don't know. But if my brief is accurate, I think the NKVD, or rather the Russians, are interested in your operation.'

'I've been told that. But why Hazel?' asked Ewan, getting concerned.

'A way of getting at you.'

Ewan looked hard at the young sub lieutenant. This was a reiteration of what had been said at the meeting with Admiral Kelly earlier.

Sub Lieutenant Starling reassured Ewan. 'Don't worry, Commander, I've got your back covered.'

'But what about Hazel's?'

'That's my job also,' said Sub Lieutenant Starling with a wry smile.

Ewan was getting changed, taking off his good day shirt and putting on a well-worn seagoing shirt. Hazel entered the bedroom, carrying two mugs of coffee. Ewan smiled.

'Thought you might want a hot drink before leaving. Being picked up in fifteen minutes?' she said.

'Sorry about this, but it's actually my fault. We don't slip until just before daybreak, but I want to go over a few last-minute issues, especially any change in orders.'

'I know. Don't need to beat yourself up over me. And anyway, I'm off tomorrow midday from Luqa. I'll spend the morning with my brood, also going over any last-minute change of plans. Shouldn't be any, but you never know.'

Ewan opened a small haversack and took out a white webbing holster and its attached belt and ammunition pouch; it contained a holstered pistol. Hazel looked surprised. He put the belt around his waist and shuffled the holster into a comfortable position to his left side. There was a lanyard trailing the pistol handgrip which he duly slipped over his head, seating it around the neck collar of his shirt. He caught Hazel's eye of concern.

'I thought you said that this was a routine operation?'

Ewan grinned slightly. 'It is, but we aren't taking any chances.'

'Is there something you aren't telling me?'

He puckered his lips and looked momentarily away.

'OK, I understand. It's confidential. Just promise me one thing—be careful and come back safe.'

'Of course. How could I not turn that down? Hopefully, we'll meet up in Brindisi in a couple of days. Check in with the Naval Shipping Control officer. He'll tell you where I am. I can tell you that I will be in Brindisi for at least three days.'

'Do you think we will get any personal time?' she asked hopefully. 'Selfish of me really, I suppose.'

'More likely depends on your itinerary. I understand that you are destined for Bari, just a few miles up the coast from Brindisi.' He chuckled.

The fifteen minutes passed quickly. A knock on their door signalled the arrival of Ewan's driver. The couple gave each other a quick tight hug and kissed goodbye.

Hazel suddenly felt lonely in their apartment; it wasn't the same without Ewan. She sat in their small lounge and started to drift off to sleep. She had a feeling of foreboding but at the same time knew that Ewan would be all right. It was a strange feeling.

She awoke later in the morning as the sun peeked its way above the horizon of apartments to throw a bright sheen into the lounge. Hazel rubbed her eyes and struggled to put her feet down firmly. She had fallen asleep in an uncomfortable position on the well-worn sofa, whose springs were moaning because someone was sitting on them.

Finally standing, she outstretched her arms and made herself ready to meet with the other nurses in an old lecture room attached to the nurses' home. All including Hazel had had a light breakfast in the canteen, except Helen Grayling, who arrived after the breakfast plates had been removed. She looked a little haggard, attracting smirks from the others.

'Did you have a good night?' asked Marjory, knowing the answer.

'Oh, sure. We went back to his hotel room and I promptly fell asleep!'

'You! You fell asleep?' said Lesley Grant in disbelief.

Helen simply nodded. 'Any tea left?'

'Have you had any breakfast?' asked Hazel.

'Sort of. I had him, or rather he had me. Such an animal!' said Helen.

'You fit to fly?' asked Lesley, grinning.

'Other than my hips and thighs aching, yes.'

'There's no answer to that,' one of the women said under her breath.

Hazel changed the subject to get on with a final briefing before they landed at Brindisi. They would be met by RAF military police and taken to a holding centre for medical staff at Brindisi casualty reception. They would then be taken by road to Bari, probably the next day. It shot into Hazel's mind that she might not be able to meet with Ewan after all; she would have less than twenty-four hours in transit.

Luqa airfield was emblazoned in brilliant sunshine with the odd wisp of dust kicked up by manoeuvring aircraft. They were boarding their aircraft, a Dakota DC-10, when an RAF airman ran up to Hazel. 'Miss, I've a message for you,' he said, handing Hazel an envelope.

Hazel sat down with Marjory Shaw, who looked to Hazel. 'What's the message?'

Hazel opened the envelope. It contained a folded signal. She opened it to find the note headed 'URGENT—Principal Medical Officer'.

'It's from the PMO,' she said. She shared the message with the others. 'We're getting another nurse, Nurse Doreen Canley, from Cyprus, RAF Akroteri. She'll meet us on arrival.' She read on. 'And I will be staying in Brindisi for an extra day, joining you ladies a day later by a different transport, I suppose. They want me to sort out some new Italian nurses who will be joining us later. Seems very odd to me, but then I suppose orders are orders.'

'You're right, it does seem odd,' added Marjory Shaw. 'Maybe you should check with Malta HQ. Could be some foul-up. Been plenty of that lately.'

'I think I will,' said Hazel. She had an uneasy feeling about this change, not that it was anything significant, but the message covered both the inclusion of another nurse and a change of immediate orders, as though the latter had been added as an afterthought.

CHAPTER 18

INCIDENT AT BRINDISI

BRINDISI WAS A bustling town with a busy port tucked away on the south-east coast of Italy, facing the Adriatic Sea. Hazel left her group of nurses at the Casualty Reception and Holding Centre, having arranged to meet them later in the early evening. Eventually, she found the Naval Shipping Control Office in a battered building at the entrance to the main harbour. She realised that Ewan's flotilla would be at least another day's sailing away. It would take thirty-six hours to get from Malta to Brindisi; at least that was what Ewan had estimated. Hazel searched for someone to help her. She wanted to get a message to the principal medical officer, Malta, to confirm her change of orders and to find out when Ewan would arrive. She caught the eye of a naval lieutenant, who approached her. He had not seen a nurse in his offices before. 'Can I help you, miss?'

'Yes, I hope so,' Hazel said. She went on to explain that she needed to contact Malta and get some idea when Ewan would be arriving.

'I can help you with the message to Malta, but I can't tell you of any naval movements,' he said. Then he asked to see her ID card.

'I understand. Bit of a long shot, but thought I would ask anyway.'

The lieutenant smiled. 'You write out your message and I'll see if I can get it to Lieutenant Commander Jones on his arrival.'

'Thank you. And Malta?' she said softly.

'Same again. Write your message on this signal pad'—he handed her a signal pad—'and I'll send it to the Communications Room immediately. You may not get an immediate reply, so where can I contact you?'

Hazel gave the lieutenant her contact details at the Casualty Reception and Holding Centre and then set about writing the signal to PMO Malta.

She was just about to leave the office when there came loud cheers and laughter from the whole office. 'What's going on?' she said.

'Confirmed. Hitler's dead, and mass surrenders of German and Axis forces. Northern German Army have stopped fighting, and General Montgomery is in discussion with German High Command for a surrender,' said the lieutenant, not containing his joy.

'Does this mean it's all over?' Hazel asked.

'Hopefully. There are pockets of Axis resistance, so we will still need to be on our toes. It's been rumoured that there's a large Jerry SS division hung up across the water from here in Albania, and another in northern Yugoslavia, and more SS on the Italian-Austrian border,' said the lieutenant. He then paused in deep thought. 'Of course, it does beggar the question of who the hell they are fighting for.'

'Yes, everything seems topsy-turvy these days. I thought things would get better, but there's uncertainty. Goodness knows what going on.'

The lieutenant agreed and then had a thought. 'Sister Jones, do you need a lift back to the Casualty Reception Centre? It's uncomfortably hot here now.'

'If there's one available, that would be good,' she replied. The idea was welcome as she had not been looking forward to the walk back in the hot, dusty atmosphere.

'No problem. I'm off duty in a couple of minutes. Be glad to drive you back,' he said.

The lieutenant drove Hazel back to the Casualty Reception Centre. She was glad of his offer as the traffic was chaotic; some roads still showed the signs of Allied bombing, with every other road junction displaying mounds of rubble.

As they neared the Casualty Reception Centre, the lieutenant posed a question to Hazel. 'A bit forward of me, but are you free for dinner this evening?'

Hazel was not surprised. She had often had such invitations, and although she had never thought of herself as attractive, she nevertheless caught the attention of several servicemen. 'You know I'm married?' she said, not refusing the invitation.

'I guessed you are, and to Lieutenant Commander Jones.'

'But he could be my brother,' she teased.

'Your wedding finger has no ring but shows the indentation that indicates you do wear a ring.'

'That's mighty observant of you. I don't wear a ring when on nursing duty—hygiene and all that,' said Hazel.

'My mother's a nurse in London; that's how I know,' the lieutenant said. He added, 'And tonight?'

'Lieutenant, I would love to join you this evening, but I have a brood of nurses to look after, and we're all going out tonight. But maybe you might like to join us.'

'OK, that sounds fine. What time?'

'I think about seven-thirty, here.' They stopped outside the Casualty Reception Centre.

Hazel slipped out of the passenger seat and turned to her driver. 'See you later.'

Hazel smiled, almost flirtatiously, and turned away to the entrance of the Casualty Reception Centre. The lieutenant drove away, wondering what he had let himself in for.

Hazel met Marjory Shaw, who immediately grinned. 'Got a sailor, have we?'

'Yes we have. I've invited him to come out with us this evening. I thought he might know the best spots to forage in this place,' said Hazel.

'Is that all?'

'I'm married, remember?'

'Oh yes, I've seen your antics with Ewan!'

Hazel and her party were allocated a room in a dormitory for medical staff at the back of the main offices of the Casualty Reception Centre. It was spartan with six beds, which looked barrack-style uncomfortable, with a shared toilet and a shower room that seemed to have been thrown together. Jo Mitchell was the first to comment on their overnight abode. 'Rough, but hopefully we'll get a good night's sleep.'

'No lock on the door,' noted Marjory.

'There never is,' added Hazel. 'Best not to wander around starkers.'

Lesley Grant and Helen Grayling were already undressed down to their underwear in readiness to fight to be first in the shower. Helen succeeded, leaving Lesley standing naked in the doorway. 'Water's cool,' said Helen.

After a minute, Helen stepped out of the shower, allowing Lesley to take her place. 'Just about cool, more like room temperature,' she said.

Hazel had her shower next. Afterwards, she redressed in the uniform she had travelled in; none of them had any real change of clothing. As Marjory left the shower, Hazel said, 'Look after the brood. I'm off to the admin office to find out when our nurse Doreen Canley is due.'

Marjory grinned. 'Find out where the bar is. I think we all need a drink.'

'You just find the bar and get the drinks in. We'll find you,' said Helen.

Hazel grinned and nodded.

'Is this Nurse Canley one of us?' asked Jo Mitchell.

'I think so. She's coming from Cyprus, so she could be PMRAFNS,' said Marjory.

'PM-what?' Jo asked.

'Princess Mary's Royal Air Force Nursing Service,' said Marjory.

'Oh, thanks. I'm still getting to grips with all these titles,' said Jo, who revealed that she had been in Queen Alexandra's Royal Naval Nursing Service (QARNNS) for only three months after having qualified at Manchester Christie Hospital. Jo was the youngest nurse in the group.

Hazel found the bar, frequented by most of the hospital staff, a few minutes' walk from the Casualty Reception Centre. Ten minutes later Helen arrived with the others after having gotten the same instruction from the admin officer. Hazel had decided on getting cool beers rather than Italian wine because of the warm atmosphere. The beer was a welcome sight.

'Did you find out when Doreen Canley will be with us?' asked Marjory.

'Yes, tomorrow morning at ten. Our transport, or rather yours, is expected at ten-thirty. Not much time for Doreen to change. Just hope she has a pleasant flight,' said Hazel.

'What about you?' Marjory asked.

'No reply to my query yet from Malta, but the admin officer says I can stay until my orders are sorted out,' Hazel answered.

They chatted and downed two more cold beers each, when the lieutenant from the Naval Shipping Control Office arrived. 'Ah, our escort for the evening,' said Hazel. 'This is Lieutenant—oh hell, I don't know your name!'

'I didn't give it to you. I'm Gary Brookes,' said the lieutenant, beaming a bemused grin to all.

'Good heavens, Hazel, you capture a handsome-looking naval officer and don't get his name! Looks like I've got a lot to learn,' said Helen, chuckling with an impish grin.

'Ladies, here I am with five gorgeous nurses. I'll be the envy of the division. So it's up to me take you to a good restaurant. Italian, I presume?'

'With an intro like that, I think you can take your pick!' said Helen seductively.

'There's also the question of money. We don't have much between us, just enough for a couple of rounds of beers,' said Hazel.

'Don't worry about that. I guessed that when I learned you were in transit, so I have arranged to cover tonight. We have contingencies for these situations,' said Brookes.

He declined a beer with them and suggested they make their way to a nearby traditional Italian restaurant. There was suddenly a relaxed atmosphere, especially as they entered the restaurant, where it was quite obvious that the owner knew Lieutenant Brookes as a regular customer. They sorted out their drinks and thumbed through the menu, which to their delight was quite varied and appealing, especially for wartime. Gary whispered to Hazel, 'No message from Malta for you yet. I can't give you your husband's arrival, but I can say he is expected sometime tomorrow afternoon.'

'Thanks. Perhaps I can repay your help in some way,' said Hazel.

She did not realise that what she had said could give the wrong impression until Gary said, 'If Lieutenant Commander Jones can get me onto sea duty, that would be great.'

'Oh yes. I'll mention it to him. Nearly gave you the wrong impression,' said Hazel, blushing. For the first time since meeting Ewan, she found herself attracted to someone else. It made her feel both uneasy and a little excited.

The evening ended with them strolling back to the Casualty Reception Centre. Hazel hung back after the nurses had thanked Gary for the evening. 'Gary, a special thanks from me, but as I said earlier, I am married and ...'

'I know. He's a very lucky man. I'll look forward to meeting him. Come around tomorrow afternoon if you don't hear from me.'

Hazel gave Gary a quick kiss on the cheek and followed the others into the dormitory.

Lieutenant Gary Brookes turned and walked slowly away from the Casualty Reception Centre and towards his own billet, not far from the port entrance and his office. He stopped for a moment and turned to peer back along the street he had walked. He got a glimpse of a figure in the shadows of a small shop. He had the distinct feeling that he had been followed. He had.

CHAPTER 19

ROAD TO BARI

THE MIDMORNING SUNSHINE was already sending sharp shadows from the misshaped buildings that made up what looked more like a shanty town than a hospital. Hazel gathered her brood of nurses at the entrance to the Casualty Reception Centre. She checked the group's orders that had been given to her in Malta and passed them to Marjory, who was notionally her deputy. 'Should be straightforward. Your transport will be here at ten-thirty, and Nurse Canley should be arriving any time now,' said Hazel to Marjory. 'Any questions?'

Nurse Helen Grayling was half listening. 'When will you be joining us?'

'Hopefully day after tomorrow. Still awaiting confirmation from Malta,' said Hazel.

'Seems odd to split us up, now we've gotten to know each other,' said Marjory.

'That's why I've asked for confirmation.'

'Anyway, you'll be able to see Ewan,' said Marjory.

'Hmm. I'm not so sure about that either. It all seems very hush-hush to me,' said Hazel.

They set about getting a cup of tea as Nurse Doreen Canley appeared, looking very tired and dishevelled. She introduced herself, recognising Hazel from her nursing sister's uniform.

'God, you look terrible!' said Hazel as Nurse Doreen Canley dropped her small case. 'You need to freshen up and get something to eat.'

'I don't think I'll have time. The transport that brought me here from the airfield is destined for Brindisi, and I guess that's all of us. Driver's reporting to the admin officer.'

'I can get that put on hold for half an hour,' said Hazel.

'Thanks, Sister Jones, but I understand that the driver is under orders to get away as soon as possible,' said Doreen.

'Well, OK, but I'll just check,' said Hazel, nodding to Marjory.

Hazel went off to find the admin officer and the driver.

Marjory approached Doreen. 'Doreen, we're fairly informal here, if that's OK. Nursing Sister Jones prefers to be called Hazel when not on nursing duty.'

'Suits me. Same with us in the RAF,' said Doreen.

Within a few minutes, Hazel returned with the driver.

'Sorry, Doreen. You're right, but the driver here says he can give you ten minutes, and the admin officer has arranged a couple of canteens of tea to take with us.'

Helen Grayling showed Doreen to a small toilet block and washroom, while the driver, Lance Corporal Smithers, backed up his truck.

'Stroll on. It's a boneshaker of a truck,' mumbled Jo Mitchell. Her despondent tone was felt by all.

Lance Corporal Smithers loaded their luggage next to some small crates and pointed to several blankets. 'The blankets will make the benches feel a bit more comfortable—best I could do,' he said apologetically, and grinned.

'Don't worry, Corporal, we're used to it,' said Hazel.

'Oh, right, miss. Just one thing though. I was told five nurses, not six.'

'That's right. I'm not going, at least not on this trip,' said Hazel. She thought for a moment. The lance corporal looked very young, probably no more than nineteen. It was a view that she and Ewan shared.

Doreen returned from the washroom.

'Feeling better?' Hazel asked.

'A lot, thanks. Look forward to meeting up properly in a couple days,' said Doreen.

'Me too,' said Hazel, turning to Marjory. 'Look after this motley crew. Don't let Helen lead you or the others astray.'

'I'll do my best. See you in a day or so,' replied Marjory, grinning. Marjory took to her role quickly and turned to Doreen. 'Why don't you sit up front with the driver? Might be more comfortable than at the back with us.'

'Well, thanks, but does anyone else want to sit up front?'

'Look, my dear, you've been travelling all day already. Your arse could do with something better. We can change around later if you wish,' said Marjory.

'Anyway, it'll keep the driver happy,' Helen put in with a grin.

Lance Corporal Smithers started the truck. They all waved goodbye to Hazel. He drove the beaten-up Bedford three-ton truck and its precious cargo of nurses out of the Casualty Reception Centre and hospital yard and onto the dusty road to Bari. For a moment Hazel felt alone. She clutched the shoulder strap on her handbag and strode off to the harbour and towards the Naval Shipping Control Office.

The journey by road to Bari was about a hundred miles, estimated to take more than two hours given the poor state of the road with potholes that had not been tended to since 1943, when Italy surrendered and joined the Allies. This assumed that there would be no hold-ups such as broken-down cars, wagons, and trucks. They were approaching a road junction with a signpost showing 7 km to Ostuni on the left; the road carried on north, signposted 'Monopoli 90 km'. Lance Corporal Smithers carefully steered the truck northward to Monopoli, the road hugging the Adriatic coast. It was hot and uncomfortable, made all the more irksome by the sun approaching midday and the blinding glare in Smithers's driver's mirror.

He did not notice that he was being followed until he rounded a long bend that momentarily removed the glaring sun from his mirror. 'That's odd,' he said.

'What's odd?' asked Doreen.

'I'm certain we're being followed. Saw the car following us on the outskirts of Brindisi. I'm sure of it.'

'Maybe it's also going to Bari,' said Doreen.

The road twisted and turned. Smithers slowed to allow the car to overtake. It didn't. But it was closing the gap between them.

'I don't like this,' said Smithers.

Helen, sitting nearest to the cab, overheard Smithers's concern. 'That car is definitely following us,' she said.

'You're right,' added Marjory.

Smithers had a sixth-sense feeling. He saw a truck on the road ahead around the bend. The land was flat; he could see no other vehicles. He drove his truck round the bend in the road and slowly brought it to a halt before an old farm wagon straddling the road. There were two men, who looked like farmworkers, standing in front of the wagon, which appeared unladen.

'Stay here,' said Smithers, and climbed down from the cab. He spotted the car following as it stopped behind them. He approached the farmworkers.

'What's goin' on. You broken down?' he asked.

They shrugged their shoulders. 'No understand,' said one.

Before Smithers could say anything else, there came a yell from the back of his truck. One of the nurses saw two men armed with pistols get out of the car. One levelled his gun to Smithers, while the other trained his pistol on the nurses.

Smithers turned sharply, only to be felled by a single shot from the approaching gunman. He crumpled to the ground and rolled partly into a ditch.

The commotion ceased as the gunmen ushered the four nurses from the rear of the truck into the farm wagon. Doreen, who was still stunned, was grabbed from the cab and also bundled into the farm wagon, whose engine miraculously came to life. One of the farmworkers, if that is what he was, drove Smithers's truck off the road, just missing his lifeless body. The farm wagon was almost a wreck; it bounced along the main road until, after a mile, lurching off onto a dirt track. The five nurses were thrown around; they held on for their lives. Two of their captors brandished pistols, which they waved at the nurses as they, too, were tossed around on the uneven track. The two occupants of the black sedan car followed, looking every part as sinister. They were NKVD agents. Eventually, the party arrived at a small farmhouse surrounded by olive trees and citrus fruits. They were met by two men and a woman.

'What the hell's going on!' shouted Marjory to one of the gunmen.

'Shut up. We'll see to you later,' said the gunman in an aggressive, sinister tone.

'He's got an Eastern European accent,' whispered Helen.

'But who the hell are they, and what do they want with us?' muttered Lesley Grant.

CHAPTER 20

THE REPLY

THIRTY MILES AWAY in Brindisi, Hazel Jones walked into the Naval Shipping Control Office within the port. She found Lieutenant Gary Brookes seated at a desk, surrounded by an untidy mess of sheets of paper and files, which was unusual for him; he was normally a very tidy administrator. He looked up with anguish, expecting yet another wad of signals. His expression changed to great delight and a wide grin. 'Hazel. You're a grand sight for sore eyes and a befuddled brain.'

'What on earth is going on?' said Hazel, sensing a tense atmosphere throughout the entire office. 'Am I interrupting?'

'Yes, you are, but it's most welcome. Let's get a coffee,' he said. He needed a break.

Lieutenant Brookes called a rating to him: 'Jameson, I'm having a break for coffee with this lady. I'll be in the cafe.'

Leading Seaman Jameson acknowledged and returned to his large wall map of Brindisi and the surrounding coast.

Hazel and Brookes strolled to the cafe much frequented by the port offices personnel. They sat outside the cafe in a garden, away from the busy, dusty road. 'Hazel, I know what you have come for. I received this signal about half an hour ago and was going to get it sent to you,' said Brookes, pulling the signal from his pocket.

Hazel unfolded the signal sheet. She was surprised by the message:

To: Nursing Sister H. Jones

Confirmed you stay in Brindisi for two days. An urgent request
has been received by Italian Red Cross to oversee reception of
a large number of civilian refugees from Albania. Work out of
Brindisi No. 2 Casualty Reception Centre. They are expecting
you. Our apologies. End.

PMO RNH Bighi Malta

'Well. That answers my query. Looks like I'll be busy,' said Hazel.

'That's my issue also,' said Brookes.

'How so?'

'All the refugees are coming into my port on various craft—in fact,
almost anything that will float,' he said.

'Sounds like an almighty tragedy.'

'It is. To make matters worse, it's rumoured that the refugees include
escaping Nazis.'

'War criminals?' Hazel asked.

'That's our guess. I've got intelligence officers arriving soon. God knows
what they'll get up to. And on top of that, we've received a signal from
GOC Italy that Russian NKVD agents are here also. Not too friendly; in
fact, downright dodgy guys.' Brookes sounded depressed.

'So I've heard. Same concern in Malta before I left,' said Hazel.

'Allies! That's a joke. Some of the stories I've picked up over the water
in Yugoslavia and Albania makes them out to be even more hated than
the Gestapo.' Brookes was still depressed, even though Hazel insisted he
drink his coffee and get another inside him.

'Thanks, Hazel. Incidentally, I think Lieutenant Commander Jones's
flotilla is expected midafternoon. I'll get a message to him as soon as he berths.'

'That'll be very much appreciated, but I'm getting the feeling we won't
have much time see each other,' said Hazel. 'Perhaps very selfish of me
given these uncertainties.' It was her turn to feel uneasy and disappointed.

'Selfish? No. But I am envious that you have someone,' he said.

They returned to Brookes's office.

Hazel said she would return to the Casualty Reception Centre and get herself sorted. She was about to leave when she had an afterthought. 'Gary, would it be possible to phone the hospital in Bari from here? My nurses should have arrived by now.'

'No problem. What's the number?' Brookes relayed the number over the phone to the local telephone exchange operator. The connection took a minute. When the call was answered, he handed the phone to Hazel.

'Hello, I am Nursing Sister Jones, leading the relief team from Malta. Can you put me through to Nurse Marjory Shaw? She should have arrived from Brindisi by now. She's part of my team from Malta,' said Hazel.

'Uno momento—er, just a minute,' replied the Italian operator.

'I am sorry, Sister Jones. They have not yet arrived. We expected them an hour ago. Must have been delayed.'

'Oh, OK. Leave a message for her when she arrives. Ask her to telephone me at the Casualty Reception Centre number two at Brindisi. She has the number.'

'Yes. I will do that,' said the operator.

Hazel handed the telephone handset back to Brookes.

'Everything all right?' he asked.

'Yes, I think so. They haven't arrived yet. I've left a message but will check again later. I suppose the roads aren't so good these days.'

'They're not too bad. The coast road to Bari from here is fairly good, but then delays are always there, especially if you get stuck behind some of the farming traffic,' said Brookes. 'I'll let you know when Commander Jones's flotilla berths,' Brookes added, more of a prompt to remind himself.

Hazel thanked him and set off for Casualty Reception Centre No. 2. It was early afternoon; the sun was searing into every nook and cranny that it could find. It seemed that there was no hiding place from the sun. Although used to the scorching sunshine in Malta, Hazel found this sun to be much more aggressive. She adjusted her hat, but it did not afford any protection. *Oh, for a large straw sombrero hat,* she muttered to herself. As she made her way through the dusty roads, she began to feel the beating sunshine on her arms also. She stopped for a moment under a large olive tree at the corner of a road junction. A slight breeze enticed her to sit on a low wall. She looked down at her feet; her shoes were laden with dust. A wolf whistle from a couple of passing soldiers alerted her to continue on to her destination. Ten minutes later, she arrived at the reception desk of the Casualty Reception Centre. A young Italian reception clerk greeted her with a big smile. 'Sister Jones, Doctor Emanuel has asked you join him in his office,' said the clerk, pointing to an open door near to the main corridor that led to the hospital wards.

Hazel thanked the clerk in Italian. She had already impressed the administrative staff with fluent Italian, something they much appreciated.

She entered the office, lightly knocking on the door first. A man wearing a white overall coat emerged from behind the door. 'Ah, Sister Jones. Welcome. I understand that you now know that your services, or should I say your experience, is badly needed here. We have a large intake of refugees due in from Albania. I guess we have a few hours before they actually descend upon us. I've called a meeting of all available staff for four-thirty. Should give us time to sort ourselves out.' He went on to explain in detail what they should expect.

'So, there you have it, Sister Jones. Our apologies for not alerting you and informing you earlier. Are there any questions?'

'Not really, Doctor Emanuel, except a personal question. Your accent. You're not Italian?' she asked.

'Perceptive of you. Yes, not Italian as such. I'm an American but from an Italian family in New York. US Army Medical Corps seconded me here, but unlike you, I am probably here until we can sort out this mess. One thing, though, I believe you must have an Italian background. I've overheard you on several occasions speaking with the staff here in fluent Italian,' said Doctor Emanuel.

'Yes, Doctor. My father is Italian.'

'Ah, that explains a lot. Come, let's get a coffee and you can tell me more about yourself,' he said.

They strode off to the small staff cafeteria at the rear of the main hospital, next to the staff residential quarters.

As they were finishing their coffees, they were joined by several Italian nurses, along with some US Army, British Army, and Italian Army medical officers. To complement the team, there were half a dozen British soldiers from the Royal Army Service Corps whose main function was to provide supplies, particularly food and clothing. Hazel noticed two British Army officers standing just inside the doorway to the cafeteria. She discerned their ranks, both lieutenants, but couldn't see clearly their insignia. They were not Royal Army Service Corps, and they were not dressed in clean uniforms, as many others she had seen recently freshly arrived from Britain. They were, however, carefully observing everyone in the room. Her instincts told her that they were either Royal Military Police or intelligence; she had been around such characters frequently to recognise the signs. *So, what are they here for?* she thought.

Doctor Emanuel finished the briefing and introduced Hazel to the nurses whom she would be leading. Hazel discussed with the nurses a quick action plan to review the empty hospital wards for those requiring hospitalisation. Thankfully, she would not be involved in billeting the majority of refugees in a tented park; this would be the job of the Royal Army Service Corps. She was about to go to the first ward with two nurses, when one of the British Army lieutenants whom she had spotted earlier approached her.

'Sister Jones. Can I have a word please?' said the lieutenant.

'Yes, certainly,' replied Hazel. She indicated to the nurses that she would join them in a moment. 'What can I do for you?'

'We noticed that you eyed us up. So, we reckon you realise we're RMP.'

'Police?'

'Yes. Our function here is scrutinise the refugees and weed out any Nazis, if you know what I mean?' said the lieutenant in a cold voice.

'I understand, but how can I help?'

'You speak fluent Italian. We've noticed that. That'll be very useful to us, that is if you don't mind.' His tone changed to almost an apology as he strained his neck round to meet with the other lieutenant joining them. 'Robin?'

'Yes, Todd. Confirmed.'

'Remiss of me, Sister Jones. My apologies. This is Lieutenant Robin Saunders, and I'm Lieutenant Mark Cross. We're both Royal Military Police.'

'Cross? I know a—' said Hazel. She was interrupted.

'Yes. You've met John Cross in Malta. He's my older brother.'

'Sister Jones, we have a problem and need to talk to you confidentially. I've already cleared this with Doctor Emanuel. We can use his office,' said Lieutenant Robin Saunders.

They went to Doctor Emanuel's office and closed the door.

Hazel was apprehensive. Her first thought was that something had happened to Ewan, but that didn't make sense; if it had, the navy would have informed her. The two officers nodded to her to sit down.

'Sister Jones, we have some strange news. Your nursing party left here at ten this morning and should have arrived in Bari by at least two this afternoon,' said Saunders.

'Yes. I tried earlier to contact them, but they hadn't arrived. Has something happened to them?' Hazel felt a cold shudder; she was suddenly concerned.

'We simply don't know. But we have just had confirmed that the lorry taking them has been found run off the road about thirty miles north of here and the driver is seriously injured. There's no sign of your nurses,' said Saunders.

'An accident?' asked Hazel, now feeling nauseous.

'No, Sister Jones. That's the problem. The driver, Lance Corporal Smithers, had been shot and at close quarters.'

'What the—!' Hazel's anxiety exploded. 'So what's happened? What are you doing to find them? Bandits? Robbery?'

'No, nothing like that. The driver was discovered unconscious, next to his lorry, by a farmer who thought he saw a car and another lorry or farm truck driving off quickly from the scene. The question is: did you see anything odd before they set off? Any car following them?' Lieutenant Saunders asked.

'No. Except I did see an old battered sedan parked across the road outside the main entrance; it seemed a bit out of place,' said Hazel.

'Yes. We have that reported also,' said Lieutenant Cross.

'I don't know what to do. I—' muttered Hazel.

'Difficult, I know. But maybe return to your ward duties and we'll keep you informed. If there's anything you can remember that might help us, tell Doctor Emanuel. He has our contact details. But at least one of us will be here when the refugees start arriving,' said Lieutenant Cross, who put a reassuring hand on her shoulder.

Hazel returned to her first ward. Her mind was bouncing around. She was completely at a loss as to what to do or expect. The two Italian nurses with her realised that she was in some distress and took over most of the ward inspection sympathetically.

CHAPTER 21

THE NOTE

THE PORT OFFICE buzzed with excitement. The news coming in from Germany was of more mass surrenders. Also reported was that the Northern German Army, facing Montgomery's army, had all but stopped fighting.

Ewan's flotilla had arrived and was manoeuvring in the confines of the harbour. MGB 650, commanded by Lieutenant James Callendar, tied up to a vacant berth on the main quay; the other boats stood off in the main anchorage. Ewan left the refuelling arrangements to Callendar and the other boat commanders while he went off to report to Captain Barent, senior British naval officer, port of Brindisi. He took with him Petty Officer Tom Reynolds and Leading Seaman Dan Perry. They approached the Naval Shipping Control Office to find a melee of people entering and leaving the offices; there was no orderly control. They spotted a group of six Royal Marines doing their best to keep out of everyone's way by sitting on a stack of old wooden crates. Ewan ordered Tom Reynolds and Dan Perry over to enquire of them as to whether they were to be joining their task force. Ewan fought his way through the throng of bodies until he found a quiet back office with a lonesome lieutenant scrabbling through a host of papers. He knocked on the door and entered. The lieutenant looked up and squeezed a smile. 'I'm sorry, sir, but whatever you want, I'm rather busy, as you can see,' he said, waving his hands at the paperwork, 'unless you are going to drag me off to a bar.' There was a pause as he regained his composure. 'So, sir, how can I help you?'

'I'm Lieutenant Commander Jones. My special force has arrived, and I'm to report to the port naval officer in charge. I believe that's Captain Barent.'

'Yes it is. And you're expected,' said Lieutenant Brookes. 'Good to see you. I'll take you to Captain Barent. He's in the next building.'

Lieutenant Brookes grabbed his cap and directed Ewan out of his office, passing a large wallchart filled with pins and stickers. He suddenly stopped. 'Oh, good God, nearly forgot. I have a couple of messages for you: one from Nursing Sister Hazel Jones and this envelope.' He handed the sealed envelope to Ewan; it was marked 'Confidential'. 'Sister Jones is at the Casualty Reception Centre. I promised to let her know when you arrived.'

'Right. While I report to Captain Barent, maybe you can let her know,' said Ewan.

After negotiating a lively corridor to the next building, they arrived at Captain Barent's office. Lieutenant Brookes knocked on the door and entered. 'Sir. Lieutenant Commander Jones is here to see you.'

'Ah, Commander. Come in, sit down,' said Captain Barent. Lieutenant Brookes left, closing the door behind him.

Captain Barent stood up from behind his desk and placed himself in front of a large wallchart of the area that included the Albanian coast. 'Commander. Your orders have changed slightly.' Captain Barent took a sealed packet from his desk drawer and handed it to Ewan. 'Everything you need to know is in your orders. I am to afford you whatever assistance I can. Things are changing quickly. Very quickly.'

'Yes, sir. I was warned that my orders might change, and I guessed this would happen when we heard that Hitler was dead,' said Ewan.

'Quite so. But the news of his death was at least seven days old. It's reported—lots of rumour; not sure what to believe—that it was on twenty-fifth April.'

Ewan proceeded to open the sealed packet to find a small map and a signal sheet marked 'Secret'. He raised an eyebrow and glanced up to Captain Barent. He then realised he had another sealed envelope, marked 'Confidential'. 'Another clandestine order,' he said, opening the envelope. He was surprised. 'What the hell!'

'What's the matter?' Captain Barent asked.

'You tell me, Captain,' said Ewan, showing him the note.

Captain Barent read out the typewritten note: 'We have your wife. If you want to see her again, come to the Napoli Restaurant at eight o'clock alone. Tell no one.'

'Is this some sort of joke? Lieutenant Brookes is contacting her now to let her know I have arrived,' said Ewan.

'I don't think this is a joke,' said Captain Barent. He picked up his phone. 'Get me the shipping control officer. It's urgent.'

Lieutenant Brookes confirmed that he had just spoken with Hazel and that she could not get away until at least seven o'clock.

Ewan thanked Caption Barent and said he would go directly to the Casualty Reception Centre. Captain Barent gave him directions and said he would alert the military police.

Ewan left the port's Naval Shipping Control Office and found Tom Reynolds and Dan Perry waiting for him. 'Sir, the six marines are for us, and there's also six naval commandos on their way. I've sent them down to the 650 boat,' said Reynolds.

'Good. Now come with me,' said Ewan. He explained about the note.

They hurried along the busy road and found the entrance to the hospital and Casualty Reception Centre. Ewan strode up to the reception desk while Tom Reynolds and Dan Perry nosed around to see if there was anyone who appeared out of place.

'I'm Lieutenant Commander Jones. I would like to see Nursing Sister Jones, please.'

'Er, yes, Commander,' said the reception clerk. She picked up the telephone and looked around to see Lieutenant Saunders. Once she had attracted his attention, he strode over to face Ewan.

'You must be Lieutenant Commander Jones. I'm Saunders, RMP.'

'What's going on? Is Hazel OK?'

'Quiet safe, sir. Can I have a word while we get Sister Jones?'

Ewan and Saunders entered an unoccupied office. Tom Reynolds waited outside the office while Dan Perry took a stroll to the outer entrance to reception, casting his eyes around for anything unusual. He saw several wounded servicemen, some with crutches, milling around and the odd nurse and medical orderly attending to patients. There was nothing unusual, or if there was, he didn't detect it.

Hazel approached the receptionist but immediately recognised Tom Reynolds. 'Tom! What a surprise? Are you with Ewan—I mean Lieutenant Commander Jones?'

Tom grinned. 'Yes, Mrs Jones,' he said, maintaining the formality. 'He's in this office with Lieutenant Saunders.' Tom knocked on the office door and opened it. 'Commander. Your wife.'

Hazel entered the office, and Tom shut the door behind her.

'Ewan. What's going on?' she asked, guessing that something was wrong and his presence must have something to do with her missing nurses.

'Lieutenant Saunders has explained about the disappearance or abduction of your team, and to cap it all I've received a note that threatens you if I don't turn up at a meeting this evening. But that's a different issue. The important thing is that you're all right and, by the looks of it, well looked after by Saunders here.'

'Yes I am, although I'm damned worried about my nurses. What next?'

'You are coming with me. Saunders is sorting out everything to do with you here.'

'Saunders, thanks for everything. No doubt we will be in touch again shortly.'

'Certainly, Commander,' said Lieutenant Saunders. He added, 'There's also a Mister Cross who will be meeting with you at the port.'

'John Cross?'

'Yes. Some sort of civvy or whatever.' Saunders smirked. 'Not too sure who he is, but he's related to my assistant!'

'Hmm. Somehow I guessed he'd be involved,' murmured Ewan.

Saunders frowned.

'It's OK. I've got a good idea what's going on,' said Ewan.

'You do?' asked Hazel as she turned to leave the office.

'Not really,' said Ewan.

'And we have an escort,' said Hazel, smiling to Tom Reynolds.

'You two can get acquainted later, along with Dan Perry,' said Ewan.

'Dan's outside, keeping a beady eye on things, sir,' said Tom.

Hazel suddenly felt safe and secure with these two old compatriots from her ordeal in the North African desert more than two years earlier.

All four rode to the port's Naval Shipping Control Office, Dan Perry driving.

CHAPTER 22

THE PLOT THICKENS

WAN INSTRUCTED DAN Perry to take Hazel to MGB 650 and explain to Lieutenant Callendar to look after her until Ewan could return from the port's Naval Shipping Control Office. Ewan and Tom Reynolds entered the port offices and immediately found John Cross and Commander Alec Gratton. With them was Lieutenant Gary Brookes, who was about to leave. 'Ewan, Lieutenant Brookes has no idea who delivered that note to you, but I think things are beginning to make sense,' said Cross. 'OK, Lieutenant, you can go.'

'You know where to get me if you need any help,' said Lieutenant Brookes, who then left the office. CPO Tom Reynolds closed the door behind him.

'Ewan, the situation is as far as we can ascertain or maybe guess at,' said Gratton. 'Somehow, your wife's nursing party has been abducted by characters, which we don't fully understand at present, but they thought they would be abducting your wife.'

'Why do they want Hazel?' Ewan was worried.

'I think we've got that worked out,' said Cross.

Gratton continued. 'They want to use Hazel as a hostage and as a threat to you if you don't cooperate with them. This is where it gets grubby. We are guessing "they" want to know about your operation across the water in Albania. Now the only desperate buggers who want to know, we are guessing, are the Russians.'

'So that's how the Russian NKVD are involved?' Ewan asked.

'Correct,' said Gratton, who then turned to Cross.

'We suspect that there's a complicating factor which we have not yet fathomed out. Our agent in Albania believes it has something to with the Nazis. He reckons that an entire SS division is involved. Several are cut off from Germany, and this particular one is fully armed and provisioned with more than ninety tanks and other heavy weapons.

'Our agent believes that the SS commander is negotiating with the NKVD to hand over all their weapons in exchange for a safe passage out of Albania to a destination not yet determined. But it involves a ship. So it could be anywhere.'

Ewan screwed up his lips. 'Hang on! Are you suggesting that the SS and NKVD, which I thought were arch-enemies, are in some sort of pact?'

'Looks like it,' said Cross. 'Our agent has backed this up with information that he has obtained from the communist partisans, most of all of whom were thrown out of Greece.'

'I'm still lost on this. So what's our involvement?' Ewan questioned.

'If it's true, then the SS weapons must not get into the hands of the communists. Their main problem is that they don't have any heavy weapons and cannot get any directly from Russia at present. Stalin seems to be a little hesitant, for once, in making an open move in the Balkans after the fiasco in Greece,' said Gratton.

'OK. Admiral Kelly briefed me on part of this. But I bet there's more to this than meets the eye,' said Ewan.

Cross shot a glance to CPO Tom Reynolds. 'No offence, Chief, but do you mind leaving us for a few minutes?'

'Yes, sir. No problem.' CPO Reynolds left the room.

'Ewan, this whole operation was set up to expose a bunch of traitors or spies—call 'em what you will—back in London. It was leaked that we were assembling a special task force to enter the Balkans, namely Albania, following the support we gave to Greece,' said Cross.

'To stop the spread of communism?' said Ewan.

'Yes. But what's complicated everything is the news about this Nazi SS division. It's a new game changer. And to add to the confusion, Hazel's nursing team seems to have been caught up in the intrigue to threaten you,' said Gratton.

'Also, the abduction seems to have been botched,' said Cross.

'You mean they haven't got Hazel to bargain with?' Ewan asked.

'That's about the size of it. It means we need to tread carefully. Your meeting this evening with these shady characters—we want you to keep the meeting. Well, you'll have to play it as it comes. But if they think that they have Hazel, then for the time being we let them continue with that notion,' said Cross.

'It will also keep those nurses safe, at least for the moment,' added Gratton.

'Do you think they're in danger?' asked Ewan.

'Seriously so,' said Cross. 'As soon as the abductors find out that they don't have Hazel or cannot compromise you, the nurses are as good as dead. There's one more thing. My younger brother, Lieutenant Cross, is here with the Royal Military Police. Hazel has already met him. He's been nosing around the refugees who have just arrived. He's confirmed from a rumour that five women dressed in military uniforms, possibly nurses, have been landed in Tirana.'

CHAPTER 23

THE MEETING

E WAN LEFT AND made his way back to MGB 650 with CPO Reynolds, who sensed that Ewan was disturbed. 'Is there anything I can do to help, sir? Without the need to know, if you know what I mean?' said CPO Reynolds. Ewan cast a glance at Reynolds and shook his head slightly. They carried on walking slowly towards the quayside. As they came into sight of MGB 650, Ewan stopped.

'Chief, we have a difficult situation on our hands. I wish I could give you the details. It's tricky, but no doubt Commander Gratton will fill you in on it later. For the time being, keep whatever you pick up to yourself,' said Ewan. He knew that Tom Reynolds had a knack for guessing accurately awkward situations, and he trusted him.

'Very good, sir. May I ask, does this involve your good lady?'

'Yes it does,' said Ewan, looking first towards the moored gunboats and then back to CPO Reynolds. 'She's in no particular danger; at least we don't think so. However, I want you and Lieutenant Callendar to keep a close eye on her. I've got an errand to do this evening and will need a couple of lads to cover me, but without being seen.'

'I can arrange that, sir. Like in the old days?'

'Yeah. Dan Perry would be useful also,' said Ewan.

CPO Reynolds left Ewan as they approached Lieutenant Callendar, who was waiting on the quayside in front of MGB 650.

'James, we need to have a quiet chat aboard,' said Ewan.

'Yes, sir. Oh, I've put your wife in the wardroom for the moment. I'm guessing you want to keep her here with us.'

'You read my mind,' said Ewan.

Ewan and Callendar went aboard MGB 650 and deposited themselves in the small, cramped chart room. Ewan closed the door.

Ewan explained to Callendar what was happening and told him about the meeting he was to have later. He left out the part about the deception plan to keep Hazel's whereabouts secret.

Lieutenant James Callendar had grown to like Ewan and guessed that something difficult and dangerous was taking place. He offered Ewan additional cover, including himself.

'Thanks, James. Much appreciated. But a low profile is needed. Dan Perry and a couple of lads should be enough. I'll explain to my wife that she is to keep as low a profile as she can aboard here, until we can find out what is going on. Chief Reynolds is also in on this. I'll leave you both to look after Hazel—er, my wife.'

The evening approached. Ewan made himself ready to make the meeting. He armed himself with a standard Browning 9 mm pistol tucked inside his tunic and a smaller .38 pistol, borrowed from Cross, concealed in the side of his sock. This was just in case the meeting 'got out of hand' as Cross had put it earlier. Ewan arrived at the Napoli Restaurant and Bar at 19:45 and sat at the back of the bar with a clear view of the street entrance and access to the rear door. He guessed that by being early, he might get a better idea of whom he was meeting and if it was to be more than one person. He nursed a small glass of beer and held the front page of the local Italian newspaper in front of himself, resting it partly on the table. He was not in naval uniform, so to any of the local bar patrons, he was just another local man. It was a simple guise suggested by Gratton. The time ticked by. There was only one local man who entered the bar, dressed in grubby overalls as a labourer, before the appointed hour. Ewan quietly and unassumingly observed the bar and restaurant. At two minutes past eight, two men arrived and sat at a table inside the restaurant, next to the street entrance.

Ewan did not move but carried on reading his newspaper; at least that was the appearance he gave. He kept his head down as though reading the paper, and by adjusting the newspaper, he was able to observe the two men. They looked around the restaurant, not giving a second look to Ewan. A couple of minutes passed and they ordered drinks. *Cognac*, thought Ewan. They began looking more discerningly around the restaurant, the bar, and the outside tables. No one else had arrived or left in those minutes. Ewan decided on making the first move.

He folded his newspaper and finished his glass of beer. The waiter came over to Ewan and was paid. Ewan strolled slowly over to the entrance, navigating slowly past several tables, and stopped in front of the two men.

'Are you gentlemen here to see me?' asked Ewan slowly, without any hesitation.

'Commander Jones?' said one of the men.

'Yes. Now what's this all about?'

The other man pulled a chair out. 'Please sit with us,' he said.

'Would you like a drink?' asked the other.

'No, thanks. Let's get down to business. What's this got to do with my wife? Where is she?' Ewan asked in a forthright tone.

'First things first,' said the man who was sitting opposite Ewan. His voice seemed sickly, like that of a sleazy gangster. 'We have your wife in a safe place. You have information that we want in exchange for returning your wife to you unharmed.'

Ewan slowly looked to each man in turn. 'What sort of information?'

'Your mission here or, should I say, across the sea in Albania.'

'Mission? It's no secret. I'm heading a patrol group to police these waters specially for escaping Nazis.'

'Come now, Commander. Your group is a special group. You have an interest in gathering intelligence on operations in Albania and the Adriatic. All we want is the details,' said the man who was apparently the leader.

'You're asking me to betray my own country and the Allies? That raises the question of who you are working for. You're not Nazis. So, who are you?'

They did not answer Ewan's question. Both men sipped at their drinks.

The leader looked up from his glass with a sickening grin. 'Think it over, Commander. We'll be in touch tomorrow morning.'

'And my wife?'

'She's safe, as long as you cooperate.'

The two men stood up sharply and left the restaurant, losing themselves in the busy evening street.

Ewan was left mulling over the short meeting and their demand. Clearly, they had not gotten Hazel; then whom had they gotten? He ordered another drink and sat quietly, contemplating the few words that he had exchanged with them. Something was not right, he thought. Hazel was safe on his boat and protected by the crew and his commandos. What did these men really want, and who were they? Whoever they had captive as a hostage was safe for the moment, but as soon as they were to find out that they don't have Hazel, then what?

Ewan's throat was dry. He needed to think and so ordered a drink. Ewan thumbed his glass of beer; it was warming in the early evening heat. Was there something that Cross had not told him? He then reviewed what he knew and, for that matter, what he didn't know. What if these characters were going to abduct Hazel? But then she was safe on the 650 boat with the crew, and Naval Intelligence knew where she was.

There was one more fact: the man said they would be in touch with Ewan tomorrow morning. Did that mean that they knew his patrol group would be leaving port later that morning? If so, then there must be a spy or traitor or whatever working within the Naval Shipping Control Office.

The presence of the patrol group was no secret, but its embarkation was. What should he do next? He finished his beer and paid the waiter.

'Anything the matter, señor?' asked the waiter, who could see that Ewan was deep in thought.

'Oh, nothing. Thank you,' replied Ewan.

The waiter left but turned around briefly, sensing that Ewan was disturbed.

Lieutenant Gary Brookes's office within the port's Naval Shipping Control Office was shrouded in a smog of tobacco smoke; Brookes was the only one not smoking. He tolerated smoking but was close to being suffocated by Commander Alec Gratton's pipe, which the commander puffed slowly, waiting for Ewan to arrive. Ewan did not go directly to the port from the restaurant but took a roundabout walk. He wanted to clear his mind and also guessed that the characters whom he had met might well have him under surveillance. His action might be viewed as that of a worried man, worried for the safety of his wife. It was a simple deception, and unbeknown to Ewan, it had succeeded. In addition, Ewan did not know that Cross had also put a couple of undercover local intelligence agents on him. Apart from Ewan's being armed, Cross had a suspicion that the men he was to meet were NKVD. One of his agents reported back, while the other tailed Ewan discreetly. The latter agent had also identified an NKVD agent following Ewan.

Ewan entered the office to be confronted by Brookes, Cross, Gratton, and a thick, suffocating fog of tobacco smoke. It nearly took his breath away.

CHAPTER 24

MISINFORMATION

THE MORNING SUN rose above the horizon of the Adriatic, bathing the port, its buildings, and the ships in the harbour in a refreshing coat of clean cream paint. It eventually turned to brilliant white. Ewan sat at the map table of his small, cramped gunboat. Hazel was still asleep in his also small, cramped cabin. He rehearsed what he would say to the NKVD agents. For good measure, Cross and Gratton had prepared a signal sheet and a small chart of Ewan's mission; it was all fictitious, but it was suitably detailed with some real facts to be plausible.

Six hours earlier, Ewan had completed his briefing with Cross and Gratton. He left Hazel to bed down in his cabin. Her only instruction was to stay inside the gunboat in case of prying eyes from the shore. To aid the deception, she was given a navy-blue boiler suit to wear and a battered sailor's cap, in case she did venture on deck. She decided to stay within the confines of the open bridge and chart radio cabin when not in Callendar's cabin. It was a cramped existence; the MGB and MTBs were not designed to be out at sea for more than a few days.

Ewan went up on deck. A rating offered him a hot mug of coffee, which seemed to be more plentiful than tea or cocoa.

Ewan leaned on the deck rail, looking forward to the horizon, the view broken only by the sheeted three-inch two-pounder gun, the gunboat's main heavy armament. The briefing and associated facts tumbled through his mind again and again. So, the characters whom he had met were known to be Russian NKVD agents, and as he recalled, their accents were Eastern European.

It was a few minutes to six. The crew were awake or awakening, to make ready to slip port. This would be in four hours, at ten o'clock. When and how the NKVD agents would contact Ewan was a mystery, but they had seemed well informed, except for Hazel's whereabouts. Ewan finished his coffee and returned to the chart radio cabin, where Leading Signaller Wilkes was shuffling a wad of signals and then set about checking his radio. It was his prize possession. He treated it personally.

'Anything new in since last night?' Ewan asked Wilkes.

'No, nothing, sir,' replied Wilkes, who rechecked his wavelength dial.

Ewan returned to the bridge. He was joined by Lieutenant Callendar and CPO Davy. They exchanged views on how to split the flotilla when off the Albanian coast. It was something they had not discussed beforehand, in case there were any last-minute changes in their orders. They also exchanged views on whether there would be any serious conflict or shooting now that the major part of the German Army had surrendered. Their orders were to keep on their guard. Their main task was to patrol the Adriatic and especially the Albanian coast for any unusual shipping and, in particular, escaping Nazis. According to Cross and Gratton, this was known to the NKVD. What was not clear was why they were interested, particularly why they were interested in the timing of the patrol and its general station.

'Anyway, sir, it seems quiet enough now,' said CPO Davy.

'Famous last words,' said Callendar.

Wilkes popped his head out from his radio shack, which was part of the chart room. 'Signal for you, sir. I've decoded it.' Wilkes handed it to Ewan.

Ewan read it and passed it to Callendar, then glanced to CPO Davy. 'You spoke too soon, Chief.'

'We're to detach most of our flotilla to patrol south. We are to head towards Tirana but keep just out of sight of land,' said Callendar. 'Why split our forces?'

'I think we are to act as a decoy or create some deception,' said Ewan.

Wilkes appeared again. 'Second signal, sir. Plain language. "You have two chicks." End of message.'

Ewan knocked lightly on the cabin door where Hazel was ensconced. She was awake and sipping a hot mug of coffee given to her earlier. Ewan closed the door behind him and gave Hazel a big hug and kiss. 'Wish we could do more.'

'I'm happy as long as I am with you. I awoke earlier and popped my head out but saw you were doing sailor's things. I didn't think we had departed yet. When will that be? And I guess I am going with you,' she said. She squeezed his hand affectionately.

'Yes. It will be safer for you to come with us. We also have a slight change of plan, but that won't affect you. Once we are out at sea, I'll explain everything to you. We slip at ten, so time for a good breakfast.'

Ewan did not interfere with the general running and making ready of the gunboat; that was Callendar's job. He did, however, pace the deck, avoiding the crew carrying out their assigned duties, looking towards the quayside. No sign of the NKVD agents or anyone else unusual for that part of the quayside. The time passed. He glanced at his watch. It was nine when Lieutenant Brookes appeared. He hurried to MGB 650. Ewan realised he had a message and strode off the gunboat to meet him.

Brookes saluted. 'Urgent message for you, sir.' He handed the folded paper to Ewan.

The message read, 'Meet at the Blue Lagoon cafe at 09:15.'

'Tell Lieutenant Callendar where I've gone. He'll know what to do,' said Ewan.

Brookes scurried onto MGB 650 to find Callendar.

Ewan walked briskly to the Blue Lagoon Café; it was about a

five-minute walk, past the port entrance. He sat at an outside street table and felt in his pocket. He had the fake chart and information.

Lieutenant Brookes told Callendar where Ewan had gone. 'Right, Gary. Get a message to Commander Gratton and let him know. Everything will be OK here.'

Brookes returned to his office and informed Gratton.

Gratton was having breakfast with Cross. 'Looks like our friends have made the next contact with Ewan. Now let's see what happens.'

'And they have no idea about the change in deployment of Ewan's flotilla?' Cross asked.

'None, I hope. The uncoded message might confuse them.'

Cross chuckled. 'I like the bit about two chicks. I'll back it up with a coded message once they're out to sea. I've had a message from our agents in Tirana that the five women in nurses' uniforms have been put on an old steamship which will be leaving its anchorage up the coast later this afternoon.'

'If they honour the agreement to let them go, how will they do it? They will be at sea.'

'I doubt that they will keep their word,' said Cross coldly.

One of the NKVD agents whom Ewan had met with approached him and sat at his table. Ewan said nothing.

'Well, Commander. What can you tell us about your mission?' asked the NKVD agent.

'You already know. So, what exactly do you want?'

'Your time of arrival and position off the Albanian coast.'

Ewan was surprised. Needing to think quickly, he gave the impression that he was worried. Why was the position off the Albanian coast and the time significant? And importantly, how and when would these agents release the abducted nurses and especially the one they thought was Hazel? 'What about my wife?'

'She will be unharmed and released when we have safely completed our mission.'

'Not good enough,' said Ewan in a tone of agitation.

'We will put her ashore near Tirana. You will be told exactly where and when,' said the NKVD agent. 'Now, Commander Jones, the information.'

Ewan hesitated but provided the plan for his flotilla, including the splitting of the group. He guessed, rightly, that someone in Allied HQ Malta or Brindisi Shipping Control was spying for the Russians. For good measure, he passed on two copy documents: one a small chart of the Albanian coast, and the other the patrol dispositions of each boat. Both were the fictitious documents prepared by Cross earlier.

Ewan took a last-minute chance to find out more about the NKVD operation. 'Tell me, whatever your name is, what the hell is going on? You are, I am guessing, Russian. We're supposed to be allies.'

The NKVD agent grinned. 'I am simply carrying out orders. Goodbye, Commander Jones. Have a good voyage.' The agent got up from the table and scurried away. He was followed discreetly by one of Cross's local agents.

Ewan returned to MGB 650.

CHAPTER 25

DIVERSION

WITH THE PORT and the harbour left behind them, Hazel clambered up the narrow companionway to the bridge and asked James Callendar for permission to be on the bridge. Ewan swung round to see her. Callendar smiled. 'Of course. How could I deny such a request from the boss's lady?'

'Thank you, Lieutenant,' replied Hazel, snuggling up closer to Ewan.

'Come up for some fresh air?' Ewan asked.

'I'll try to enjoy this cruise. So, what have you been up to? What are you not telling me?'

Ewan explained what he had been up to. Coxswain CPO Davies and Leading Seaman Tanner, on the helm, also listened with some surprise.

'Sir, if the Ruskies know where we are going, then what's it all about? If they're our allies, then why are they so secretive?' CPO Davies asked.

'That's a good question,' added Callendar.

'Not sure. But I'm guessing that they're up to something else and not just spreading communism here in the Balkans. Anyway, we have a special pickup to make, which the NKVD don't know about. Then there's the abducted nurses.' Ewan looked to Hazel. 'Somehow they still think they've got you and your nurses. They're going to let us know where we can pick them up. That's where we are sailing to first, after we split the flotilla. I just hope they keep their word and that the nurses are unharmed.'

'That's the worry. Isn't it?' said Hazel.

'But what makes them believe they have, er, you?' asked Callendar, looking to Hazel.

'Could be the nurse from RAF Akroteri. Cyprus. Her uniform is different from the others. It's a little more formal than ours. She would probably look to be in charge. They've guessed wrong.'

'Let's hope they don't discover their mistake,' said Ewan.

It was a sobering thought. Cross had made it clear to Ewan that he thought the nurses' lives would be in jeopardy should the NKVD discover the truth.

MGB 650 cruised slowly towards the Albanian coast with MTB 702, commanded by Sub Lieutenant John Marsden, trailing five hundred yards off on MGB 650's aft port quarter. The other MTBs had been detached to patrol the southern Albanian coast adjoining Greece. In overall command was Lieutenant Tony Thornton, skipper of MTB 703. This part of the plan had been confirmed with the NKVD agents, except Ewan was taking his boats closer to the harbour of Tirana first. He wanted to find the merchant steamer that had left Bari two days earlier. There was something odd about it, and both Gratton and Cross were convinced that the five nurses had been taken on board.

Hazel found the high-speed boats exhilarating even though they were cruising at twenty-five knots and not their top speed of over forty knots. She was mesmerised as the other MTBs departed company from them. She could now understand why Ewan loved to be out at sea on these small craft. They were a microcosm of the much larger warships with their own way doing things but with the same navy traditions as battleships.

Ewan suggested that Hazel should rest before they reached the coast. He added that hopefully her nursing skills would not be needed. The gunboat had a sick berth attendant as part of the crew, but Ewan had an uneasy feeling that everything may not be as straightforward as Cross or Gratton had said. There was something missing in the whole affair, something that the Russians did not want their allies to know about. The discussions with Cross indicated that the Russians did not have the full capacity to support the communist insurgence in Greece and the other Balkan states; indeed, the communists in Greece had been defeated by the nationalists with British help. With this tumbling around in Ewan's mind, his thoughts returned to the abducted nurses and his beloved Hazel.

Ewan knocked lightly on the door to the cabin where Hazel was dozing. He popped his head in through the door as she propped herself up on the bunk.

'Come on in,' she said. Her smile glowed, inviting him to her.

He shut the door. 'I can guess what you want,' he said softly.

She purred and grinned.

'Sorry, love. Not quite the time or place, but highly tempting.'

'Are we near the coast?' she asked.

'Yes. Just about in sight.'

She tidied herself and followed him to the bridge.

'Marsden's detaching now, sir,' said Callendar.

'What's happening?' asked Hazel.

'I'm detaching MTB 702 to search the coast south of the Tirana inlet while we prowl around here. We're about ten miles north of Tirana,' said Ewan.

CHAPTER 26

DRIBBLES OF SWEAT

THE SS *MARINO* was tied up to a long stone jetty that just about accommodated her length. It had been used as a ferry crossing point to Bari in Italy before the war and during Italy's invasion of Albania. It had relatively good road access for heavy vehicles. Nurse Marjory Shaw peered through the small scuttle of the cabin to view the jetty. The cabin was designed for four passengers. Along with the other nurses, she had made the best of their accommodation since leaving Bari. It was stiflingly hot, and they were all suffering the high temperature with little water. What was of concern was the fate of Nurse Doreen Canley. She had been singled out for interrogation and had not been seen or heard of in more than three days. Nurse Lesley Grant thought she had heard a woman scream the day they were herded onto the SS *Marino* outside Bari. As the others had not heard anything, she dismissed it. Nevertheless, they were all scared. Nothing seemed to make sense, especially the need for their captors to find Hazel Jones. As a group, they had debated the issue several times over. It was early in one conversation that Marjory Shaw commented on Doreen Canley's uniform; it was different from theirs. Maybe their captors had drawn the conclusion that she was Hazel as they certainly knew that Hazel was in charge of them.

'Where are we?' asked one of the nurses.

'Alongside a quay, but I don't think it's Italy. Must have sailed across the Adriatic,' said Marjory, who then took another look out of the scuttle. Helen Grayling joined her. They could both just about make out what was happening.

Marjory turned her head away, leaving Helen to get a full view of the quayside.

Helen seemed to be suddenly quiet and transfixed by her view.

'Helen. What's the matter?' Marjory asked, sensing that something had captured Helen's attention.

'There's soldiers on the quay. Four of them. And they're coming aboard.'

'Great. Maybe now we will be released,' said Lesley Grant, who was curious to see for herself.

Helen turned to face the others. 'It's not what you think.' She hesitated and looked starkly at them. 'I think they're Germans. Nazis. Black uniforms of the SS!'

'What!' said Marjory, pushing Helen aside to see for herself.

They were SS. Marjory's heart sank. 'God, what are we involved with?'

'More to the point, what are the SS doing here? I thought the Germans had left this area a couple of months ago,' said Lesley.

'That was my understanding too,' said Helen.

They were suddenly fearful of their future. Nothing made sense. Then, after a few minutes' silence, Marjory returned their thoughts to Nurse Doreen Canley. What had happened to her?

'Do you think there's a connection with the interest in Hazel?' said Lesley.

'The only thing I can think of is that the interest is in Hazel's husband,' said Marjory.

'Ewan?' Helen queried.

'Yes. I think they, whoever they are, want to get at Ewan by kidnapping Hazel,' said Marjory. She turned away from the scuttle and peered at the others.

Jo Mitchell had been relatively quiet up to this point, but she was analysing the conversation. 'I think they're Russians and they're up to no good. I'd put money on it that they want to know what Ewan's mission is.'

'Now that's a thought,' said Helen. 'But where does that leave us?'

'More to the point, what happens when they realise that they don't have Hazel and that we've been telling the truth?' said Marjory.

'So, what have they done with Doreen?' asked Jo.

James Callendar looked ahead with his binoculars. The Albanian coast was in view. He ordered the coxswain to reduce speed and called Ewan to the bridge. Hazel nudged Ewan to leave the cabin and asked if she could join him. Ewan, unable to refuse, escorted her to the bridge. The wind caught her hair; she shook her head to clear the hair from her eyes. She settled herself to the back and starboard side of the small bridge, next to Able Seaman Peters, who was nursing his Vickers machine gun, the belt of ammunition already fed into position. It looked sinister and businesslike, Hazel thought. She put a smile to the gunner. Callendar spotted her gaze at the Vickers. 'Just in case we run into any bother,' he said.

'Are you expecting trouble?' she asked. The question was not really addressed to anyone in particular and could have been interpreted as being a little naive.

Callendar shot a glance to Ewan, realising that Ewan had not told Hazel about the coded signal received earlier from Malta.

'If we run into trouble, I suggest you stay in your cabin,' said Ewan. It was not so much a suggestion as it was an order. Hazel began to see the other side of Ewan, something she had experienced only once before, three years earlier in the North African desert. She had learned to do exactly what he ordered. This was their loving relationship as Ewan rarely made any commands or demands. She felt safe with him.

Suddenly, Leading Seaman Dan Perry appeared from the radio cabin. 'Sir. Signal from Malta. I've decoded it.' He gave the signal message paper to Ewan.

Ewan read the message: 'Chicks embarked on ship leaving Tirana.'

'Does that mean the nurses, sir?' Callendar asked.

'Yes it does. This complicates matters. We have to rendezvous with a special patrol farther up the coast.' He looked hard to Callendar. 'Signal 702 to intercept. And add "Be careful." Something's not quite right here.'

Callendar passed the instruction to Dan Perry.

'What's going on?' asked Hazel.

Ewan explained that he had had no further contact with the NKVD agent who was supposed to let him know where to find Hazel or, rather, the person who the NKVD thought was Hazel. The signal from Malta must have been relayed from the commando party who had infiltrated the Tirana coast and were now the subject of the pickup.

Ewan went on to say that their primary mission was to pick up the commando surveillance team as they held vitally important information on the whereabouts of the Nazi SS division and the communist partisans.

Hazel felt a cold bead of sweat run down her spine. She realised that her party of nurses were in grave danger, especially once the NKVD discovered that they did not have her and that Ewan had played them.

CHAPTER 27

FEAR

THE SS *MARINO* began manoeuvring away from the quayside. There was a moaning of the steel hull grating along the stone quay as the ship swung out its bow to point to the open sea; the stern lazily slammed into the stonework of the quay once more. SS *Marino* was impatient to get away from Tirana harbour. The four nurses gazed at each other in turn. They also guessed that the ship was not hanging around. There had been much commotion half an hour earlier as they heard the steam derricks working hard to load a variety of cargo; most of it was boxed crates of weapons, explosives, and ammunition, in addition to a large tracked fighting vehicle, which was a German Panzer Tiger Mark IV battle tank. The nurses said nothing at first; they simply wondered what was to become of them. Nurse Marjory Shaw kept her thoughts to herself, but the earlier sight of a Nazi SS officer and the sound of German voices had led her to believe that she and the other nurses were not being returned to Italy. Whatever plan they were part of had changed.

'Why are they in such a hurry to get out of here?' said Helen Grayling.

'And why haven't they put us ashore?' chipped in Lesley Grant.

'I suppose they will put us off in an out-of-the-way place once they clear of this area,' said Jo Mitchell, trying to convince herself that they were in no danger.

They all looked to Marjory. 'What are you thinking?' Helen asked.

'I'm still concerned for Doreen,' Marjorie said. Although this was not entirely a lie, she still had a bad feeling about their own fate.

The minutes passed by as the SS *Marino* tumbled through some large waves as it cleared the mouth of the harbour and caught a strong coastal current, its increased cargo weight making its presence felt.

'There's some commotion outside,' said Helen, straining to look through the small scuttle. She could see open sea. She stepped back into the centre of the cabin as the door swung open and an Italian crewman stepped inside. Behind him was Nurse Doreen Canley. She stumbled over the door coaming and was caught by another Italian crewman, before striking the deck. She was dishevelled, her uniform torn and undone. Her reddened face showed that she had been struck several times. There was a little dried trickle of blood on her lower lip.

'Christ's sake, what happened to you!' blurted Helen.

Marjory turned on the Italian crewmen. 'What have you done to her?' she demanded.

'Not us, señoras,' muttered one of the crewmen.

Behind him entered a large hulk of a man dressed in an ill-fitting dark suit and looking as sinister as any character in a Boris Karloff horror movie. The nurses peered at him and tried to tamp down their fear, only to have it compounded by another figure in a military uniform. Marjory immediately recognised him as the German officer she had observed on the quay, but now his uniform was clearly that of a Nazi SS officer. It made her shudder.

Jo and Helen took support of Doreen, who could barely walk unaided.

The sinister-looking NKVD agent growled at them. 'As this is not Hazel Jones, which one of you is?' he said with rising aggression in his tone.

'None,' bawled the SS officer.

The NKVD agent was surprised. 'But, Herr Obersturmbannführer Kranz, one of them has to be. The British know she is missing.'

Kranz gazed at the nurses in turn. 'You fool. The British have worked out that you have bungled everything. You captured these women as part of the operation to get Hazel Jones,' said Kranz.

'Then what do we do?' the NKVD agent asked.

'First, get as far away from this area as quickly as possible,' said Kranz, stepping back outside the cabin doorway.

'And what about these women?'

'Do what you originally planned with them,' replied Kranz ominously.

They left the cabin. The two Italian crewmen were fearful for the nurses and looked very nervous. Their fear infected the nurses.

MGB 650 found the quiet cove nestling beneath high-sided cliffs. There was a small pathway down to the beach; a lookout could just about make out some figures at the water's edge. The party of commandos spotted the gunboat. The radio on the gunboat crackled to life. The commando signaller made contact. 'Switch to Aldis.'

'Why switch to Aldis lamp?' asked Callendar, shooting a glance at Dan Perry.

'Radiolocation stuff. This position can be tracked,' said Perry.

Callendar did not like to be pulled up or corrected, but on this occasion he realised the sense behind it.

Ewan grinned. Callendar was a good officer but sometimes lacked common sense, he thought. 'OK. Make to shore. Closing,' said Ewan.

'Everyone be alert for any movement on the cliffs and around us. Yell out if you see anything. Gunners, make ready,' ordered Callendar.

The clicks of the ammunition loading into the breaches of the Vickers machine guns and Oerlikon heavy-calibre guns were distinctive, just like a conductor bringing his orchestra to play. Hazel ducked below decks as ordered. So this was what it was like when a fight at sea was about to take place, she thought: pent up nervous tension on the edge of exploding.

The gunboat steadily made its way into the cove. The water was deep enough for the gunboat to close within a few feet of the water's edge of mixed shingle and sand. A short scrambling net was lowered onto the shore side. Almost immediately the commandos began wading into the water and climbing the scrambling net.

'Three more covering our rear,' bellowed a voice that seemed to be familiar to Ewan.

The remaining three commandos scrambled aboard. 'We have company, sir,' said one of the commandos.

'Where?' shouted the familiar voice.

'Top of the cliff path,' came the reply.

'Let's get the hell out of here,' said Ewan.

'Damned good idea, Ewan,' said the familiar voice.

'Bloody hell! Henry Blackwell,' croaked Ewan.

'The very same,' said Blackwell.

Henry Blackwell made his way onto the gunboat's bridge. 'Excuse me, gentlemen.' The bridge was crowded, but space was made for him. 'No time for formalities. Your radio man, signaller, quickly,' snapped Blackwell.

Dan Perry appeared.

'Ah, Dan,' Blackwell said, recognising him. 'Good man. Send this message plain language, open to all,' said Blackwell, slightly out of breath.

'Good to see you again, sir,' said Perry, opening his message pad.

Blackwell gave Perry two sets of map references prefixed with the ominous word *target*, then added, 'And everything between.'

No sooner had Blackwell finished his message than firing came from the shore, especially from the clifftops.

Callendar ordered to return fire.

Ewan put in his additional order: 'Engines. Everything you've got!'

Within a minute, Dan Perry reappeared. 'Signal sent, sir.'

'Right. Send again and again until acknowledged,' said Blackwell anxiously.

Ewan, Callendar, and the coxswain in unison stared at Blackwell.

'I'll explain as soon as we're out of range of those bastards.' There seemed to be deep emotion and urgency in his voice.

The gunboat turned to the open sea and suffered its first hit near the aft Oerlikon gun mounting. Two seamen fell to the deck. Although they suffered wounds that bled, they were able to reattend their gun.

Another shell burst near the bow, raining some shrapnel, but fortunately no one was injured. The gunboat was quickly out of range. 'What guns were those?' asked Callendar rather nonchalantly as the gunboat's armaments ceased firing.

'Eighty-eights, I think,' said Blackwell.

'What the hell are they doing mounted on those cliffs? Did they know we were coming?' asked Ewan.

'Sort of,' replied Blackwell. 'Now that we're clear, I wouldn't mind a cup of tea. Then I'll explain.'

Hazel, along with the leading sick berth attendant, tended to the injured seamen and a commando who had a clean bullet wound in his arm. A rating appeared with a mug of tea for the injured and then passed several more mugs to the bridge.

Blackwell was about to explain what had happened, when Signaller Dan Perry interrupted them. 'Sir. Signal from Malta.'

'Read it,' said Ewan. His hands were cupped around the mug.

'Message received. Insurance with you shortly. End.'

'Good. Now we can relax, and I'll explain,' said Blackwell. He sipped at his tea. 'We've known for some time about an SS Panzer division held up in the hills around here. It was a rumour at first, until we intercepted a message in Bari from an Allied Command HQ officer to a Soviet general in Budapest. We were able to decode it back in London. It confirmed our suspicions that we had moles, spies, maybe not traitors, in our midst passing information to the Russians.'

'Our allies?' Callendar asked.

'Yes. Except Joe Stalin has ideas of expanding the Russian sphere of influence politically through Europe. This gave us a chance to track these, er, spies down. Ewan, this is where your antics became important. The

Russian NKVD, secret police like the Gestapo, were in discussion with certain Nazis, mostly SS, to hand over their weaponry in exchange for a safe passage out of Europe. We rightly guessed South America. One ship had already been intercepted by the Americans, who kindly kept it quiet.

'Now comes the interesting bit. The NKVD didn't have any agents to infiltrate our shipping control offices in Brindisi, but we had let it be known that a flotilla of patrol boats was headed for the Albanian coast to intercept another ship laden with Nazi SS goodies and some high-ranking characters. They needed times, dates, and places. The NKVD knew that you'—he looked at Ewan—'were to be put in command and so conjured a plan to blackmail you into revealing your action plan by abducting your wife.'

'Bloody marvellous. It was a giant set-up from the beginning,' grumbled Ewan.

'Precisely, but with a few bonuses, such as using the Russian agents and identifying their sources.' Blackwell coughed. 'Incidentally, Ewan, where is Hazel?'

'Down below, tending the wounded.'

'Here?! Well, what a turn-up. She might be needed to tend to the abducted nurses when we intercept the SS *Marino*. That's the Italian ship we believe they're on.'

'What will happen to the nurses once they find out they don't have the commander's wife?' asked Callendar.

'That's a good question,' replied Blackwell, looking longingly out to sea. 'That's a bloody good question. But I guess they never intended to release them!'

CHAPTER 28

INSURANCE

MTB 702, COMMANDED by Sub Lieutenant John Marsden, motored steadily along the coast of Albania, south of Tirana, keeping six miles from the coast so as not to attract any undue attention from the shore or fishing boats; this was Ewan's order. They had also picked up the open radio message from MGB 650 but, as briefed, maintained radio silence unless they had something of interest to report. Marsden recalled from his briefing in Malta that Admiral Kelly was providing some 'insurance'. He wondered what this insurance was. He was about to find out.

His radar operator squeaked his voice through the intercom to the bridge. 'Bridge—radar. Large contact west of us. Ten miles. Moving at about twenty-five knots. I don't think it's a merchantman. Too fast. I think it's a large warship.'

'Destroyer?' Marsden asked.

'Bigger than that, sir. A cruiser maybe.'

'A cruiser? What's her direction?'

'North-north-east. She'll be visible to the 650 boat in less than thirty minutes. She'll also be on their radar soon.'

'Right. Keep an eye it, and let me know if it changes direction,' said Marsden.

'Hold on, sir. We have another contact. Smaller. Freighter maybe. Ten miles astern of us. Doing about fourteen knots. Must have come out of Tirana.'

'Chief, slow to ten knots. We'll let her catch us up,' said Marsden to his chief coxswain.

Marsden's MTB sloshed lazily along at ten knots, striking the occasional large wave without much of a ripple throughout the boat. The minutes ticked by. The sun gleamed overhead as the heat of the afternoon began to make its presence known. It was early May; the weather was like summer, except the Adriatic Sea that had not yet warmed up from the winter spell. The sea temperature was a cool 17 degrees Celsius. *Just like back in England during the summer,* thought Marsden. He was thinking about home, Winchester, not far from Portsmouth, where he did most of his training and completing at Britannia Naval College, passing out as a sub lieutenant at the age of twenty-two. He had gone to engineering school near Portsmouth as a student after leaving school but then set his heart on the navy, much to his mother's anxiousness. However, a year earlier on the run-up to D-Day, he had proved himself as a good officer and was quickly put in charge of his own boat, a small craft. This suited him as it gave him a level of independence without the rigours of strict discipline of a larger warship. His daydreaming was suddenly shattered.

'Bridge—radar. Second contact. Another small ship following the first. Must have also put out from Tirana. Same course.'

Marsden thought quickly. They had been advised about one ship, but now two? 'Could it be MGB 650?'

'No, sir. She's still well out to west and getting near to the large contact. The cruiser?'

'Signals! Break radio silence and advise MGB 650 of second ship,' ordered Marsden. 'Radar, how far away is the first ship?'

'Six miles, sir. She should see us soon,' replied the radar operator.

'Chief. Gun crews close up!' roared Marsden.

'The war's almost over and here we are about to start shooting,' said the coxswain.

'I know, it's crazy. But this whole bloody war has been madness,' said Marsden.

Signaller Dan Perry popped his head out of his radio cabin. 'Sir, open signal from MTB 702. They have a second ship that has left Tirana following the first,' said Perry to Callendar. He added, 'The skipper is asking for orders, sir.' He looked to Ewan.

'Intercept. Stop and board. And add "Be careful",' said Ewan.

'I think Marsden will be careful, sir,' said Callendar.

'I know. That's why I chose him to cover us. Now it looks like we're to cover him.'

Hazel came onto the bridge and squeezed up alongside Blackwell. 'Hello, my dear. See you've been busy,' said Blackwell, noting the smear of blood on her uniform.

'Yes. One of your commandos has a nasty gash on his arm. Grazed by a bullet, but he'll be OK,' said Hazel, trying to hide her distrust of Blackwell. She remembered the last escapade she was involved with him in the North African desert.

Suddenly all hell broke loose as Callendar ordered full speed ahead. MGB 650 bucked up as she raced at more than thirty knots to join MTB 702. A sudden thunderous booming echoed from the direction of the cruiser. This was followed by a screaming screech as the air was torn apart above them. 'What the hell was that!' someone shouted.

'Naval gunfire. Sounds like six-inch shells to me—twelve of 'em,' said the coxswain, who was a well-seasoned Royal Navy regular.

Blackwell chuckled. 'The *Bermuda*. HMS *Bermuda*, I believe.'

'You know about this?' asked Ewan, guessing that Blackwell did know.

'Yes. Those map references were of the SS division armour and other stuff hidden in a valley just inside the coast. They'll never know what's hitting them.'

Hazel felt the cool and coldness of Blackwell. She knew only too well how devastating artillery gunfire could be, especially a naval bombardment.

'So, is this Admiral Kelly's "insurance" for us?' Ewan asked.

'Yes. And it's the main purpose of this mission. We need to stop the communists in the Balkans from getting their hands on that Nazi hardware. Took some convincing of high command until they heard the rumours about the Russians' behaviour in Poland and the Balkans. It also means we've plugged a gap in our intelligence, hopefully.' Blackwell's concluding remark was made in a tone of apprehension.

'How will you know if the bombardment has been successful?' asked Callendar.

'RAF and Americans are overflying in about an hour and mopping up anything left. They couldn't find it by normal reconnaissance. Well camouflaged and all that.'

'So, that was your mission, to find it?' Ewan enquired.

'Among other things,' replied Blackwell. He added nothing more.

Ewan cast an eye to Hazel. Both felt there was more to come.

Hazel's thoughts returned to her nurses; the war had become personal.

CHAPTER 29

SECOND SHIP

THERE WAS COMMOTION on the deck of the SS *Marino*. Several of the crew and their SS passengers were at the deck rails, straining to see a small dot emerging from the horizon. At a distance of six miles, it was but a tiny image, but it seemed to grow bigger by the minute. Its colour changed from dark grey to lighter grey. There were flickers of light from the reflection of the sun on the glazed parts of the boat: the scuttles, screens, and shining metal.

Marsden yelled to his radar operator, 'Where's that second ship contact?'

'Seems to have backed away to the north. It'll be visible to the 650 any minute now.'

'Right. Signal the 650 what's happening. We'll intercept the first ship.'

MTB 702 ploughed on. They were gaining on the second contact.

'Chief, action stations,' ordered Marsden. He wasn't taking any chances. He felt that there was something not quite right. Was the first ship a decoy to throw off the patrol from the second?

'Sir, signal from 650. Confirming intercept. And expect trouble,' said the signaller.

'Nice to let us know,' muttered Marsden, who seemed unsurprised.

The lookouts of MGB 650 found the ship as reported by MTB 702, but it was already visible on their radar. They increased speed to intercept and were converging fast on the unidentified ship. Callendar ordered, 'Action stations.'

Ewan sensed that something was unusual. Two ships had left Tirana. He turned to Blackwell. 'Henry, we have two ships. We're intercepting the first, and the 702 boat is tackling the second. Is there something we should know?'

'I'm not sure, but the second ship is the SS *Marino* and definitely has SS on board and likely some tanks that could be on the main deck. This first ship is a mystery, but I'll guess that it set out before we could observe operations in Tirana,' said Blackwell. He sensed Ewan's concern.

'Tanks on deck! Could they fire on the 702?' Ewan asked.

'Yes. If it's what we think, they could be those big Tigers with 88 mm guns.'

'Christ's sake. They could blow us out of the water!'

'Had better warn your chap to hang back,' said Blackwell in a low voice, 'just in case.'

'Hazel, this could get messy. I'd feel happier with you under cover, in your cabin,' said Ewan.

Hazel realised Ewan's concern for her, but also there was a thrill flowing through her veins. She was observing Ewan at his best with the others. This was real combat. Not ceremony, just hardened drill, the crew manning their guns with metal shields raised around the bridge to give some protection from shell splinters, she was told. She wanted to stay at his side but realised that this could distract him from his duty. She went below decks and found the leading sick berth attendant (SBA) getting his surgical instruments and other medical paraphernalia ready. She assisted, laying out everything needed to deal with wounds. The sight of the constrictor bandages used as tourniquets made her feel sick; most of her nursing was not surgical but was general nursing of postoperative patients.

The minutes passed by, and then the boat eased off its speed. Hazel and the leading SBA felt the boat swing. It was levelling up as it approached the ship a mile away. 'Any minute now,' mumbled the leading SBA.

'You've experienced this before?' Hazel asked.

'Yes, ma'am, several times. Maybe there won't be any shooting now that the war's over, but the boss isn't taking any chances.'

No sooner had he finished speaking than they could hear the shrill sound of the forward-deck 76 mm gun as it thundered a shot. Ewan had ordered a shot across the ship's bows.

There seemed to be a deafening silence. The seconds marched by.

'They're slowing,' someone said.

The distance between the two vessels lessened.

'Signal them to stop,' commanded Ewan to Leading Seaman Perry.

Perry manipulated his Aldis lamp, flickering the message as ordered.

They waited for a response.

'Got her name,' said CPO Davy. '*San Campello.*'

Blackwell strode to the edge of the bridge to observe the ship more closely.

'What is it?' Ewan asked.

'SS *San Campello*. She's Spanish. Now that makes sense,' replied Blackwell.

Perry shouted, 'They're replying, sir. They're saying they are Spanish and neutral. We have no jurisdiction. They are in international waters.'

Callendar looked to Ewan, who looked to Blackwell.

'Tell them to stop and prepare to be boarded,' said Blackwell.

Before Perry could signal, a machine gun opened fire from the *Campello*, raking MGB 650. Then another machine gun opened fire. Splintering metal and fragments of wood ravaged the smaller gunboat. Several of the gun crews, who were exposed to the firing, fell wounded. Callendar didn't wait for any orders from Ewan.

'Coxswain, open the distance bloody quick,' ordered Callendar.

MGB 650 swung crazily to starboard, lurching over sharply, throwing almost everyone off their feet.

'Get the wounded below,' bellowed Callendar. 'All guns, open fire!'

Ewan, spotting the wounded gun crew of the 60 mm Oerlikon, made his way over some wreckage to the gun mount. A seaman dragged away the last wounded gunner. Ewan seated himself in the gunner's firing position. Instead of another seaman who was loading the racks of 60 mm rounds, he glanced round to find Blackwell and one of his commandos loading the other ammunition racks. 'Ready!' shouted Blackwell and the commando.

Ewan aimed the gun at the *Campello* and pushed his foot on the unlock pedal. He pulled on the firing trigger. The 60 mm Oerlikon pounded away—*thump, thump, thump, thump, thump*. Blackwell grasped more clips of 60 mm ammunition from his commando and thrust them down hard into the firing-feed racks. Again, Ewan emptied the rack into the *Campello*.

Callendar manoeuvred his gunboat to come about on the opposite side of the *Campello*. All his guns were firing, pouring deadly shot into their target. As the distance was closed, Ewan deliberately aimed his gun at the waterline.

It worked. The *Campello* stopped.

While the fire was being exchanged, Hazel and the leading SBA treated the wounded. Thankfully there were no life-threatening injuries, but there was a lot of blood, which inevitably found its way onto Hazel's uniform.

The gunboat stopped and drifted slowly to the SS *Campello*. Hazel went up on deck carrying a first aid medical kit. There were several lightly injured crew remaining at their stations. She popped her head up, looking over the bridge screen. There she saw Ewan, Blackwell, a commando, and a sailor clinging to their 60 mm Oerlikon gun. The sight of Ewan manning the gun, a machine of destruction and death, made her feel humble. It sent a shiver through her spine. This was the man she loved so dearly, and now she was seeing him in another light. It was a contrast between the humanitarian she had learned to live with and the fighting sailor she now saw. He had bloody patches on his shirt and arms where he had been struck by splinters. She made her way to him as he unmounted himself from the firing position. He smiled to her.

'These lads need your attention. I'm all right,' he said, pointing to two wounded sailors lying next to an ammunition locker.

Callendar closed to port side of the *Campello*, his guns pointed menacingly towards the decks of the *Campello*. Those of his crew not at a gun position were armed with sub-machine guns, their fingers soothing their triggers in readiness to shoot.

CHAPTER 30

DECOY

WHILE HAZEL TENDED the wounded on deck, Ewan was getting ready to board the *Campello* with Blackwell and his commandos. Hazel momentarily looked up to see Ewan check his Thompson sub-machine gun. It again took her back to the North African desert in 1942, when he was attached to the Special Air Service special forces who had rescued her from the SS. Hazel thought that Ewan looked comfortable, but he was not. As she was tying off a bandage on a sailor's arm, she took a second glance up at Ewan and noticed that he and Blackwell were talking quietly with each other. She had the uneasy feeling that something was wrong. There was. Blackwell was about to mount the rope ladder to the *Campello*, when he turned.

'Ewan, on second thought, stay here. Let my lads sort things before you rummage aboard. This isn't the ship I was expecting,' said Blackwell. There was an ominous tone in his voice. Although they had originally decided that Ewan should get to the *Campello*'s bridge quickly to grab any documents that might be useful, Blackwell now thought differently. He did not believe that the party of nurses was on board.

'Henry!'

'No,' interrupted Blackwell. 'Ewan, I'm guessing that our nurses aren't on board.'

'We don't have time to argue. I'm coming with you,' said Ewan.

'Very well, but don't take any chances. And one more thing: who fired on us?!'

Blackwell reached the top of the ladder and was climbing onto the deck when a volley of shots rang out, followed by two quick bursts in succession. Ewan recognised the snarling cacophony of a Thompson sub-machine gun. He momentarily froze on the swaying ladder, then looked up. Blackwell appeared over the edge of the deck and grinned. Ewan continued to climb the ladder. The gun crews of MGB 650 tightened their grips on their weapons. Hazel was filled with fear as she saw Ewan clamber over the edge of the deck of the *Campello*. There were more shots fired.

A commando sergeant appeared over the edge of the deck rail and shouted down to Lieutenant Callendar: 'Sir. We're secure up here. No casualties. Checking the rest of this tub.'

Callendar acknowledged with a short salute and then glanced at Hazel. She was relieved.

The mid-deck of the *Campello* beneath the bridge was strewn with six bodies, only one of which was moving; the others were dead. A couple of the commandos took away the German Schmeisser sub-machine guns from the dead and dragged the wounded man away from them. The others started to comb the ship, while Ewan and Blackwell made their way to the bridge.

They were confronted by four men who appeared in shock. One stepped forward. Judging by the insignia on his cap, they surmised he was the captain. The helmsman was shaking and kept looking over his shoulder to one of the other two men. One was dressed in greasy overalls; the other, in a shabby but clean light-grey suit. Blackwell's instinct kicked in. He pointed his pistol towards the two men. 'OK. Who are you two?'

The captain looked at the man in the suit, who was concealing a Luger pistol behind his thigh. Blackwell aimed his pistol at the man and, without any warning, shot him in the leg. The man fell to the deck of the bridge, dropping his Luger pistol, which Blackwell quickly kicked away.

'Right, Captain. Time for you to explain, firstly, why you fired on us, and secondly, what the hell you are up to and where you are headed,' said Blackwell.

'And what is your cargo and who are the passengers?' added Ewan.

'I am Captain Marcelus, Italian Navy. I and my crew are not fascists. We have been forced into working for the Nazis,' said the captain.

Captain Marcelus went on to quickly explain what their mission was. They had been ordered at gunpoint by the SS to sail along the Dalmatian coast from Trieste in Northern Italy, mainly sailing by night to avoid any patrolling Allied aircraft. Once in Tirana, they were to take on board a number of German vehicles, including tanks, and a contingent of German SS. Their destination was to be South America, but that was all he knew.

Blackwell asked how many SS were on board.

Captain Marcelus estimated sixty but wasn't sure. He went on to say that one of the SS officers believed they could sink or at least severely damage the gunboat with their Panzer Faust antitank weapons and machine guns.

The commando sergeant appeared. 'We've bagged a number of Jerries, some in SS uniform. We have one minor casualty, but, er, the SS—well, their number's a bit less.'

'Anyone else on board other than the crew?' asked Ewan.

'No one, sir. We've accounted for eight crew,' said the sergeant, looking to Blackwell and then Captain Marcelus.

'That's right,' said Captain Marcelus. 'And are my crew all OK?'

The sergeant nodded.

Blackwell stroked his chin.

'Anything the matter?' Ewan asked.

'Er, yes. What do we do with our prisoners?'

'Lock 'em up in the forward hold,' suggested the sergeant.

'That might be a problem,' said Ewan, looking at the clinometer on the back wall of the bridge. It indicated a six-degree list to port.

Captain Marcelus also looked at the clinometer and then to the other crewman. 'My engine room crewman here reported that we are making water as you boarded. Your gunboat fired onto our waterline. We are holed and sinking.'

Ewan said nothing at first, as he had indeed fired on the waterline of the *Campello*. 'How long have we got before we founder?' he asked.

'Two, three, maybe four hours,' said Captain Marcelus. The engine room crewman, who understood English, agreed.

'Lifeboats should take everyone. We can escort them into Brindisi,' said Ewan. 'So, let's get moving.'

They evacuated the bridge. The ship's lifeboats were lowered. The SS prisoners were filed into three lifeboats and tethered to a fourth, which held the Italian crew. The lifeboats were roped to MGB 650. They were about to act as a tug for the lifeboats and head to Brindisi, when Ewan ordered them to stop.

'What's the matter, Ewan?' asked Blackwell.

'Radio. Radio operator and radio room.'

'Christ's sake, forgot about that in all the excitement,' said Blackwell.

Ewan, Blackwell, and two sailors from the gunboat reboarded the SS *Campello*. The list was much greater and the ladder was well away from the side of the ship. They made their way to the radio room.

'They're cutting it a bit fine. She's sinking faster than we thought,' said Callendar.

'Why is Ewan going back on board? Can't someone else go?' asked Hazel. She was fearful for his safety again.

'I can answer that,' said Leading Seaman Perry. 'They're looking for any info on the other ship, and the boss'll know what he's looking for.'

'He'll be OK,' added Callendar.

The boarding party scrambled, with difficulty, towards the cabin at the back of the bridge where the radio room was located. Ewan quickly rampaged through the radio log and message pad. 'It's in Italian and German,' said Blackwell.

'Not a problem.' Ewan chuckled.

'Anything?' Blackwell queried.

'The other ship is the *Marino*. Same as this except more SS, as you might expect. I'm guessing this ship is a decoy for the *Marino*.'

'Decoy? That would make sense. The *Marino* must be carrying senior SS and Nazis and maybe a special cargo,' said Blackwell. 'And our nurses!'

'Cold-blooded bastards. They know we would tend to this ship first. They knew this would also move our attention away from their armoured division.'

'Yes, but I think Admiral Kelly's action will scupper that.'

'You mean the *Bermuda* shelling the location you radioed,' said Ewan.

One of Ewan's sailors appeared. 'Water's up to deck, sir.'

'Time to get off of her,' said Ewan.

Ewan and Blackwell grabbed a pile of message papers and the logbook.

They darted to the main deck. Waiting for them was a rubber dinghy from the gunboat. They dumped the papers and logbook into the dinghy and scrambled aboard. It was a close run. As the sailors paddled the dinghy away, the *Campello* lurched and began to settle rapidly. The men climbed aboard MGB 650 as the *Campello* finally slipped beneath the surface.

CHAPTER 31

ONE DOWN, ONE TO GO

ALLENDAR SKILFULLY NUDGED his gunboat westward towards Brindisi. He kept a watchful eye on his towing charges, while CPO Davy, along with a couple of machine-gunners, kept an eye on the prisoners. Two of the German SS had been transferred onto MGB 650 because their injuries needed Hazel's nursing attention. Both were still in their SS uniforms, something that brought a shiver to Hazel as she recalled her ordeal three years earlier in the North African desert. Nevertheless, she went about her nursing service as though they were ordinary wounded men. Ewan could not help but notice her hesitation when confronted by the wounded SS.

Within minutes of setting out, Ewan sent two signals to MTB 702. The first was in plain English that they were heading back to Brindisi with survivors from a ship that they had engaged. His second signal was encoded and repeated to the Admiralty and their Malta HQ. Sub Lieutenant Marsden read the decoded message. It was simple: 'Shadow the second ship. Expect trouble.' Although Marsden had been advised earlier to expect trouble, he now realised that he was on his own, at least for an hour or so. Their original plan of splitting the flotilla included the main force to back up MGB 650 and MTB 702 if needed. He knew that the main force would have received the same messages.

The main flotilla, led by Lieutenant Tony Thornton, skipper of MTB

175

703, was already motoring at full speed north to join Marsden as MTB 702 was closing on the SS *Marino*. The messages were also picked up by HMS *Bermuda*. Their job done in bombarding the SS Panzer division, they turned to meet with MTB 702. However, both the supporting flotilla of MTBs and HMS *Bermuda* were at least one hour away. Marsden guessed he was on his own. He ordered a reduced speed and to keep no less than two thousand yards. They could clearly see the activity on the decks of the *Marino*.

The five nurses heard the commotion outside their cell of a cabin. 'Something's stirred them up,' said Helen Grayling.

Marjory Shaw was uneasy. 'They seem agitated. I wonder what that means for us?' There was an ominous tone in her voice. Doreen Canley looked to Marjory and said nothing; she had already been interrogated by their captors. 'Is there something bothering you?' asked Marjory.

Doreen gathered her thoughts together. 'They've got a senior SS man. He's nasty, but he believes me that I'm not Hazel.'

'That's good, isn't it?' Helen asked.

'I don't know. He was very angry with the men who captured us. I felt he knew Hazel, but that's impossible. Isn't it?'

Marjory knew a little about Hazel's past experience of being tortured by the Gestapo in North Africa. Could there be a link?

'The boat's moving again,' said one of them.

'Why did it stop, and where the hell are they taking us?' asked Helen.

'More importantly, what do they want with us?' said Lesley Grant.

'We can't be of any value to them,' said Jo Mitchell. She hoped they would be released. It was a naive thought.

A few minutes passed by. The engines took on a more labouring sound. Through what little window space of the scuttle, the nurses realised that they were out in the open sea.

The ship began to roll as it headed out of the bay, away from Tirana, then it settled into a throbbing rhythm. There was the occasional jolt as it was hit by a large wave.

The five nurses began to settle down, but this was short-lived. An Italian sailor entered the cabin. 'You are to all come on deck,' he said.

'Now what?' muttered someone.

They were about to file out of the cabin into the fresh sea air, when in came an SS officer. His uniform gave his rank as an Obersturmbannführer, although only Marjory could guess at his rank. He was tall and sinister-looking. His right hand was gloved, hiding a bad scar from an injury some years earlier. The Italian sailor stood aside as the SS officer strode into the cabin. He looked glaringly at each of the nurses.

'Take your uniforms off,' he ordered.

'What!' came a sharp rebuttal from Helen.

'I won't tell you again,' said the SS officer as he moved his gloved hand to the pistol in his holster.

They removed their uniforms, which were of single boiler-suit style, except for Doreen, who was wearing a shirt and skirt. They began to remove their shoes to allow them to pull off their boiler suits. 'Leave your shoes off,' said the Italian sailor. He was hesitant.

Dressed only in their underwear, they walked slowly out into the brilliant sunshine and onto the deck below the bridge. The sunshine momentarily hurt their eyes; they had been cosseted in near darkness for several days.

They were ordered into a line before the SS officer and several Italian sailors. No one was pointing a gun at them, which at first Marjory thought was a good sign. Captain Carlo, the master of the *Marino*, looked on from the high vantage point and sanctuary of his bridge. He scanned the horizon and shifted his eyes to the sky. He was apprehensive. Anytime now an Allied ship or plane, or both, might appear. He reset his gaze to the line of nurses and the uniformed SS officer.

All five nurses were worried.

The sinister stance of the SS officer cast a shadow onto the line of nurses. 'I am SS-Obersturmbannführer Kranz. You will be split into two groups of two and another single. You two will go over there.' Kranz pointed Doreen Canley and Lesley Grant to an open area on top of the main cargo hold. He turned to Jo Mitchell and Marjory Shaw. 'And you two, up onto the foredeck. Move!'

They departed for their positions, escorted by Italian sailors. 'You will go to the rear deck,' the SS officer said to Helen Grayling.

Helen was escorted by a junior SS officer and an Italian sailor to the deck aft of the bridge and funnel. There she found a large towel laid out with a small table holding a jug of water and a glass. Helen was bemused. What on earth were they up to?

She stood at the edge of the towel and waited for the next order.

Captain Carlo quizzed Kranz. 'Do you think it will work?'

'Why not?' said Kranz. 'Our war is finished, and any Allied planes would simply think that we are now enjoying it.'

'With attractive girls—bella bambinos—sunbathing and a relaxed crew. It might work,' said Captain Carlo. He hesitated before adding, 'And if it doesn't?'

'We will face that if it doesn't,' said Kranz in an icy tone.

'What will you do with the women when we have no more use for them?'

Kranz grunted, turned on his heel, and left the bridge.

Captain Carlo and two sailors on the bridge with him stared at each other. A sick feeling was shared by them. Kranz would kill the nurses.

'What can we do?' said the helmsman.

'We're not fascists,' said the other sailor.

Captain Carlo looked thoughtfully at his two bridge crew. 'Nor I, but there have been threats against my family. Then there's the rest of the crew. I just don't know what to do.'

Kranz approached Helen on the afterdeck and stood intimidatingly in front of the SS officer and the Italian sailor.

Helen suddenly had a nauseous feeling.

'Take your underwear off,' said Kranz slowly and sickeningly.

Realising that she shouldn't protest, she began to remove her brassiere.

The two onlookers provided a sneering grin. Helen focused her eyes on Kranz, whose expression showed no emotion. He was cold and calculating. She slipped her knickers off.

'Lie down on the blanket and soak up the sun. You will get a good tan. You will stay here on your back or front. It doesn't matter. And you will, of course, wave to any aeroplanes that might fly by.'

'Is that what I am, a decoy?' said Helen, feeling the glaring eyes from her two onlookers.

Kranz turned away and said to the SS officer, 'I am going to sort the others out. You will keep an eye on this one. Get out of that uniform.'

Helen lay on the blanket, face down. The sun-baking heat from the steel deck passed through the towel. It was uncomfortable, but she had no intention of revealing too much of herself. She felt humiliated and vulnerable. She was no stranger to being nude with a man, but this was different.

Marjory saw Kranz approach. She put aside her fearful thoughts for a moment and realised that Kranz must be the same SS officer whom Hazel had encountered in the North African desert in 1942. He was.

'You will lie down on these towels, giving the impression that you are sunbathing, and will wave to any aeroplane that flies over us. Is that understood?' said Kranz.

'Er, yes,' said Marjory. Jo nodded.

'Make sure the other two do the same,' said Kranz to the guarding crewmen.

Marjory and Jo did as they were told. Jo looked up to the searing sun that beat down upon them. 'Marj, we can't take too much of this sun.'

'I know. And that's all we need,' said Marjory.

'Quiet. No talking!' came an aggressive order from one of their guards.

The radar operator of MTB 702 reported to Marsden. 'Sir, we're just on two thousand yards from the target.' He added quickly, 'Sir, radar contact north of us. It's a plane. One of ours. Six miles out.'

The radio operator interrupted before Marsden could acknowledge the radar contact. 'Open radio message from approaching plane. "We'll overfly ship ahead. Any other orders?" That's all?'

'Yes. Tell them to circle the ship and let us know what they see,' replied Marsden.

Captain Carlo was suddenly shaken by one of his crew shouting wildly that a plane was approaching; he was pointing to the starboard bow. All eyes on the bridge and the deck below turned to the approaching aircraft. Kranz yelled at the crew to get the nurses to wave at the aircraft. The plane screamed past the starboard side of the ship to get a good view of the people on deck. The pilot and his navigator spotted the near-naked women waving. They flew on, dipping their wings in friendly recognition.

'Seen enough?' said the pilot to the navigator.

'Certainly have.'

'Right. Radio base on what we have seen. Add that we've flown on.'

The plane disappeared from view quickly.

A couple of minutes passed, when the radio crackled. The radio operator spoke to Marsden, 'Sir, RAF recon flight report that it looks normal with some women sunbathing on the deck. They waved. Typical Itie behaviour.' The term Itie was used by the British for Italians.

'Right. Tell them to fly on by and not to circle,' said Marsden.

'Are you thinking what I'm thinking, sir?' said his chief petty officer.

'Yes. Our missing nurses. Sparks, send a message to the boss on 650.' He thought for a moment. 'Morgan, get that big telescope thing of yours and scour the ship,' he said to his leading lookout.

Morgan joined Marsden on the bridge, the highest part of the boat. He set his long telescope to the SS *Marino*.

Kranz appeared on deck. He had hidden from view of the plane as he was still in his SS uniform. 'Good. Very good. But we must keep up the pretence. That was a fighter-bomber—probably used for patrol and reconnaissance as it was alone.'

'It worked!' bleated someone on the deck below.

Kranz was not so sure.

Although only twenty minutes in the sun, Marjory and Jo were glad to move their bodies as they were now suffering the effects of exposure. So were Lesley and Doreen. 'I wonder how Helen is faring?' said Marjory. She and Jo looked upward to a point beyond the bridge where Helen had been placed.

Helen had not been in direct view of the passing plane but had played her part in waving, which meant she had exposed her nakedness to her guards. Helen was not the bashful sort, but here at her present predicament she drew a line. She had the feeling that her fate was not good—and neither was that of her companions.

Kranz approached Captain Carlo. 'Captain, I think we should increase our speed and get well away from this area before any more inquisitive eyes find us,' Kranz said. He was not entirely buoyant with their success. He was looking forward to getting into the open seas of the Mediterranean. He took Captain Carlo to one side. 'Captain, I am concerned that our whereabouts and entire mission may have been compromised. The British are not fools. Far from it.'

'What do you mean, Herr Oberst?'

'My general made our arrangements with the Russians to leave this area. They were to find out the disposition of the British naval patrols here in the Adriatic. The Russian NKVD were told by me that they should abduct the British naval commander's wife and use that to pressure him to reveal where their first patrol would be deployed.'

'But that's worked, hasn't it?'

'I don't know. You see, Captain, we have five nurses on board, taken by those bungling NKVD agents. None of them is Lieutenant Commander Jones's wife, who is Nursing Sister Hazel Jones. She was supposed to be in charge of the four nurses.'

'But we have five,' said Captain Carlo.

'Yes, and that bothers me,' said Kranz, turning to look out to sea.

'How do you know none of them is Sister Hazel Jones?'

Kranz stared out to the horizon. 'I encountered her some time ago.'

Captain Carlo guessed that the encounter was not good for Kranz.

Kranz continued to stare at the horizon as though he were expecting trouble. 'Have we heard anything from the *Campello*?' he asked.

'No. Nothing. They must have slipped passed the British patrols,' said Captain Carlo.

'You could be right. Yes, that is good. They would have sent our prearranged code word if they were boarded,' replied Kranz, feeling more confident.

Captain Carlo thought for a moment. Kranz was very sure that Hazel Jones was not among the nurses whom the Russian NKVD agents had captured. It was a simple and clever plan to coerce a British naval officer into giving them the disposition of the naval patrol area in the Adriatic and the dates and times. However, what was now important was that since they did not have Hazel Jones, it meant that the British had not been fooled. Captain Carlo felt uneasy. Everything seemed to be working well other than the failed kidnapping.

CHAPTER 32

ENGAGE!

H MS *Bermuda* started for Brindisi, leaving MGB 650 to rejoin MTB 702. Lieutenant Callendar was happier now that he had transferred his injured crew and several survivors from the SS *Campello*. Ewan and Callendar pored over a chart of the area, discussing the location of the second vessel and where MTB 702 was likely to meet up with her. Ewan tapped the chart with a pencil. He was about to mark the chart when Henry Blackwell joined them. Henry handed Ewan a slip of paper; it was a signal. Callendar looked to Ewan, who read the signal. 'So, there is a second ship. It left Tirana thirty minutes after the SS *Campello*.'

'Yes. One of my agents has confirmed it,' said Blackwell. 'Pity we couldn't have had this earlier, but my agents we left behind were checking on the destruction of the SS Panzers.'

'What's the problem?' asked Callendar.

'The *Marino* took four Panzer tanks on board on the main deck, sheeted over to conceal them. They're armed with eighty-eight guns. That makes the *Marino* a deadly armed ship,' said Blackwell.

'Too bloody right,' said Ewan. 'James, warn the 702.'

'Yes, sir. Shall we also crack on?' said Callendar.

Ewan nodded in agreement. He drew Blackwell's attention to the point on the chart that he had marked.

MGB 650 bounced and shook as she picked up speed to forty knots.

Hazel appeared. 'Ewan, we've increased speed. More trouble?'

'Sister Jones, you're staying with us?' queried Blackwell. He thought that Hazel might be transferred to HMS *Bermuda*.

'Yes, Hazel's staying with us to take care of her nurses when we find them,' Ewan answered.

'Do you believe they're on this other ship?' Hazel asked Blackwell.

'Er, yes. That's our guess.'

'I hope they're unharmed, but I get the impression that you are concerned,' said Hazel. She detected that Blackwell was uneasy and thought that he might be holding something back. Ewan looked up from the chart to Blackwell.

Blackwell hesitated. 'There is something you should know. Both of you.'

Ewan and Hazel cast uneasy looks to each other.

'My information is that there may be several German SS on board. Escaping from us. Heading to South America probably.' Blackwell paused and stroked his chin. He looked momentarily down at the chart, then lifted his gaze to both of them. They knew something of concern was about to be revealed. 'One of the SS officers is believed to be Otto Kranz—SS-Obersturmbannführer Kranz.'

Hazel shuddered with fear. 'Oh God! How? I thought he had been arrested and put in prison in Tripoli.'

'He escaped to Italy and then went back to Germany. We first became aware of him six months ago when the Nazis massacred a village in Czechoslovakia. He's a ruthless bastard and is on our most-wanted list. The Yanks want him also. He could be connected to the murder of American soldiers in the Ardennes. He took command of the SS-Panzer division we've just beaten up. They were supposed to be deployed to protect the southern flank of Austria, but things moved quickly and they were cut off here. We had good intelligence that several high-ranking Nazis were getting out of their precious Third Reich. That's when we came across Kranz again.'

'But how does this involve Hazel?' Ewan asked.

'Chance, Ewan. Chance,' said Blackwell. 'As far as we can ascertain, the Russian NKVD wanted to get at you by holding Hazel for ransom, that is blackmailing you into giving away the patrol area plans to allow the escaping ships with their cargo of Nazis in exchange for the SS Panzers and other weapons for their communist partisans in various areas of the Balkans. That bit we've scuppered.'

'And?' said Hazel.

'And if Kranz is aboard this other ship, the *Marino*, which we believe has your five nurses as hostages, then he is likely to realise that you are not among them.'

'I don't give them much of a chance if he finds that out,' said Ewan in a low voice.

'Are you sure they're on the *Marino*?' asked Hazel.

'Almost certain. One of our RAF recon planes overflew the *Marino* and reported that there were at least four women on board—sunbathing—who waved to them. We ordered the plane to overfly so as not to arouse any suspicion. It's highly unlikely that there would be any Italian women aboard,' said Ewan.

The forward lookout on MTB 702 reported a ship on the horizon. This backed up the earlier radar report. Marsden took the signal from his radio operator; it was from MGB 650. He sent a reply signal advising Ewan that he had a ship in sight and that it was probably the SS *Marino* from the information received from Blackwell. 'Chief, slow ahead to fifteen knots. Approach target ship as though we're just on patrol and checking,' said Marsden to his coxswain.

'That should allow the 650 to catch us up, shouldn't it, sir?' the coxswain asked.

'I do hope so, Chief. If that ship is what we think it is, it is armed with eighty-eights, which could give us a bit of problem,' said Marsden in a matter-of-fact tone.

'Christ's sake, they could blow us out of the water!' uttered a sailor manning a Vickers machine gun aft of the bridge.

The minutes ticked by.

The radar operator reported, 'Range, two thousand yards, sir. Second contact, north, closing fast. I think it's the 650.'

'Action stations!' ordered Marsden.

A bridge lookout on the SS *Marino* turned to Captain Carlo. 'Captain, patrol boat closing on our port bow.'

'Act normal. Get those women under cover,' ordered Captain Carlo.

Kranz appeared with another SS officer, but this time they were in civilian clothes. 'Why hide the women?' he asked.

'If challenged, I'll say we are in international waters carrying machinery to Cyprus. They should be satisfied.'

'But the women would give it more of an Italian feel,' said Kranz.

'No, Herr Oberst, their skin is too white. They could be looking for the women.'

Kranz grunted with disapproval. 'They should have seen them on deck anyway.'

'Get the Panzer guns ready to shoot, but keep the covers on until I order to open fire,' said Kranz to his junior officer.

Captain Carlo was about to protest but was interrupted by Kranz. 'Captain, we have more than enough armed men to take on the English patrol.'

MTB 702 closed the range quickly, but Marsden kept his boat almost bow on. He signalled by Aldis Morse lamp to the *Marino* to stop and be boarded. He repeated the message in Italian. Captain Carlo replied that he did not understand and was in international waters. Marsden repeated his message to stop. Captain Carlo ignored the order. The range diminished to fifteen hundred yards.

'Chief, we're within range of their guns. Come up on the port side for a couple of seconds, then turn sharply back under their bow. That should mess up their gunnery if they have those eighty-eights trained on us,' said Marsden.

They made their manoeuvre.

As MTB 702 came into full view of the port side, Kranz ordered the Panzer guns to fire. Two shells screamed out, plunging within yards of the gunboat. MTB 702 turned sharply, throwing almost everyone on board off their feet. Two more Panzer guns fired. One shell overshot and plunged harmlessly into the sea. However, the fourth shell tore through the afterdeck and shattered much of the superstructure, passing through the side of the boat into the sea. It had not exploded. It was an armour-piercing round that harmlessly shot through the plywood structure. MTB 702 raced away ahead of the *Marino*'s bow. The Panzer guns were unable to train on their target.

'Chief, check for damage. Signal 650 that we've sustained damage,' ordered Marsden.

The range opened to three thousand yards.

Marsden reported that they were still seaworthy and could attack but that they had seen five women on board on an upper deck. He added, 'Do I attack?'

Ewan threw a glance at Blackwell and Callendar. 'Send. Sink her!' he said.

The reply from Ewan was devastating to Hazel. Here was the man she loved so much ordering the almost certain death of those on board the *Marino*, including the five nurses.

'Ewan. You ca-can't!' stammered Hazel.

'James, get your best swimmers to be ready to dive into the water to rescue our ladies as soon as they jump ship,' said Ewan.

'I'll get a couple of my commandos to help,' added Blackwell.

'Signal 702 what we're going to do—cut in close as the *Marino* sinks. They're to be ready also,' said Ewan.

Marsden studied the signal from Ewan.

'Chief, prepare torpedoes. We'll put the first in the bow and the second into her stern, and then we'll close fast to pick up survivors,' said Marsden.

MTB 702 lined up to attack and increased speed to twenty-five knots.

'Engage!' shouted Marsden.

Captain Carlo's worst fear was realised. 'They're going to attack us with torpedoes!'

'What!' yelled Kranz. 'Tie the women to the rails!' It was his last desperate order to put off the attack.

Suddenly, an SS lookout turned momentarily to the starboard side. Racing towards them was MGB 650. 'Schnellboot! Englischer schnellboot!' screamed the lookout.

Everyone on the bridge turned to see the heavily armed motor gunboat cutting violently through the water towards them.

CHAPTER 33

RESCUE

CAPTAIN CARLO TURNED to his helmsman. 'Hard a starboard!' he roared. There was a chance, a slim chance, he could avoid the torpedo. The SS *Marino*, beginning to answer to the shift of the helm, started to turn. Kranz could hardly believe what was happening. He always thought, and had been indoctrinated, that the British would always put the protection of life first and would act as gentlemen. He had contempt for the German Kriegsmarine, the German Navy, except for maybe the U-boat service. This feeling had endowed him with the same contempt of the Royal Navy. He was wrong. He stood transfixed at the distant approaching white wake of a torpedo heading on a collision course for them. It was too late.

The first torpedo struck fine on the port bow, exactly where Marsden wanted; he had anticipated the *Marino*'s turn. Almost everyone on board was thrown off their feet by the shattering explosion. The SS *Marino* ploughed on, causing her forward bulkheads to be crushed by the water, which was charging in with greater destruction, than a side beam-on assault owing to the forward motion of the ship.

'Stop engines!' shouted Captain Carlo. No sooner he had given the order than he could see that the bridge clinometer was registering a list to port by a few degrees. SS *Marino* was a well-built robust cargo freighter of French origin. She would founder slowly at first, until enough water entering the forward compartments would succumb her to being pulled under the surface.

His next order was the worst command any ship's master could give. 'Abandon ship!' His heart was heavy with dismay.

As he ordered his crew to leave their engine room and lower lifeboats and rafts, he spotted Kranz gripping the side of the bridge railing. He was looking down at the nurses whom he had ordered to be tied to the railings. A sailor began to untie them.

Kranz was enraged. 'Leave them!' he bellowed. There was hatred in his voice.

'Mama mia! For God's sake. Let them save themselves,' shouted Captain Carlo.

'I said leave them,' said Kranz, pulling his pistol from its holster and pointing it towards Captain Carlo.

The helmsman grabbed Captain Carlo's arm and pulled him away. They began to leave the bridge, when they heard a crewman shout, 'Torpedo! Another torpedo!'

The second torpedo struck aft, blowing off the entire stern. Debris spewed out. A fire started. Kranz was thrown off his feet again; he fell down the gangway to the deck below. The helmsman fell headlong down his gangway but luckily was able to stand. Captain Carlo returned to his bridge. The clinometer now showed a list of ten degrees to port and it was increasing. The ship was settling fast.

Nurse Helen Grayling fumbled with the cords that had haphazardly been tied around her wrists. She had already freed one hand and now worked on the other. The water was almost up to the edge of the deck. Nurses Jo Mitchell and Lesley Grant cried out for help, tugging hard at their ties, which only caused the knots to tighten further. Nurse Marjory Shaw struggled with her bonds. She looked down as the water began to seep at the edge of the deck and tease at her bare feet. She felt panic setting in.

Nurse Doreen Canley was slumped onto the deck with only her bound wrists holding up her arms. Helen freed her last restraint and began to untie Doreen. The others shouted, pleading for help.

Marjory prayed for a miracle as the seawater began to lap at her knees.

Jo and Lesley stared at each other, tears rolling down their cheeks. 'This is it,' gurgled Lesley.

'Oh God! Yes,' answered Jo, choking on her words as the water reached her waist.

Marjory's prayer was answered.

They were suddenly surrounded by sailors, cutting at the cords. MGB 650 had raced onto the foundering port side and delivered several sailors, who dived into the sea to free the nurses. The MGB was dangerously close to the sinking side of the SS *Marino*.

CPO Davy, at the helm, expertly nudged the boat as close as he could. The main deck of the SS *Marino* was now deluged with water. The five nurses were being thrust aboard MGB 650. At the same time, two commandos and another sailor grabbed crew members from the SS *Marino*. With all safely on board, CPO Davy nurtured the boat away from the sinking ship, just avoiding loose wires from the superstructure.

Hazel and the sick berth attendant tended to the nurses. Hazel, almost in tears with joy, smiled. 'Fancy meeting you here,' she said to Marjory.

'Take a look at Doreen. She's in a bad way. The rest of us have a few scrapes and bruises,' said Marjory.

'Will do. But what about that gash on the back of your hand?'

'That was from the sailor who freed me. His knife slipped, I think.'

'Let's get some hot tea inside you,' said Hazel as the sick berth attendant appeared with blankets. 'I think these are just as important. It's not every day that we get near-naked ladies to look after,' he said, handing out the blankets.

The nurses huddled into their respective blankets.

'She's going, sir,' said Callendar.

Ewan had been almost mesmerised by Hazel's nursing skill. Her caring nature was evident. He looked over to the SS *Marino* as she finally slipped beneath the waves, disgorging her last breaths of air, leaving a mess of flotsam.

MTB 702 joined them, and they pulled several more survivors from the floating wreckage. Ewan, Callendar, and Blackwell viewed the damage to MTB 702.

'Looks like you've been in the war,' said Callendar. 'Any casualties with your lads?'

'Luckily only minor cuts and bruises. We can make Brindisi,' replied Marsden.

'Incidentally, John, I think you might have made a bit of history,' hailed Ewan.

'How's that, sir?'

'I do believe that you might have fired the last torpedo in anger here in Europe.'

'Crikey. Hadn't thought about that. One to tell the kids back home.'

'I hope so,' said Blackwell, who then disappeared to the cabin where the chart of the area was laid out.

Ewan joined him. 'Anything the matter, Henry?'

'I guess we'll be trailing after Nazis and the like for several weeks to come, if not months. Now begins the long road to recovery. Some might say it will be more difficult than actually fighting. The world's changed.'

'And that leaves Japan,' added Ewan.

'Yes. But you'll have your work cut out here for a while, no doubt. You and your command have done well. It will certainly be shown in my report,' said Blackwell.

'Thanks, Henry. Please make sure my crew gets a good mention. All I want is to get back to some sort of sanity and to have some time with Hazel.'

Blackwell nodded in agreement.

CHAPTER 34

THE BRINDISI PARTY

MGB 650 AND MTB 702 motored slowly into the inner harbour of Brindisi. They passed HMS *Bermuda*, where the majority of the survivors of the SS *Campello* had been transferred from the gunboats or picked up directly. Ewan stood quietly by himself on the bridge of MGB 650. Hazel saw him, his right hand crossed behind him and held by his left hand, as though standing at ease. She wanted to sidle up to him and give him a big hug, but she could see he was deep in thought. Something was bothering him. She was about to interrupt Ewan's thoughts when Callendar joined her. He stopped and glanced at Hazel. 'Anything the matter, sir?' asked Callendar, also detecting that Ewan was deep in thought.

Ewan turned and smiled at them both. 'Oh, nothing really. Once we've put our injured ashore, I'll address the crew. Let Marsden know also, would you?'

'Yes, sir.'

'Can I stay until you're free?' asked Hazel.

Ewan nodded approval.

Hazel left Ewan with his thoughts and made her way to see her nurses.

'Marjory, Lieutenant Callendar has told me that there will be transport to take you and our brood to the nurses' quarters at the Casualty Reception Centre and hospital. I'll join you in about an hour. If that's OK.'

'That'll be fine, Hazel. We're just glad that this whole affair is over. Is it right that we will be returning to Malta in a couple of days?' said Marjory.

'Yes. We all will. How did you know?'

'Henry Blackwell mentioned it. He's not navy or army. So what is he?'

Hazel chuckled. 'I'll explain later.'

The boats tied up at the quayside. Military police, recognisable by their red cap covers, were waiting for them to take charge of the *Marino*'s crew and SS survivors. Blackwell said goodbye to his commando detachment and joined Ewan. They stood alone talking about their next steps. Blackwell explained the twists and turns in the operation, which thankfully had worked out satisfactorily. He also commended Ewan for having split his flotilla to continue patrolling the southern straits of the Adriatic. Ewan pointed out that as soon MTB 702 was repaired, it would return to the Albanian coast with MGB 650.

'Will you be sailing with them?' asked Blackwell, but he knew the answer.

'For the first foray. But then I've been summoned back to Malta. Flying back in a week's time.'

'Get some time off with your good lady. Hazel is an exceptional woman. She needs you now more than ever,' said Blackwell. This was a new side to Blackwell that Ewan had not experienced before. Blackwell's coldness seemed to have thawed a little.

'Yes. That's what's been bothering me,' said Ewan.

'I guessed that. She's seen first-hand just how committed you are to your command.'

'Will she understand?' Ewan asked, looking directly at Blackwell.

'Oh, no problem there, my old son. She's also seen how you care for your men. And you've seen her in action as a nurse. Right?'

'I fancy getting drunk with her tonight and anyone else I can get. You?'

'Good idea, but I have a quick job to do first, which I'll explain later.

Let me know where and when to meet. I'll be at the Shipping Control Office.

Blackwell went ashore, and disappeared among the throng of uniforms and grubbily dressed dock workers.

Callendar approached Ewan. 'Sir, I'll be forming up my crew in a few minutes. Sub Lieutenant Marsden is getting his crew ready also.'

While waiting for the crews to be paraded, Ewan took the opportunity to look around both gunboats. Their engagements had battered each of the boats. The worst damage was to MTB 702, but Ewan believed that it could be repaired within a few days.

He stood near the gangway to MGB 650 as the crews formed up. Some were tidying themselves as best they could. Several had rips and holes and blackened marks on their work uniforms. Some sported bandaged dressings over light wounds. Those who were wearing caps had grubby white covers. They look dishevelled but were smiling.

Lieutenant Callendar spoke with his chief petty officer, who stood to attention, facing the crews. He gave the command to stand easy, and then quickly followed the main command to attention. He did a right about-turn and saluted Callendar. 'Naval crews present and correct, sir.'

Callendar returned the salute. 'Thank you, Chief.'

He turned, faced Ewan, and saluted as normal. 'Sir, our crews are present and correct—er, as best we can.'

Ewan returned the salute and threw a glance to Sub Lieutenant Marsden, who stood before his crew. 'Thank you, Mister Callendar.' He then took a step forward. 'Stand at ease,' commanded Ewan. 'Stand easy.'

Ewan paused for a moment, eyeing the crews. He grinned. 'Well done, everyone. We've had an unusual operation, and you have conducted yourselves in the best traditions of the Royal Navy. I'm proud of you, and you should be proud of yourselves. And one final thought. As you are all aware, it has now been confirmed that the war here in Europe is over. Hopefully there will be no more escapades like this last one.'

Someone shouted 'Hooray!' followed spontaneously by others.

Suddenly Callendar bellowed, 'Three cheers for the boss!'

Ewan thanked them.

Coming up to his side, Hazel joined him. She was very proud of her husband.

Ewan and Hazel sat at a bar table waiting for others to join them, which soon happened with Hazel's nursing party. Lieutenant Brookes arrived a few minutes later and arranged for the waiter to sort out their drinks. Marjory guided Doreen Canley to sit next to Hazel. Helen Grayling sat next to Ewan. They settled down with a variety of drinks posing before them. Hazel spotted Marjory's concern for Doreen.

'Doreen, do you want to talk about what they did to you? Not now, but maybe later?' whispered Hazel, leaning her head towards Doreen.

Doreen squeezed out a smile and nodded. She sipped at her large gin, as ordered by Marjory. 'Marjory told me that you had a similar experience more than two years ago.'

'If what happened to you was anything like what happened to me, then we need to talk. One thing,' said Hazel. 'I haven't gotten over my experience—just learned to manage it. If that's any help.'

'Marjory told me a little,' said Doreen.

Hazel lightly clutched Doreen's hand. 'Tomorrow, when you're ready. But don't let it linger for too long. You need to get it out of your system. It won't fully go away, but it will get easier with time. Believe me, I know.'

Gary Brookes snuggled in between Helen and Lesley. Ewan shuffled towards Helen to give Gary more space. Lesley at first thought that Ewan was getting amorous, but then she saw Helen's gaze at Gary. She had a mental giggle and wished it was Ewan.

CHAPTER 35

MALTA HOMECOMING

THE PLANE TOUCHED down at RAF Luqa airfield. The journey from the old Italian airfield outside Brindisi took less than an hour. It was a DC-10 transport plane, the workhorse of the Allies. This particular DC-10 was designed mainly for cargo and only ten passengers. Hazel's nursing party numbered six, including herself; Ewan and three soldiers made up ten. It was cramped with several crates of goods and mailbags taking up the last vestiges of space. An RAF airman sat on a seat at the back of the plane, keeping an eye on the passengers. The cargo crates were tied down. He had made a couple of cursory checks on the security of the cargo. He ensured that everyone was strapped in for landing. Few words were exchanged with any of them. They were all glad to be safely on the ground.

The soldiers helped the party of nurses to alight. Individually, the nurses thanked the soldiers and the airman, who guided them onto the short stepladder. Ewan approached the doorway and looked down to the concrete runway to see two military policemen, recognisable by their red cap covers, hence the colloquial term *redcaps* used by the army. In addition, there was a leading seaman regulator from naval police, identified by the white armband with the letters *N* and *P* separated by a crown. Ewan set himself down from the ladder and was greeted by the leading seaman. Ewan returned the sailor's salute.

'Lieutenant Commander Jones?'

'Yes. You're our escort, I believe,' said Ewan, eyeing the three redcaps.

'Yes, sir. Please follow us. We have three staff cars for the nurses and you. There will be an MP with each car for the nurses to take them to RNH Bighi, and I will be taking you to Naval HQ.'

'Very good. But can I see your orders?'

'Certainly, sir,' replied the leading seaman, taking his pass from his pocket.

Ewan examined it. It was bona fide. Ewan nodded and returned the pass.

'Sir, we've been briefed to look after you and your party,' said the leading seaman.

The three cars drove in convoy to Valetta. Ewan's car split off to the Naval HQ in Valetta, while the others continued on to the Royal Naval Hospital.

Ewan went directly to Admiral Kelly's office; he was expected.

Hazel and her nurses were led to a small conference room that doubled for training. One of the redcaps informed Hazel that they would have a guard on them in the nurses' quarters and that Captain Williams would be with them shortly. Hazel guessed rightly that it was Captain Mark Williams, as she remembered he was responsible for much of the military policing in Malta. They did not have long to wait.

The door to the room opened. Mark Williams entered. 'Good afternoon, Hazel, ladies. I'll quickly explain why we are providing you with a guard, and then we'll let you go to your quarters and resettle in.'

'Mark, are we still in danger?' asked Hazel.

'We don't think so, but Admiral Kelly is not taking any chances. From what I have learned, I think he's right. We're in the process of tracking down foreign agents.'

'Russian NKVD?' asked Lesley Grant.

'Yes.'

'One last thing. We want to interview you all to get an idea of who was involved in your kidnapping. But that can wait until tomorrow. Nurse Doreen Canley,' Mark Williams said, looking to Doreen, 'it's been agreed with your matron in Akroteri that you should stay here for a few days.'

'Captain, I'm all right, really,' said Doreen.

'That may be so, Nurse Canley, but your welfare is very important to us. From what I've been told, you've been through a harrowing ordeal. Rest up, relax, and take it easy.'

'Doreen, Captain Williams is right. I will be looking after you with my matron, Margaret Stanton. Believe me, you will need this rest,' added Hazel.

'Does Matron Stanton know what has happened to us?' asked Helen.

'Yes. She certainly does,' said Hazel. 'And the recuperation applies to all of us.'

Hazel thought a minute. After saying goodbye to Mark, she added, 'And that applies to me also.'

'What about Ewan? Will he be off again?' asked Marjory.

'Hmm, yes. I'm afraid I must put up with your company for a few more days. I think he's going back to Brindisi tomorrow afternoon.'

Helen chuckled. 'Hazel, are we all going out tonight?'

'I guess we can. Unwind, eh! Probably we will get an escort,' said Hazel.

The suggestion seemed to be warmly received. Doreen grinned. This was probably what she needed, but her ordeal had left its mark in her mind, even though she was hiding it.

'I'll let Ewan know. I think he's with the admiral. It may be a long meeting.'

'At least you've got a man to look after you,' said Jo.

'Do I detect some envy?' Marjory asked, grinning.

'Not really, but I could do with a man,' replied Jo. Her comment attracted glaring eyes from everyone except Doreen.

'Oh, I think I can arrange that,' said Helen.

'Now that I can believe,' mumbled Marjory.

Sub Lieutenant Andrew Starling stood at the bar with two sailors from Admiral Kelly's staff, all three in naval uniform whites. Andrew Starling's role in Naval Intelligence was ideal for providing an escort and serving as guard for the party of nurses. They had before them pint glasses of beer. For all intents and purposes, they were simply having an evening out with some nurses, although they were on duty acting as a guard. When Hazel and her party arrived, Andrew guided them to reserved comfortable armchairs and tables. As they sat down and Andrew summoned the barman, WRNS Third Officer Kate Davies arrived. She attracted Hazel's attention.

'Kate. Are you joining us?' asked Hazel.

'Yes, if you don't mind. And I have a message for you from Ewan,' said Kate.

'He'll be late?' Hazel sighed.

''Fraid so. The admiral has him in deep conversation with Henry Blackwell, John Cross, and Commander Gratton.'

'Now what are they cooking up? I hope he's not being talked into another dodgy mission. You know what I mean,' said Hazel with a sense of foreboding.

'No. I don't think so this time. But I can say it is quite complex,' said Kate.

CHAPTER 36

EWAN'S NEW ORDERS

THE EVENING BEGAN to liven up with an accordion playing and the odd song by whomever contributed. It was as this began that Ewan arrived, appearing at the doorway and scanning the crowded bar and lounge. Hazel spotted him and waved her hand to attract his attention. It worked. He found Hazel and the party occupying a corner of the lounge bar that was also open to the street. There was a haze of tobacco smoke, which was very much diluted by the opening to the outside atmosphere. Behind Ewan was Commander Alec Gratton.

'Looks like the party is well under way,' said Gratton.

Ewan chuckled. 'Do you think we can handle this lot?'

'We'll have a damned good try!' said Gratton.

They quickly settled in with Ewan squeezing himself in between Hazel and Marjory.

Gratton eventually got to sit with Kate. Hazel and Kate exchanged approving grins.

'So, are you off again?' asked Hazel, half whispering to Ewan and trying to hear above the humdrum of conversations.

'I'll explain later,' said Ewan.

Eventually the party broke up with Hazel's nurses being escorted to the nurses' home, except for Helen, who surreptitiously left with Andrew Starling, and Kate, who left with Alec Gratton.

Hazel and Ewan sat in their quarters on a well-worn settee, part of the original furnishings. Hazel hastily made two mugs of cocoa. They nurtured their cocoa as she tucked herself into Ewan's arms. It had been a long working day for Ewan, and although he desperately wanted to make love to her, he was tired. Hazel sensed this. She too wanted him but realised that simply holding each other was basically all they needed of each other at that time. Ewan drank half his cocoa and felt himself dropping off to sleep.

His slumbering was interrupted. 'Ewan, my love, are you able to tell me what you will be doing from now on?'

Ewan was drifting in and out, therefore paying only partial attention to Hazel.

'When will you be returning to Italy?'

Ewan grunted.

'Are you awake?'

There was no reply. Ewan had slipped into a deep sleep. Hazel kissed him on his forehead and tucked a blanket around him, letting him sleep.

Ewan awoke as daybreak arrived to find that he was covered with a blanket and no Hazel. There was a waft of freshly brewed coffee emanating from the kitchen. He struggled to stand and stretched out his arms. Hazel appeared with the coffee. 'Ah, you're awake,' she said.

'You let me sleep,' he said.

'Well, you were not in any condition to do anything else.'

Ewan laughed. 'I remember you asked me something, I think.'

'Oh yes, just wondered when you're returning to Italy.'

'Day after tomorrow. So, we've got all day today and tomorrow to ourselves,' replied Ewan, shooting her a leering look.

'We have this morning also. I don't have to see Matron until midday.'

'So, what about breakfast? There's the officers' club, unless you've got something else in mind.'

Hazel thought quickly. 'How about we go to bed?'

Within a minute they were nestling together and feeling each other.

'Ewan, are you doing anything dangerous again? Alec Gratton was with you last night, and I'll bet he was at your meeting with Admiral Kelly.'

'It's doubtful whether there will be anything more dangerous than the last few days. The war is really over, and now it's a matter of getting to grips with the transition to peace, I suppose. It's been a long war. God knows how long it will take to get back some sort of sanity. Anyway, I guess you want to know when I'll be back.'

'You read my mind.'

'Back in about a week, and then only away on the odd day or so. The admiral wants me to set up a training school here for coastal patrols, among some other bits and pieces,' said Ewan. 'This could be a three-year posting. How do you feel about that?'

'Well, that will be good. We both love Malta. No need to worry about where we go next for a while then,' said Hazel. She thrust herself on top of him.

Hazel left Matron Stanton's office and headed off to meet Ewan in the hospital reception; he had suggested they meet for lunch.

The restaurant was more of a backstreet cafe that overlooked part of the Grand Harbour. Their lunch consisted of salad, cold ham, and rabbit with a glass of cool beer each.

They talked about how their lives would progress. Ewan had had his new role confirmed by Admiral Kelly. Hazel smirked. 'Do you believe in coincidences?'

'Sometimes. Why?'

'Matron has asked me whether I would like run the new nurses' training school here in Malta.'

'And you said yes,' said Ewan gleefully.

'Actually, I did. I knew you would approve.'

'I certainly do approve, as long as it is what you want. Does this also mean that you don't need to take a party of nurses back to Bari?' said Ewan.

'Yes. The high command believe we've been through enough.'

'Oh. Nearly forgot. Alec Gratton has a team rounding up foreign agents,' said Ewan.

'Russian NKVD and the like?'

Ewan looked into his empty beer glass. 'And hunting down Nazis.'

'Kranz included?'

'You know about him,' said Ewan.

'Yes. Marjory, Helen, and Doreen told me,' said Hazel uneasily.

'His body wasn't found after we sank the *Marino*, but then the daylight did fade fast as you know. There is an area-wide alert for him. Just in case he survived. But I bloody hope not.'

Ewan took hold of Hazel's hand to comfort her. They began to walk to their quarters. After several minutes, Ewan steered Hazel to walk along the battlements that overlooked the Grand Harbour. He reminded her that when they had returned to Malta, they had planned to spend a day exploring Valetta, which had been scuppered by their respective escapades.

They stopped at a bench and took in the glorious sunshine.

'Is there anything else you would like to do? Not the obvious right now, but over the next three years maybe?' said Ewan. There was a soothing and warming tone in his voice.

Hazel stared into his gleaming eyes. 'Sort of connected, my love. How would you feel about starting a family?'

'You're not, er—are you?' stuttered Ewan.

'No. Not yet!' Hazel's cheeky grin captured Ewan's imagination.

'So, shall we try?'

'Let's go.' Hazel did not need any persuasion.

CHAPTER 37

THE NEW LIFE BEGINS

THE WEATHER HAD suddenly changed. Although June was almost always warm and sunny in Malta, there were occasions when a storm would arrive and last a couple of days. This was one of those occasions. The rain, albeit not heavy, brought on a humid and generally uncomfortable atmosphere. Ewan had gone off to his flotilla of patrol boats berthed in St Julian's inlet. Hazel left their quarters a few minutes after Ewan and made her way to RNH Bighi via the daily naval transport bus.

She set down her handbag on her desk in the training room. It was eight-thirty. Her first main intake of trainee nurses was due at nine. Hazel began arranging the lecture room to accept ten student nurses; four were training as auxiliary nurses, and the remaining six were undertaking further training to become registered nurses. Their basic training, which would amount to thirteen weeks, was the same for both types of nurses. To the side of Hazel's desk was a wall-mounted blackboard cleaned and ready for use. On the other side of the blackboard was a dangling full-size skeleton secured to a stand at the top of the skull. To the rear of the room was a hospital bed containing only a mattress with a neat pile of linen stacked at the foot of the bed. Other than storage cupboards for a range of hospital equipment, dressings, and manuals, there were only small tables, allowing two people to sit behind each of them in the uncomfortable-looking metal-framed canvas chairs.

Hazel sat at her desk and opened a folder of notes for the first training lesson. After a few minutes she let her thoughts drift to Ewan. She contemplated the past six weeks. Ewan had returned from Italy and had been away on several occasions with different patrol boats. His initial approach to the training of the crews was to work with them to find out what their existing capabilities were. In this way, he could coordinate their training more effectively. This was different from Hazel's training role; she was dealing with young women with no or very little training in nursing.

Hazel's thoughts stepped back to Ewan. For a substantial part of the six weeks, she had Ewan all to herself and they both enjoyed the intimacy without their war duties getting in the way. Today the minutes drifted by. As Hazel set out her notes and forms for the student nurses, the training room door opened and the first student entered.

'Nursing Sister Jones?' said the student.

'Yes. That's me. And which one are you?' said Hazel, smiling.

'Student nurse Patricia Buckley.'

A chattering of voices emanated from the corridor.

'Is that the rest of my class?' Hazel asked.

'Yes, Sister. I think they're excited,' said Buckley, grinning.

'Good. I wonder if they'll be as excited by the end of this week. It's a tough course.'

As the student nurses filed into the room, Hazel directed them to sit at the tables. 'Good morning, everyone. My name is Hazel Jones. Nursing Sister Hazel Jones. I am your tutor for the next three months. There will be other lecturers and specialists. Firstly, let's get to know each other. Starting with you,' Hazel said, nodding to Patricia Buckley. 'Tell us your name, a little about yourself, and, importantly, why you want to become a nurse.'

The small harbour inlet of St Julian's only had one motor torpedo boat (MTB) berthed at the quayside. Ewan stood at the quay eyeing up the

MTB. He noted that there were two guards, one on the quay itself and the other adjacent to him, standing on the main deck of the MTB. Ewan guessed, rightly, that both guards had seen him approaching. He stopped and stood still, observing them and MTB 712. Out of the corner of his eye, he spotted a chief petty officer appearing from the flotilla's small office at the back of the quay. It was CPO Davy. 'Good morning, sir. MTB 712. She arrived earlier this morning,' he said.

'That's good, Chief. She'll take the place of the 702 boat until it's repaired. Does Sub Lieutenant Marsden know?'

'No, sir. He phoned earlier to say that he would be late this morning.'

Ewan smirked. 'That makes sense. I guess the party he went to last night didn't finish until late. I won't go aboard her just yet. I'll wait until he arrives. In the meantime, I need to work out the next patrol rota. Maybe you can give me a hand with that, Chief.'

'Yes, sir. Fresh coffee is on in the office,' said CPO Davy.

After an hour had passed, Ewan had finished the patrol rota.

'Chief, can you make copies and distribute to each boat skipper? Oh, and don't forget a copy for the admiral,' said Ewan.

Sub Lieutenant Marsden appeared, looking a little fragile.

'Good morning, John. Good night, was it?' said Ewan.

'I feel wrecked, sir,' replied Marsden, clutching his head.

'You look it,' quipped Ewan. 'Get a coffee inside you, then we'll look over the 712 boat. Incidentally, Sub Lieutenant Clements brought her in. He'll be remaining with us, and as you are the senior sub, he will act as your number one.'

The next hour passed quickly. With the inspection of the 712 boat completed, Ewan, Marsden, and Clements returned to the quayside office.

They were greeted by CPO Davy. 'Message from the admiral, sir. Would you pop over to his office? I think we have some new orders.'

'Right, Chief. Had better make all boats, when they return, ready just in case the admiral has something special planned,' said Ewan.

Sub Lieutenant Clements looked a little startled. 'I thought that this is a quiet station now, sir.'

'Oh, that's just a rumour. We get our share of excitement even though the war is over out here,' replied Ewan. Then he grinned.

'You'll soon get used to this posting. Most of the awkward stuff seems to come our way to Malta,' added Marsden.

Ewan was directed to Admiral Kelly's office by WRNS Third Officer Kate Davies. He was soon confronted by Henry Blackwell, John Cross, and Commander Alec Gratton. He knew immediately that they were cooking up something and that it involved him. Admiral Kelly saw the expression of dismay on Ewan's face. 'Ewan, come, sit yourself down. Don't worry, they're not getting you involved in one of their nefarious jaunts. At least I don't think so,' said Admiral Kelly.

'Oh, that's good, Admiral. Er, so, why am I here?'

Admiral Kelly nodded to Alec Gratton. 'Commander, over to you.'

'Ewan. You have a special quality insofar that you can pass off as an Italian naval officer, which of course you've done before and very successfully too. We simply want you to board a ship berthed in Catania posing as an Italian naval officer inspecting the ship for its seaworthiness before it sets sail for South America. You'll be looking out for the passengers. We believe there could be several. The cargo is Fiat engine parts and anything else a port official might want to look into. Not dangerous. Just have a look-see and report back here.'

'That's it?' said Ewan, slightly surprised.

'Yes. That's it. Simple and quick,' answered Cross.

'When do I go?'

'In two hours. Plane ready for you. Back later tonight,' said Gratton.

'There's no one else?' asked Ewan.

'No. Not at such short notice,' said Gratton.

Henry Blackwell was his usual quiet self. Ewan looked suspiciously to him. 'Am I looking for anyone or anything in particular?'

'Use your instinct,' said Blackwell.

'I'll let Hazel know that you're tied up and won't be back until later tonight. She'll be having dinner with me and Kate this evening,' said Gratton.

'You've got it all worked out, haven't you?' said Ewan. He then turned to the admiral, who smirked.

CHAPTER 38

CATANIA

HAZEL MET WITH Kate and Alec Gratton at the officers' club. Kate had sent Hazel a message earlier saying that Ewan would be arriving later, probably after ten. Hazel was not unduly concerned until she realised that her husband was doing something for Alec Gratton, which meant it must be to do with naval intelligence. Their dinner finished, Alec led Hazel and Kate into the lounge bar for late-night drinks. Hazel noticed Alec glance at his watch. The time on the clock above the bar was ten-thirty. 'Ewan's late,' said Hazel.

'Yes he is. Plane must have been delayed,' said Gratton.

'Plane! What plane?' retorted Hazel.

'Oh, nothing dodgy. He's flown to Sicily for quick job for us. Should be here by now.'

'But he isn't,' said Hazel nervously.

'Let me check,' said Gratton, who then went to the bar to use the telephone.

'Did you know Ewan was flying to Sicily?' Hazel asked Kate, insinuating that maybe Kate had misled her or at least had failed to tell her what was happening.

'No I didn't,' said Kate. 'Don't worry, the admiral wouldn't sanction anything dubious involving intelligence.'

'Sorry. I believe you. It's just that I don't trust these intelligence operations. I don't mean any disrespect to Alec. It's Henry Blackwell who really bothers me.'

'Ah, Blackwell,' muttered Kate.

'Don't tell me. He's involved?!'

'Er, yes he is, and with John Cross,' said Kate, feeling Hazel's rising concern.

'You know, I could scream at Ewan sometimes. He shouldn't get himself involved in their dirty tricks. And now they've got him flying to Sicily,' said Hazel with a rising sickness in her voice.

'Here's Alec. He'll explain what Ewan is doing, if he's allowed to.'

'No worries. Ewan's plane has been delayed in Catania. He should be here in the morning,' said Gratton.

'Catania. Why on earth do you want him in Catania? And where does Blackwell and Cross fit into this?' Hazel was agitated.

'Oh, don't worry, Hazel. We simply want Ewan to inspect a ship in Catania and return with a report to us. Quick and simple—really,' said Gratton convincingly.

'But why Ewan?'

'He speaks fluent Italian, and we don't have anyone else.'

'Hmm. I'm not convinced that you're telling me everything. Then I suppose you can't tell me,' said Hazel, pushing her empty glass towards Gratton.

'How about large brandies all round,' plugged in Kate.

Gratton agreed.

The RAF transport plane, a Lysander, landed on the rough dusty airstrip that was made up from crushed volcanic ash from nearby Mount Etna, which overshadowed Catania and the north-eastern side of Sicily. Ewan was met by two Royal Air Force military policemen. They whisked him off to their building, situated away from the airfield's main building. Catania airfield originally had been an Italian naval airfield that had been overrun by the British Eighth Army in the 1943 invasion; it was generally intact except for the volcanic ash runway. It was dusty; the gravel crunched underfoot; and the runway was generally inhospitable.

Ewan was guided to a small office, where two RAF officers and two Italian policemen greeted him. They handed him a large box and a bundle that contained an Italian naval officer's uniform. He was then given an identification card with a battered photograph that would just about stand up to scrutiny, thought Ewan.

'So, I am Tenente di Vascello, Giorgio Bonetelli,' said Ewan, mustering an Italian accent. He chuckled.

'Something amusing?' said one of the RAF officers, a wing commander.

'Not really. It's just that I know this character,' said Ewan. 'Maybe I can explain later if we have time.' Ewan took the bundle and changed into the uniform, which was in near-pristine condition. As he changed clothing, the wing commander explained that the two Italian policemen would take him to the port where the ship he was to inspect was berthed. The ship's master was expecting him, and the Italian policemen would wait to return him to the airfield.

In full Italian naval uniform, Ewan spoke with the two Italian policemen. 'You know what I am doing here?'

'Yes, Tenente, we have been fully briefed. I am Sergeant Cruzo. I am to assist you in your inspection.'

'Good. Then let's get on with it,' said Ewan. They departed for the port.

The two RAF officers exchanged their views after Ewan had left. 'He speaks fluent Italian. In fact, I would definitely take him for a native Italian from the north,' said the wing commander.

'I wonder what he's looking for?' said the other RAF officer.

'Something important, I'll bet, but best we don't know.'

'Oh, definitely, sir. I'll be here when he returns. I will have the plane ready.'

The Italian police car stopped on the harbour quay near a rusty, almost derelict crane and opposite a merchant ship.

'This is the ship, Tenente. The SS *San Gabriel*. Her master is Captain Lopez. I believe there will also be a port official here to meet us,' said Sergeant Cruzo.

'This will be interesting,' said Ewan.

'Do you know what you are looking for? Anything in particular? Contraband?'

'No. I'm supposed to be inspecting the ship for its seaworthiness and noting anything unusual. I'm not even sure what cargo it is carrying,' said Ewan.

Ewan and Sergeant Cruzo climbed the gangway onto the SS *San Gabriel*, where they were met by Captain Lopez and two other men. One was the captain's first officer; the other, the port official who was introduced as the harbour master. The first officer led the party to the captain's cabin, where a host of documents were already laid out for inspection. The captain offered them a glass of wine, which Ewan and the sergeant duly accepted; it was a courtesy that Ewan had expected. He was able to clear through the documentation, pausing only on the manifest and route; he noted that the final destination for the main cargo was Buenos Aires in Argentina. Ewan set about inspecting the ship, starting with the engine room. He explained that the engine room was the heart of the ship and that the ship's seaworthiness was mainly dependent on the proper functioning of the engine room.

Ewan did not note any defects in the engine room, much to Captain Lopez's delight. It was clean and tidy with an auxiliary generator quietly chugging away in the background. Ewan did wonder, however, why the generator was apparently running at near full capacity. What was there on the ship that required it to do so when the main engines were already fired up and ready for departure within thirty minutes of being given clearance? He noted that there were sixty passengers on board, including women and children, described as family of the businessmen passengers. The cargo holds were nearly full to capacity with machine parts labelled as from the

Fiat motor company, which Ewan had anticipated from his briefing in Malta. The SS *San Gabriel* was due to stop on her way to Argentina in the Canary Islands to take on more cargo; it was not clear what this would be. Since the Canary Islands were part of Spain, a neutral country, there was no cause to query any further.

Ewan had also inspected the bilges and pumps, which were satisfactory. He was happy for the SS *San Gabriel* to leave port. He left the ship with Sergeant Cruzo after advising the harbour master that it could safely leave port. He stood for a moment by the police car with Sergeant Cruzo.

Ewan looked at the hull of the ship, not aware that he was being watched from a darkened porthole.

'Tenente, is there something wrong?' asked Sergeant Cruzo.

'Not sure.'

'Everything seemed in order,' said the sergeant.

'Yes. That's just it. What am I supposed to be looking for?'

'Your higher command did not give you any indication?'

'No. I suspect that they wanted an unbiased sea safety examination.'

'Tenente, since we have some time before your return flight, shall we stop by my station? We can have a drink there,' suggested Sergeant Cruzo.

'Good idea. I need to clear my mind and think. What am I missing?'

The local police station was well aged, built in the mid nineteenth century with no visible signs of any war damage, but it was in a poorly maintained condition, if maintained at all. The sergeant's office was small with little furniture, a filing cabinet, and a wall map of Catania and Sicily in general. Sergeant Cruzo produced a bottle of Italian red wine and invited the other policeman to join them.

Sergeant Cruzo topped up their glasses and peered at Ewan. 'Tenente, something is bothering you. Did you see something that didn't make sense?'

'I really don't know. I guess this has all been a wild goose chase,' said Ewan, grinning. He explained the English expression.

'I'm not sure we could have done anything to stop the ship sailing if we had found anything wrong,' said the sergeant.

'True.'

'Anyway, at least it's a weight off our minds and we can look forward to getting our island of Sicily back to normal one day. And you can return to your home also,' said the sergeant, who had revealed earlier to Ewan that they were still under the effects of the war, even though Italy had surrendered in 1943 and gone over to the Allies.

Ewan pondered on the words as he was about to get up in readiness to leave. Sergeant Cruzo and the other policeman, their driver, began to move towards the door with Ewan.

Ewan suddenly stopped. 'Weight?'

'What?' said Sergeant Cruzo.

'Weight. Weight off my mind. No. It's the weight the ship is carrying. It didn't dawn on me then when we stood at the quayside.'

The sergeant looked puzzled. 'I don't understand.'

'The weight the ship is displacing for its size and the waterline. The Plimsoll line is showing that the ship is overweighted for the Mediterranean. There's something heavy—very heavy—aboard. Telephone. Can I use your telephone?'

Sergeant Cruzo directed Ewan to the only telephone in the small police station. Ewan asked him to phone the RAF office at the airfield. Ewan got through and spoke with the wing commander, asking when his plane would be ready and if it could fly over the port and spot the SS *San Gabriel*.

Twenty minutes later, the plane carrying Ewan was turning in a wide arc to bring in the port of Catania as it approached. The RAF had reluctantly agreed to his request. The wing commander sent a radio message to his counterpart in Malta advising of the slight change in flight plan.

The pilot spotted the SS *San Gabriel*. 'There she is.'

'Yes. That's definitely the SS *San Gabriel*,' said Ewan. 'Make another turn and let's see if it is keeping to its course, because it doesn't look like it. It's too close to the shore.'

'OK,' said the pilot, who then let out a yell. 'Christ's sake, we're losing oil pressure.'

The single engine of the Lysander began to run very rough and then cut out. The plane was going down.

'Hold on, we're going down,' said the pilot.

'Can you land on that beach ahead?' barked Ewan.

'I'll try. Brace yourself.'

The pilot crash-landed by gliding the small flimsy craft onto the beach. It was short and included protrusions of rocks. However, he made it, ripping half the fuselage away.

'Let's get out before the fuel tank goes up!' yelled the pilot.

Within seconds, they were both lying face down twenty yards away as the remnants of the Lysander burst into flames.

'That was bloody lucky!' said Ewan.

'Better than you think, Commander. Had we been out over the sea, I might not have been able to ditch in one piece. Good job you got me to make another sweep of that ship.'

CHAPTER 39

SEARCH AND RESCUE

THE OFFICERS' CLUB was beginning to thin of patrons. It was eleven-thirty. Hazel was concerned, and Kate could see her anxiety. Hazel asked Alec to recheck with the airfield. The frozen look on his face said it all. Hazel's heart sank. She had had a feeling of foreboding most of the evening. A couple of minutes later, Gratton returned. 'Alec, what's the matter?'

'The RAF have lost contact with Ewan's plane. It apparently took off OK but then went off radar, but not before circling, which doesn't make sense. They're getting an air-sea rescue patrol to go to their last known position, but it will be daylight before they can make any meaningful search,' said Gratton.

'Oh God, no!' squeaked Hazel, close to tears.

'It sounds like there was something wrong with plane. It circled. Must have lost power slowly and ditched. We shall have to wait for first light before the search can start.'

Hazel was suddenly distraught.

'Kate, take Hazel back to her quarters and stay with her. I'm off to brief the admiral. I'll keep in close touch with the RAF,' said Gratton, who was feeling sick to his stomach, afraid that something awful might have happened to Ewan. He knew that the light Lysander would break up easily if it landed on water.

Gratton entered the admiral's office and somehow was not surprised to find Henry Blackwell and John Cross with the admiral. 'Come on in, Alec. I can guess why you're here,' said Admiral Kelly.

Gratton cast a disapproving glance at Blackwell and Cross. 'I'll bet you two know what's going on.'

'No. Not really. Although I do admit something might happen, but I didn't think it would put our man in any danger,' said Blackwell in a matter-of-fact tone.

'Your man!' retorted Admiral Kelly. 'He's my man.'

'So, would someone like to tell me what's going on?' said Gratton indignantly.

'Ewan's plane has gone down near the coast of Catania. That's all we know,' said Admiral Kelly.

'Did you expect something like this?' Gratton asked Blackwell accusingly.

'No, I did not,' replied Blackwell.

'We thought that our man, er, Ewan, might be given the runaround—maybe misled or lied to and so on. At the moment, we're guessing that it's an ordinary plane crash—engine failure. It does happen,' said Cross.

'I'll grant you that, but we don't get many crashes these days. And I understand from RAF Luqa that the pilot is experienced—one of their best. It's too much of a coincidence. Did Ewan send any message before take-off?' said Gratton. He was still agitated.

'Strange that you mention that. He made a telephone call from Catania Police Station to the RAF airfield to say he was on his way back. And then he added something about "It's too heavy in the water." The pilot also reported that they were making a deviation to fly over the harbour of Catania,' said Admiral Kelly.

'Does that mean anything to you?' Blackwell asked.

Gratton eyed up Admiral Kelly. 'Hmm! "Too heavy in the water" could be something to do with the displacement of the SS *San Gabriel*,' said Gratton.

'Yes. That's my belief also,' added Admiral Kelly.

Blackwell thought for a moment. His silence was characteristic when he went into deep thought. 'John, get a hold of RAF Catania and ask them to check whether anyone went near the plane before it took off. It would have been near sunset, but their security should have checked on anyone going near it,' said Blackwell.

'Yes, it's dark out there. Won't be able to search for them until daybreak, but at least they'll be in the right area,' said Gratton.

'I've ordered our RAF air-sea rescue patrol to get there as soon as possible too. The one based at Catania is on its way also,' said Admiral Kelly.

'One thought, Admiral,' said Gratton. 'I think two of Ewan's boats are heading back here from Taranto. Not sure exactly where they are, but they could be there by daylight.'

'Good idea. Get on it right away. I'll stay here in my office,' said Admiral Kelly.

Gratton was about to leave with Blackwell and Cross, when Blackwell stopped for a moment. 'Has anyone told his wife, Hazel, about what's happened?' asked Blackwell.

It was a sudden interruption, not quite the coldness that Henry Blackwell usually portrayed when it was anything to do with his intelligence work. Admiral Kelly and Gratton were surprised. They realised that there was genuine concern and sympathy, something neither had thought was possible from him. John Cross was not surprised. He knew that Blackwell not only trusted Ewan but also liked him very much.

They left the office, but Admiral Kelly called Gratton back. 'Alec, whatever happens, see that Hazel gets anything she needs. I've gotten to know Ewan as though he were my own son. For a moment I nearly forgot that he is also Hazel's man.'

Gratton nodded. 'Yes, sir. Will do. He's also like a brother to me,' said Gratton, who remembered that Admiral Kelly had lost his son on a North Atlantic convey three years earlier.

CHAPTER 40

DAWN

THE DARKNESS SURROUNDING Ewan and Flight Lieutenant John Bromley seemed to invade them. The flames from the burning Lysander aircraft had finally dwindled away, leaving a wisp of smoke to betray their plight. The smoke was almost imperceptible in the darkness, only barely visible when blown across the surf of the waves on the beach. Although the summer was encroaching Sicily, the night-time was much cooler than the sun-drenched daylight. The two men huddled close together to keep warm. Bromley nursed his bruised forehead where he had taken a frontal blow as the plane first struck the beach. Ewan clutched his left arm close to his body. He was in pain and for a while thought that he had broken his arm, but the pain eased to an uncomfortable ache. Either way, they were lucky to be alive. They needed to rest and wait for dawn.

'How's your arm, Commander?' asked Bromley.

'Hurting a little. What about your head?' said Ewan.

'Feels as though I've been on a binge all night.'

'Once we get out of this mess, I'll be buying you the biggest thank-you drink I can.'

'Thank you for what?'

'A superb bit of flying and landing. We're both alive thanks to you.'

'Thanks, but if you hadn't asked me to make another turn, we would be down in the drink. And in such a light plane as the Lysander, I wouldn't have given much for our chances, especially as I had no power at all.'

Ewan thought for a moment. 'No power at all?'

'Right. The engine simply cut out with virtually no warning,' said Bromley, who turned his gaze from out to sea to Ewan.

'Just sudden loss of oil pressure?' queried Ewan.

'Actually, a catastrophic engine failure. Yet I personally checked the plane over before we left Malta,' said Bromley.

The minutes drifted away, leaving a thought in Ewan's mind. 'Could it have been tampered with in Catania?' he asked.

'It would have to have been immediately before you boarded. I left the plane for only a few minutes. I was called over to the RAF office. It was a call for me about your wanting to deviate; well, that's what the ground controller said. Come to think of it, the caller rang off before I could answer it. Do you think that someone wanted me away from the plane?'

'That's my guess,' said Ewan, 'which raises the issue of what it was that had caused an alarm in someone's mind.'

'If that's the case, do you think we're safe here?' said Bromley.

'I think so. If anyone was awake on the that ship, they would have seen us crash. The plane exploding into flames—no survivors, eh?'

They stared out to sea, waiting to be found.

The officers' quarters where Ewan and Hazel had been billeted until they could find something better were relatively quiet for midnight. There were the odd groups of servicemen and servicewomen who could be heard chattering as they returned from their evenings out or as they were coming off duty. Hazel fumbled with her door key.

'Do you need a hand?' asked Kate.

'No, I'm all right. Just shaken, I suppose.'

'I think I should pack you off to bed with a large brandy. You'll have news in the morning.'

'One way or the other,' muttered Hazel. 'Anyway, I'll be OK.'

'I'm staying with you all night. And don't worry about your duty shift tomorrow. Leave that to me,' said Kate.

Hazel didn't argue. She slipped off her uniform and climbed into bed. Kate brought in a large glass of brandy; she knew Ewan always kept a couple of bottles of gin or brandy in their apartment. 'Here you are. Get this down you.'

Hazel nodded and tried to smile but could not.

'Take your bra off. You'll be more comfortable,' said Kate.

A trickle of tears emerged from Hazel, and she grinned.

'Something tickle you?'

'Yes. That's what Ewan says, except he usually removes my bra,' said Hazel.

Kate giggled. Now there was a thought to sleep on. Hazel settled into the bed. Kate made sure that the sheet and blanket were snuggled up around her.

Kate took a spare blanket and covered herself on the small sofa. She dropped off to sleep, unable to help herself from worrying about Ewan also.

The morning sunshine beamed into the bedroom and lounge. Hazel did not stir. Suddenly there was a banging on the door. Kate rolled off the sofa and flopped onto the floor. She scrambled for the door. Standing before her was Alec Gratton with an ecstatic grin.

'He's safe!' said Kate, rocketing out of sleep.

'Yes. They're both safe. Ewan and the pilot have been found.'

'Hazel. Hazel!' shouted Kate. 'They're safe!'

Hazel emerged from the bedroom wearing only her knickers. She rubbed her eyes.

Kate repeated, 'They're both safe, Ewan and the pilot.'

'They're on their way into Malta on one of our air-sea rescue launches.

Due in at about one o'clock,' said Gratton. He added slowly. 'Er, Hazel, don't you think you had better get some clothes on!'

The full light of dawn arrived at four. One of the RAF air-sea rescue launches had spotted a little smoke on a beach a few miles from the last reported radar contact with the Lysander. As there was no debris in the area, they guessed that the plane had made a landing on the rugged beach. Ewan and Bromley had awakened with the dawn. The cold morning air had been kept at bay by their flying suits, but it nevertheless gave them a shiver. After an hour, they noticed a craft low in the water on the horizon. It seemed to get closer and closer until, with wild cheers, they shouted and Ewan waved his uninjured arm. They were spotted. The launch closed towards the shallows of the beach. A dinghy was already being paddled towards them as they waddled to the water's edge. They were cold as they waited for the dinghy crew to help them aboard. Five minutes later, they were on board the RAF air-sea rescue launch clutching a hot mug of cocoa each in the warmth of the crew's mess room. 'We've radioed Malta and told them we have you safely aboard,' said the skipper. 'Suggest you both rest up. We estimate to be in Valetta at about thirteen hundred.'

'Thanks, Skipper,' said Ewan, wrapping his hands around the mug of cocoa.

Flight Lieutenant Bromley spoke up. 'Cocoa's good. Skipper, I need to talk to HQ.'

'Are you sure?' asked Flight Lieutenant Donaldson, the boat skipper. It was an oddity of the services that the crews of RAF air-sea rescue launches kept their RAF ranks at sea, except for the flight sergeant, who was sometimes referred to as the coxswain—maybe to preserve the maritime element, thought Ewan.

'You're worried about that sudden loss in oil pressure, aren't you?' said Ewan.

Bromley nodded.

The radio operator called up RAF Luqa in Malta and handed the microphone to Bromley. 'Flight Lieutenant Bromley speaking. Get a message to my CO.'

'He's here. Just a mo,' said the Luqa radio operator, who handed over the microphone.

'Wing Commander Bentley here, John.' It was Bromley's CO. 'What happened?'

Bromley explained, concluding, 'It was good fortune that my passenger, Lieutenant Commander Jones, instructed me to fly around a merchant ship to observe it better as the night had caught up with us. If we hadn't have done that, we would have ditched much farther out to sea. In fact, sir, the sudden loss of engine power would have caused us to crash like stone. We were circling for the second time when it all happened, so I was able to glide onto the beach because of the turning effect. Lucky, I suppose.'

'We're already investigating. Is Commander Jones with you? I have someone here who wants a word,' said Wing Commander Bentley.

Bromley handed the microphone to Ewan. 'Jones here.'

'Ah, Ewan, glad you're safe,' came the dulcet tone of Henry Blackwell.

'Oh, thank you, Henry. Did you expect this?' said Ewan. His statement was a surprise to Bromley and the RAF crew listening.

'Not exactly. Your message about weight—was that to do with the displacement of the SS *San Gabriel*?' Blackwell asked, getting straight to the point.

'Yes. I'm guessing she's carrying a much heavier load than the manifest shows. And another thing. Her course, although close to shore to start with, as best I could judge was farther out to sea to well and clearly skirt Malta. Is that any help?' said Ewan.

'Brilliant, Ewan. Knew I could rely on you,' said Blackwell.

'Really. What about my wife—how much does she know?'

'We're looking after her. She'll be here to meet you.'

Ewan signed off, handing the microphone back to the radio operator.

'Who were you talking to?' asked the skipper.

'You really don't want to know,' replied Ewan with a smirk. 'He's part of the cloak-and-dagger brigade, if you know what I mean.'

The skipper nodded and grunted. 'Guessed it was something like that.'

CHAPTER 41

APOLOGY

HAZEL WAITED IMPATIENTLY for the RAF air-sea rescue launch to tie up at the jetty. She saw it enter Minola Bay. It seemed like an eternity until it tied up, but it was actually less than five minutes. She soon spotted Ewan standing at a side rail, one hand on the rail, the other bandaged. He was injured, but it seemed minor, or so was her hope. Ewan also saw Hazel and waved to her with his unbandaged arm. He knew how protective she was of him and wondered what she had been told about his escapade. Standing a few yards away from Hazel was Henry Blackwell. This was not good for Ewan as she would have guessed that he was involved with one of Blackwell's jaunts. She had urged Ewan not to get involved in anything remotely dangerous, especially as the war in Europe was now ended.

Blackwell approached her. 'Hazel,' he said.

She turned to face him. 'I should have known that you were behind this,' she said sarcastically with disappointment.

'Sorry, Hazel, but truly this should have been straightforward. Nothing dodgy at all. I, er, have a favour to ask,' he said, anticipating a tone of disapproval.

'What sort of favour?'

'I need a few minutes with Ewan before you whisk him off to tend his injury.'

It suddenly occurred to Hazel that Blackwell would not have asked unless it was important. 'Right-o. I guess it's important.' She wasn't entirely convinced.

'Yes it is, and there's no need to disappear while I speak with him.'

The RAF launch tied up, and Ewan stepped ashore. Hazel shot forward and gave him a big hug, neglecting any of the formalities of rank and protocol and forgetting his injured arm.

'God, it's good to see you,' said Ewan as he pulled his bandaged arm away.

'And you. I love you very much. But before I can take you off to bed, this, er, gentleman wishes a few words with you.'

'Both of you, join me in that cafe across the road,' said Blackwell, looking to the cafe.

Blackwell order three coffees and looked around to see when the waiter was out of earshot.

'Ewan. Run by me exactly what you saw on the SS *San Gabriel*,' said Blackwell.

'It's as I told you on the radio. Nothing untoward, except I thought she was riding low in the water—heavy. The Plimsoll mark was barely visible. She must have been carrying something heavy—very dense. No signs of her shipping water. Dry, in fact. Little or no sign of any large steel cargo. I also reckon her displacement was about four thousand tonnes. A small freighter that's seen better days. She was also flying an Italian flag, but I thought I heard Spanish being spoken.'

Blackwell thought for a moment. 'That's interesting in itself. Any indication of how she came to be in Catania or this area at all?'

'Olive oil. That was her previous cargo, and she took on more.'

'That doesn't account for the much-increased weight, does it?'

'No. The passengers all seemed genuine. No sign of escaping Nazis, whatever they look like. Businessmen mainly, with their families. I guess looking for a better life away from Italy.'

Hazel was left out of the conversation but felt she needed to interject. 'What can have such a high density that could be mistaken for a lot of steel?'

It seemed a simple question, but Blackwell picked up on it and tossed a quick grin to Ewan. 'Your lovely wife here has hit the nail on the head!'

'I don't follow,' muttered Ewan.

'Neither do I,' added Hazel.

'Mercury,' said Blackwell. 'Mercury.'

'Mercury? The stuff found in thermometers?' Hazel asked.

'And those special barometers for measuring air pressure,' said Ewan.

'Right. But in this case, it's for another use. All I can tell you is that the Nazis were accumulating a lot of the liquid metal for a top-secret research project. The Russians would also like to get their hands on it. And so would we,' said Blackwell.

'Was it loaded in Catania?' said Ewan.

'Yes. It had been stored in Sicily for some time, but we had no idea where. It's actually extracted from cinnabar, mercury sulphide, which is found freely in Sicily. One of the world's biggest sources, all thanks to Mount Etna, which has been very active here for at least the past ten years with the big eruption two years ago,' said Blackwell.

'Oh, I remember that. Didn't it cut off a retreating German Panzer unit, leaving it to us to bombard them at will on the coast road?' Ewan said.

'It sure did. Our concern is where that hoard of mercury is going,' said Blackwell.

'Our?' queried Hazel.

'London and Washington,' replied Blackwell. He finished his coffee.

'Enough said,' muttered Ewan.

'Certainly out of my league. Anyway, you two get off to bed or whatever you do on homecomings.' Blackwell chuckled.

'That's one way of embarrassing me,' said Hazel.

'Really. What about the one-handed bra removal expert?' said Blackwell.

'What's that all about?' said Ewan, looking puzzled.

Hazel squirmed. 'Is there nothing that gets by you?'

Blackwell grinned. 'Not a lot.'

CHAPTER 42

NEW ASSIGNMENT

THE TENSION AROUND Ewan's crash and apparent sabotage of the aircraft was all but forgotten when Ewan was summoned to Admiral Kelly's office. It had been four weeks. The warm fair June weather was now making its mark on Malta. Ewan had a good idea of what the admiral wanted, and he was right. Admiral Kelly got right down to the issue. 'Ewan, I won't beat around the bush. You are well versed with what's been going on, and I understand that Commander Gratton has briefed you. We want to change your role slightly. Your group will retain its training role but will include more coastal patrols. Gratton will keep you informed of the latest intelligence, and I will have detailed orders for you by tomorrow morning.'

There was now growing black-market trading in almost any commodity, especially in the former occupied Nazi territories, and Italy was no exception. Malta was relatively free of the black marketeers, but nearby Sicily was not. To make matters worse, the Mafia was also very active in this area. The Americans had used the Mafia against the Nazis and Italian fascists, but now they were free to roam almost freely, unmolested by the Italian police and Allied administrations.

Ewan quickly took in the significance and importance of his patrol group's role. 'Admiral, I'll need to set up a robust command structure. Am I free to work it out myself?'

'Yes, of course. Just let me know as soon as possible,' said Admiral Kelly. 'One more thing, Ewan: have you given any thought as to what you want to do—your future, that is? You can leave the service whenever you like starting next year.'

'Not really, Admiral. Hazel is already enjoying her new nursing role. Not really sure what I want to do. For the time being, I think I would like to stay here in Malta, but then I suppose things will change, especially as our empire will start to shrink. It's a changing world.'

'You're right there. I've been summoned back to Britain and will be replaced at the end of August. I think the new Maltese administration would welcome your continued service here, and I'm more than happy to recommend that you should stay on.'

'Am I likely to be posted elsewhere?' asked Ewan. It was an inevitable question. He had wondered when this might occur. The war in the Pacific and Malaya was still raging, and the Royal Navy was playing an ever-increasing role. Ewan had discussed the future with Hazel, but neither had come up with any firm plans. Perhaps now was the time to give some serious thought to it.

Ewan returned to their married quarters early, having visited a local solicitor to discuss the possibility of buying their own home in Malta or at least renting privately away from the naval base. He thought that getting some groundwork on the possibility of setting up their life by staying in Malta might be an option. It was a starting point for a serious discussion when Hazel came off duty.

The balcony door to their apartment was open, letting in a warm draught. Ewan sat in an old, well-used lounger, soaking up a little of the evening sun while waiting for Hazel.

CHAPTER 43

SETTLING INTO FAMILY LIFE

T HE SUMMER OF 1946 heralded changes in Ewan and Hazel's life in Malta. Hazel was well settled into her nurse tutoring role and enjoyed the occasional hands-on nursing when the hospitals were put under pressure. Matron Margaret Stanton was relying more on Hazel, who by now was seen by many of the nursing and medical staff as the matron's deputy. Margaret had discussed with Hazel how their nursing functions were changing. The residue of the war, notably that involving refugees and displaced persons, had reduced significantly. This left what appeared at face value to be an excess capacity of medical services for Malta. The governor of Malta suggested that the Royal Naval Hospital could take on more of the general civilian requirements. This was agreed. Although the reducing military commitment had led to the downsizing of military nursing, one area was deemed important for Malta's health and medical services. This was the training of nurses. Hazel's input was seen as very important. For the first time in Malta's modern history, the island was able to train and produce their own qualified nurses without recourse to external support. However, the British War Department in London recognised that it was still an important asset to permit the enhanced training of qualified military nurses from Britain in an overseas role. Hazel easily adapted to these changes and enjoyed her work.

The motor torpedo boat flotilla under Ewan was similarly being wound down, although there was still a need for high-speed interception craft in the area, at least for the near future. Much of Ewan's nontraining role was taken up with intelligence gathering, reporting shipping movements, and the occasional intercepting of contraband running between Italy, Sicily, Malta, and North Africa. There was still a glimmer of political conflict in Greece, Cyprus, and Crete.

It was on one of the hot summer days that Ewan and Hazel took a day off from their routine duties to have a break. They went to the north part of the island of Malta, which partly overlooked the island of Gozo. They aimed for their private spot, a small cove accessible from the landward side by a steep pathway down the cliffs that guarded its privacy. It was where they had spent their short honeymoon in 1943, and it remained their small treasure and place of escape when they needed it. Hazel set out a towel to act as a tablecloth and arranged their basket of food and drinks.

Ewan, having already decided to get into the sea, swam around for about five minutes. He plodded up the short sandy beach to be greeted by Hazel offering him a bottle of beer. He sank onto his knees and took the bottle. He took a large slug of the beer and jemmied the bottle into the sand to keep it upright.

'Are you going in for a swim?' he asked.

'In a moment.'

'Hmm. What are you thinking?'

'Nothing of any significance really. Just wondering if you're happy with what we are doing now. Or have you any ideas of what we should be planning to do in the future?'

Ewan thought for a moment. He took a pilchard and tomato sandwich from the basket and took a bite. He cleared his mouth and turned to Hazel.

'No ideas or thoughts about our future?' she asked again.

'Not really. It's more about what you want, isn't it?'

Hazel raised herself onto her knees. 'I suppose you're right. But then I'm not sure what I want,' she said.

'You're not bored with me, are you?' Ewan asked.

She stood up and flaunted her body in front of him. 'More to the point, are you bored with me?'

Ewan went to stand up and go to her, but she quickly ran into the sea, splashing the water as she immersed herself in the warm water, which seemed like ice because the sun had baked her body. Ewan charged after her and took a long lunge towards her, almost throwing her off her feet.

He stood up next to her. 'Bored, is it!' he said.

Before she could reply, he was capturing her body in his arms.

She reciprocated by wrapping herself around him.

'Now what shall I do with you?' he said.

'I'm all yours.'

They kissed and hugged each other. The minutes rolled by as the waves began to beat onto their bodies. Ewan released her bikini top. She removed it and cast it back towards the beach. They stripped off their remaining swimming costumes, throwing them up onto the beach. Ewan grabbed her to make love, only to topple over with Hazel on top of him. After half drowning each other, they waded back onto the beach, where Ewan settled himself onto her. The hot sunshine soon dried their exposed skin. No words passed until they finished lovemaking.

'Are we bored with each other?' Ewan asked.

'Not bloody likely. And anyway, you're still an animal when you get going. A bit slower this time though,' she said.

'What?' said Ewan, wondering what she meant. 'Slower?'

'A little bit. Remember when we first came here on our honeymoon?'

'Er, yes,' he replied, unable really to recall the detail.

'You stripped me before we got into the sea and shagged the living daylights out of me. God, I'll never forget that!'

'I made love to you. I didn't shag you as you put it,' said Ewan, looking deeply into her gleaming eyes. '*Shagging* is a crude term.'

'It's also an accurate word. Ewan, I could hardly walk after you did me,' she said, sporting an alluring grin. 'At least now I'm used to it. Anyway, you're still an animal.'

Ewan chuckled. 'OK, you win that. Er, do you want me to do you again?'

'Let's a have a bite to eat and drink, then we can decide how you're going to have me again,' she said, and laughed. 'Of course, I might decide how I want you.'

Ewan caught a glimpse of her flirtish grin and then aimed his hand into the basket of sandwiches.

The time seeped by. They both began to feel the burning effects of the blazing sunshine. 'Time to cover up, I think,' said Ewan.

'Good idea. Anyway, I think someone is coming down the path,' said Hazel. 'Don't want to upset the locals and their strict laws, etcetera.'

'You mean their law against you being nude,' he said, chuckling.

Hazel dressed in her bikini just as two men and two women appeared from behind a large boulder that guarded the entry to the small cove. Ewan had already dressed and gathered up the basket and towels. He viewed the four clambering around the boulder and recognised one of the men. It was Lieutenant Andrew Starling, Naval Intelligence, who was attached to Admiral Stanley's command, with Stanley having replaced Admiral Kelly.

'Andrew. What a pleasant surprise,' said Ewan.

'And you, Commander, and your wife,' replied Andrew.

'Haven't seen you around for months. What have you been up to?' Ewan asked.

'Oh, the usual stuff. Been on secondment to Cyprus, but back now,' said Andrew.

'Ah yes. And I heard that you got your promotion—well deserved.'

'Thanks. And that was a lot to do with you. In fact, this is fortuitous.

I was going to contact you to arrange an evening out with you and your wife. I also have some other news for you,' said Andrew.

Ewan agreed that they would sort out an evening within the next few days. Andrew then apologised to his party and introduced them to Ewan and Hazel. His three companions were all from Naval HQ.

Hazel climbed over the large boulder to the path. Ewan was about to follow her, when he stopped and asked Andrew what news he had that would interest him.

Andrew threw a glance at Hazel and made sure she was out of earshot. 'Commander, we have it on good authority that Otto Kranz survived the sinking of the *Marino* last year and somehow has ended up in either Argentina or possibly Spain. I'll tell you more when we meet.'

Ewan felt the news like a cold knife stabbing him. Otto Kranz alive and escaped again! Would he ever be held account for his war crimes? More importantly, was Kranz still wanting revenge on Ewan and Hazel? It seemed from what little intelligence could be gleaned from the captured SS soldiers, following the sinking of the *Marino*, that Kranz had an obsession to get Hazel. Of course, Ewan had not revealed this to her. He had hoped that Kranz had gone forever.

CHAPTER 44

REMEMBERING THE PAST

S EVERAL DAYS PASSED after Ewan and Hazel had met with Andrew
Starling. Ewan had almost forgotten about Andrew's suggestion
that they should have dinner together, when he received a phone call
from Kate Davies. She informed Ewan that Admiral Stanley had called a
meeting, along with Andrew Starling and Alec Gratton. She added that
Andrew was also arranging a night out and provided a number of dates. He
suggested that as Hazel rarely worked nights, there should be no problem,
telling her to pick an evening.

The meeting with Admiral Stanley concerned naval intelligence matters
and the future of Malta as a command hub for the British Admiralty.
Ewan's involvement became clear in the first minutes of the meeting. Ewan
was to take command of all shore patrols around Malta and would reach
out to the North African coast of Libya and Tunisia, and Sicily. Most of the
patrol work would involve intelligence gathering and interception of vessels
suspected in contraband smuggling, including weapons and ammunition
for political insurgences. Admiral Stanley, reiterating that the Admiralty
would not get involved in any political activities, then turned to Gratton.
'Alec, have you briefed Ewan on the latest Russian communist activities?'

'Not yet, Admiral,' said Gratton, who turned to Ewan. 'We'll get
together after this meeting. Shouldn't take long. Andrew will also apprise
you of the latest we have on Kranz.'

The admiral turned to Ewan. 'Good. Ewan, as regards your patrol group, I will need a weekly update on operational capability. And include boats that will be nonoperational for whatever reason. The, er, Admiralty like these sort of reports,' he added coyly.

'And the government.' Gratton smirked.

'Quite so,' said Admiral Stanley.

The meeting broke up. Ewan joined Alec and Andrew in a small dingy room tucked away in another part of Naval HQ.

The three sat around a small table, upon which Gratton had opened a chart showing the islands of Sicily and Malta. He explained what they wanted but said he would leave the detailed arrangements to Ewan to sort out patrol strength and patterns. Ewan pointed out that he would adopt a random patrol regime with respect to locations and in particular dates and times. He didn't want undesirable observers to get a patrol routine as he thought it would jeopardise the operation. Gratton and Starling agreed.

'One more thing on that matter,' said Gratton. 'I think your reporting should be random dates also. It's important. I think if we can give the impression that the patrol activity is not too serious and perhaps lackadaisical, it might reveal the hand of adversaries.'

'Adversaries, eh! Thought we once called them enemies,' noted Ewan.

'Times are changing,' said Gratton.

'And one day Malta will become an independent, self-governing state, I guess,' said Starling, who up till now had remained fairly quiet.

'True. So, is there anything else?' Gratton asked.

'Yes. What's this news you have for me?' Ewan asked, looking first to Gratton and then at Starling.

'Ah yes, Kranz,' said Starling.

'Don't tell me! He's really alive somewhere,' said Ewan, feeling a little depressed.

'Yes. He was reportedly in Spain but left before he could be gotten at by the Allies' war crimes tribunal investigators. They now believe he is in South America—Argentina or Paraguay.'

'Well, at least he's well away from here. And I hope it stays that way,' said Ewan.

'I'll second that,' said Gratton, who knew how much Ewan and especially Hazel loathed Kranz.

Andrew Starling stood from the table. 'Sirs, I've got a duty inspection before we meet this evening, so if there's nothing else, I'll shove off.'

'See you later, Andrew. By the way, who are you bring along this evening?' Gratton asked.

'My secret until later,' said Starling, who slipped on his cap and left.

'Nice lad, that,' said Gratton.

'Yes. I'm guessing he's grabbed a nurse. Is there anything else?' Ewan asked.

'No. Not really,' said Gratton.

They carried their caps, only putting them on as they left the Naval HQ, and walked slowly towards the centre of Valetta. Their idle chatter was mainly directed to Ewan's new intake of crew for training from Britain and Gratton's revealing that he was to be posted back to London in the near future. Kate would be going with him. They would be getting married in England. Alec asked if Ewan would be his best man. Ewan eagerly agreed.

'Thanks, Ewan. And Kate will be asking Hazel to be her matron of honour. Keep that to yourself until Kate gets hold of Hazel this evening.'

'Certainly. She'll definitely accept. So, when do you expect to do the deed? Set a date yet?' said Ewan.

'Probably next January in Epsom. I'll sort out the details with you both later.'

'Is there something else on your mind?' Ewan asked.

'Perceptive of you, as ever,' said Alec.

'I understand that you and Hazel are considering, or have considered, staying on here in Malta after you leave the service,' said Alec.

'Yes. That's right. Any issue on that?'

'No. Quite the opposite. I've heard a rumour that the new Malta administration are looking for someone to take charge of the island's coastal defence forces, within RN operations here. Your name has been mentioned. Interested?'

Ewan was taken aback. 'Yes, I'm interested. Mind you, I'm not sure whether we will stay in Malta. Hazel's happy here, but in some respects we miss Britain.'

Alec nodded in agreement. They continued strolling along the battlements that overlooked the Grand Harbour, before finding a pub for a drink.

The Royal Malta Yacht Club was relatively quiet for a Friday evening. Alec Gratton and Kate Davies were sitting at the bar, nurturing a couple of gin and tonics. They had reserved a table and were waiting for Ewan, Hazel, Andrew, and his friend to arrive. Alec commented to Kate about the secret partner whom Andrew was bringing. Kate had no idea but suspected that it would be a nurse, which is what Ewan had thought and what he'd told Alec earlier. Alec had just about finished his drink when Ewan and Hazel arrived. 'That's a good cue for another drink. What are you two drinking? Kate, another?' said Alec.

Alec gave up his bar stool for Hazel. Ewan stood next to Kate and nudged her.

'Hazel, before we get engrossed in all sorts of gossip, I've got a question for you. It's an important question,' said Kate, sporting a grin.

'I'm intrigued. Fire away,' said Hazel.

'You know that we've decided to get married. And now we've set a date. There's only one problem. I don't have a bridesmaid, and we—that is Alec and I—were wondering whether you would do us the honour?' said Kate.

'Honour. So, I would be your maid of honour?'

'Is that a yes?' Kate's voice bounced with joy.

Alec rejoined them and immediately guessed that Hazel had agreed.

He nodded approval to Ewan. Hazel spotted Ewan's grin. 'You knew Kate was going to ask me? Why didn't you tell me?'

'Not for me to commit you to such an important role, my dear.' Ewan chuckled.

'Really? And what about our escapades at the end of the war?'

'Aargh. OK, you win that.' Ewan felt a little uncomfortable.

Kate and Hazel began discussing the wedding arrangements. Alec and Ewan moved themselves to stand at the bar to talk about the changes that were taking place in their naval command. The talk about wedding arrangements did not appeal to Alec. Ewan was of the same mind.

After ten minutes, Andrew Starling arrived with his partner for the evening; it was Helen Grayling, which was of no surprise to Hazel. Andrew directed Helen to Hazel and Kate.

Andrew approached Alec. 'Apologies for being late, sir, but I had some urgent information to digest,' he said. He added lightly, 'Helen nearly gave up on me.'

'What was so important to almost miss an evening out with us?' Ewan asked.

'Or the date with the delectable Helen?' quipped Alec.

'Hmm. I need to have a chat with you both, but not with our ladies present.'

'I think we have another ten minutes before our table is ready. How about more drinks? I'll sort out our ladies,' said Ewan.

'Good idea,' added Alec.

Ewan placed a tray of drinks before the women. 'Sorry, girls. A bit of men's talk, then we'll join you. Table's ready in a few minutes.'

'We understand. You don't want to be bludgeoned with wedding chat,' said Hazel, who grinned.

'So, it's on then? You're getting married to Alec,' Helen said.

Ewan left them and returned to the bar. The men positioned themselves at the end of the bar, away from the barman and other passing guests.

Andrew explained about the important information that he had received. A report had been received by Allied Command in Rome that SS-Obersturmbannführer Otto Kranz had been seen in mainland Italy near Naples. Confirmation was awaited by the Italian police, but US Army Intelligence were fairly certain as the original alert had been made by the Italian police after they arrested a black marketeer and smuggler. The smuggler had given them a strange story involving his activity on the North African and Spanish coasts. He had been taking so-called refugees from Italy to Tunisia and Spain. He guessed that they were Nazis and fascists escaping from the searches by Allied Intelligence and war crimes investigators. He didn't care as the money was good. Everything had been going well until one of the so-called refugees, who was part of a larger group, demanded that he be taken to Malta first and then be collected a few days later. The smuggler overheard a conversation in German that the man was ex-SS as he had a tattoo of his SS number on his forearm. The SS man said that he had some unfinished business, an old score to settle involving a woman who was possibly based in Malta. From the way the man talked, the smuggler thought that it might be a medical doctor or a nurse.

US Army Intelligence were not particularly interested, but when they interviewed him, as a matter of routine, they learned from the smuggler that the SS man was a survivor from a ship sunk by the Allies off the coast of Albania and near to Brindisi the previous year.

A member of the US Army Intelligence unit remembered the incident and knew it involved a special Royal Navy flotilla. The US Army decided to pass on the information to the Royal Navy in Malta. However, this had been four weeks earlier and the smuggler said that other smugglers had already taken the SS man to Malta.

'Didn't want your wife to know, if you know what I mean. Or Helen for that matter. Did I do the right thing? It does sound like Kranz. The circumstances and description fit him,' said Andrew.

'Yes,' said Alec, 'it certainly sounds like Otto Kranz. He must have survived. I'll lay on some surveillance without Hazel or Helen knowing. Andrew, get additional surveillance set up on some of our black-market characters here in Malta.'

Ewan took a slow glance at the three women and especially Hazel. Hopefully, it was not Kranz and hopefully Hazel was not in any danger.

Hazel caught Ewan's smile and realised that the three men were talking about something serious. She hoped that Ewan was not getting involved in anything dangerous again. Putting her misgivings aside, she returned to the talk of Kate's wedding arrangements. It was, after all, a special evening.

CHAPTER 45

KATE

AZEL AND KATE sauntered along the main street of Valetta towards the bus station, where they planned to get a taxi to Kate's apartment. Unbeknown to them, they were being followed and not by any of Alec Gratton's intelligence team. They reached the taxi stand and quickly found a vacant taxi to whisk them away. A car followed them. Kate's apartment was next to the main officers' quarters, where she had lived for five years, but now that peace had arrived she wanted her own place, albeit a rented one. Alec would often stay with her even though he had a room in the officers' quarters. Kate invited Hazel for a late-night drink with a view to staying the night. Ewan had no objection as he needed to return to his command following the discussion with Alec and Andrew. He assured Hazel that it wasn't dangerous, just routine. It was partly a lie, and she half believed him. Kate poured two large gins with tonic water, adding handsome slices of lemon.

'We should do this more often,' said Kate.

'A girls' night out. Yes. Ewan won't mind. More likely to encourage me. What about Alec? Will he mind?' said Hazel.

'No. Like Ewan, he, I think, will very much approve. And anyway, it stops me worrying about what he gets up to—intelligence stuff and all that.'

'I know what you mean. I do hope that Ewan isn't being dragged off into more clandestine stuff.'

'But you trust him. I think he's learned his lesson. And Alec certainly won't put him in harm's way.'

Hazel took a sip of her gin. 'Yes, I know. My main concern is Blackwell. God knows what he gets up to.'

'He's gone back to London, so don't worry,' said Kate.

They carried on drinking slowly and chatting about their respective futures. Kate expected to return to England with Alec within a couple of months.

'I'll miss you,' said Hazel.

'Me too. I'll also miss you. So. What about you? Any plans on a family?'

'Don't know. We have discussed it. I suppose it depends on how long we stay here,' said Hazel.

They were just about settling into an all-night drinking session when the telephone rang. 'Who on earth can that be at this hour? HQ know that Alec isn't here,' muttered Kate. The gin was taking effect.

'Didn't know you had a telephone,' said Hazel, surprised.

'Yes. Alec had it put in for when he stays with me. He's always on call. I suppose I'll have to get used to it.'

'If he stays in the service,' noted Hazel as Kate lifted the handset.

'Good heavens! It's for you, Hazel,' said Kate, turning to Hazel. 'Who's calling? Oh, right. Hazel, it's Matron Margaret Stanton.' She handed the telephone to Hazel.

'Matron. How did you get this number?' Hazel asked.

'Got it from Ewan,' said Margaret Stanton. 'Sorry to upset your evening, but I have a problem. Is it possible for you to cover a duty shift? I've got three nurses sick. Can you get in as soon as possible?'

'Well, er, yes. I'll get a taxi. See you in about twenty minutes,' said Hazel.

'That's great. Anticipated you could make it. I've booked a taxi to pick you up from the officers' quarters. Should be there in ten minutes. Majestic Taxis. Thanks, Hazel.'

Hazel handed the telephone back to Kate.

'I guess that's buggered our night!' said Kate.

''Fraid so, but I'll finish this gin first,' said Hazel.

Hazel left Kate after arranging another night out.

The Majestic taxi was waiting for Hazel at the entrance to the officers' quarters. It took her to RNH Bighi.

Kate settled down on her bed. She had finished her gin and was about to switch off the bedside lamp when someone knocked on her apartment door. *It must be Hazel,* she thought, so she hurried to open the door, anticipating that Hazel wasn't needed until the morning. She opened the door and was ready to greet Hazel, but to her astonishment two men confronted her. Without any warning, they pushed her back into her apartment and grappled her to the floor. She tried to scream for help but was quickly gagged and wrapped in a blanket from her bed. She was helpless. She was bundled down the stairway and then thrown into a waiting car. Her terrifying realisation was that she was going to be assaulted. She could not see where the car was being driven to. Several minutes and a bumpy, very uncomfortable car journey culminated with her being rebundled out of the car and taken inside a dilapidated warehouse.

Kranz, having heard the car stop outside the warehouse, strolled to where the bundle containing Kate had been deposited. The lighting was dim from an old lamp with a single bulb. Kranz approached the bundle as the two men began unravelling Kate from the blanket. She tumbled out of the blanket, wearing only her nightdress. She was shaking with terror. What the hell was happening to her?

The two men handled her roughly. She was unsteady as they stood her up before Kranz. They steadied her and ripped open her nightdress, pulling back her shoulders. She was terrified as Kranz approached her. Kranz was ready to defile her but suddenly stopped. 'What's this?' he bellowed.

The two men gazed at each other, not knowing what he meant.

'This isn't the Hazel Jones woman.' His gravelly voice cut the atmosphere. 'You bungling fools. Who is this?'

'We followed the woman you spoke of to her apartment. There were two women. As soon as one of them left, we took this one,' said one of the men. They appeared just as terrified as Kate.

'She's the wrong one. This is the second time this has occurred,' said Kranz, leering at Kate. 'So, who are you?' His voice was bullying.

She could hardly speak, half choking with panic. 'I'm Kate. Kate. Kate Davies,' she said, squeezing out the words.

'Where's Hazel Jones?' demanded Kranz. His gravelly voice sounded menacing and also made his two thug cohorts nervous.

'I-I-I, er!' whimpered Kate.

Kranz moved closer to Kate. His eyes were piercing, glaring at her part-naked body. He took an object from his pocket and raised it to Kate's face. There was a *click* as the knife blade appeared. It was a flick-knife or, as Kate remembered it by its American term, a switchblade. She shuddered. The two men holding her relaxed their grip on her shoulders and arms. Her body began to sink; she slumped. 'Hold her up,' bellowed Kranz.

The two thugs obeyed his order and clamped their hands tightly to her arms, pulling her arms back and thrusting out her chest.

Kranz pointed his knife to Kate's throat. She flinched as the tip of the blade touched her. Her eyes followed the blade, but Kranz's sickly grin drew terror to her stomach. He slid the tip of the blade slowly down to the top of her sternum. Was he cutting her? It felt as though he was. Kranz, adept at torture, continued crawling his blade down to the cleavage of her breasts. She felt sick with fear.

'So, Kate, where is Nurse Hazel Jones? Where has she gone?' he said in a more controlled yet authoritative Germanic voice, quieter this time.

She realised that this must be Kranz. She wanted to say nothing, but the tip of the blade was now edging towards her navel. The muscles in her abdomen flinched as the blade felt as though it were scratching into her skin. 'I don't know,' she muttered.

Kranz nicked the tip of the blade into her contorted abdomen.

She flinched. 'Argh!'

'Try again,' said Kranz in an almost consoling tone. He nudged the blade onto her pubis. 'Well?'

This is it, she thought. Her mind raced to self-preservation. 'Hospital.'

'What about the hospital?' he said, continuing to move the tip of the blade into her.

'Her hospital, RNH Bighi!' She had given away Hazel's location.

Kranz was not entirely satisfied with the answer. He removed the blade from Kate's body and replaced his invasive instrument with his finger. 'Why the hospital? She is not on duty.'

'Matron called her in. They have several nurses sick.'

Kranz thought quickly. It made sense. He said nothing more to Kate, then turned away, leaving her with the two thugs. He dissolved into the shadows of the derelict warehouse.

'What do we do with her?' said one of the thugs.

'Do what you like with her,' came the dismissive voice from the darkness.

Kranz left. The crunching of his shoes echoed into the voids of the warehouse.

The two thugs let go of Kate and sharply turned to hear more crunching footsteps. They fumbled to retrieve pistols from their belts and then waved them towards the shadows. There were other people in the darkness of the warehouse.

Kate slumped to the floor. Suddenly, the silence was shattered by two shots ringing out and echoing. The two thugs crumpled down, their pistols clattering to the floor. Kate, still terrified, lifted her head to see armed MPs (military policemen) coming towards her. Two were pointing their pistols to the felled thugs. Emerging from behind them was a naval officer; it was Commander Alec Gratton. He sprinted forward, took hold of Kate, and pulled her torn nightdress around her.

'You're safe now. I'm here,' he said, cuddling her up to his chest and closing his arms around her.

'They're dun fer,' said one of the MPs.

'Thanks, lads. I'll look after Miss Davies,' said Alec.

'The other bugger's got away,' said another MP.

'I think it was Kranz,' croaked Kate.

'What!'

'Kranz. He's German, I think. I heard someone say that Kranz might be here,' said Kate. 'And I've told him that Hazel has gone to the RNH. I couldn't help it.'

'Right. Don't worry.'

'But I've let down my best friend,' Kate whimpered.

'No, you haven't, but I need to get the bastard. Sergeant, get to RNH Bighi and alert Lieutenant Commander Jones at the MTB base as to what has happened,' Alec shouted to the MP sergeant.

'Alec, how did you know where I was?' Kate asked.

'An alert naval guard recognised you and spotted those two sods taking you. He contacted the MPs. They were able to follow you here. And, yes, it's Kranz,' said Alec.

CHAPTER 46

KRANZ'S ENDGAME

THE NURSES' OFFICE and ward station, located between the two main trauma wards, was dimly lit to help the patients get to sleep. Hazel sat at her desk reviewing the patients' notes. She had relieved the only other nurse on duty so the latter could have a break. There was another nurse, at the far end of the first ward, tending to a patient who was unable to get comfortable; he was a new arrival after minor surgery for a broken arm.

Hazel heard the double doors to the connecting corridor swing open and felt a slight breeze of warm air waft in. She looked around, anticipating that someone had entered the wards. There appeared to be no one, so she went to investigate. The corridor and entrance to the wards were also dimly lit with several shadowed areas. Suddenly she was confronted by a man in a dark suit brandishing a 9 mm Luger pistol that was pointed towards her. He stepped out of the shadows to reveal his face. Hazel recognised him immediately. It was SS-Obersturmbannführer Otto Kranz. Her heart thumped deeply, dropping to her feet.

'Nurse Jones, we meet again. Come with me,' he said in a low voice, gesturing with the Luger. He didn't want to arouse any of the patients or other staff on the wards.

'I have patients to attend to,' she replied.

Kranz waved the Luger again.

Hazel slowly stepped forward nervously.

He nudged her with the Luger through the main doors and directed her outside. She turned occasionally. He waved the Luger, pointing her into the shadows of the buildings. They stopped near the main entrance to the hospital complex, remaining in the darkened, unlit buildings that made up the entrance. When Kranz was satisfied that there was no one about, he pushed Hazel into an old damaged building. Hazel recognised it as the original mortuary that had been abandoned after it was severely damaged in an air raid in 1942.

SEAN (State Enrolled Auxiliary Nurse) Tomlinson strolled slowly through Ward 4 to the nurses' station and the sisters' office to report to Hazel. To her surprise, Hazel was not present. She looked around the adjoining utility rooms, but to no avail. A patient in his bed next to the entrance of the ward called out as loud as he dared, without disturbing the other sleeping patients. SEAN Tomlinson approached the patient. 'What's the matter?' she whispered.

'I'm sure I've just seen the sister being escorted out by a man with a gun,' he whispered.

'You must be dreaming,' said SEAN Tomlinson, guessing that the patient's medication may be causing him to suffer hallucinations. 'Not to worry, I'll check,' she said reassuringly. She turned away, looked over the ward, and went back to the office. She noticed that there was a patient's record open on the desk. This was something that she knew would not be left open by Hazel. In addition, Hazel's nurse's uniform was lying on the end of the desk. Hazel had not yet changed. She must have been interrupted. This caused her to be concerned. She was about to phone the hospital reception and administration office, when two military policemen arrived.

'Nurse, is Nursing Sister Jones about?' asked the MP sergeant.

'Well, no. I was about to phone our reception. I don't know where she is. A patient reckons he saw her being taken away by a man with a gun a few minutes ago. What's going on?'

The MP sergeant turned to the MP soldier with him. 'Go to the reception and check. I'll contact security HQ.'

'Sergeant, what's going on?' SEAN Tomlinson was almost shaking with fear.

'Not sure, Nurse. Stay here. I'm getting help.'

Several minutes had passed before Captain Mark Williams arrived with more MPs. He ordered them to seal off the hospital, guessing from what the sergeant had reported that whatever had happened to Hazel, she was still within the hospital grounds. There was only one way in and out, and that was via the main entrance. In addition, the main entrance guard revealed that two men in white medical staff coats had entered fifteen minutes earlier and were not challenged; there seemed to be no reason to do so.

Mark Williams spoke with the patient who believed he had seen Hazel being ushered away by an armed man. The patient described the man and was certain that the pistol was a Luger. The patient was suspicious as it seemed that the tall man was pushing Hazel out of the doors to the ward. Mark had no doubt it was Kranz. He explained to the MP sergeant that the man was very dangerous and asked him to tell his men only to report back for the moment and not do anything to antagonise him, adding that Hazel's life was in deadly danger.

Unbeknown to Kranz, Ewan was told of Kate's demise and of the fact that she had been tortured to reveal Hazel's whereabouts. Within minutes, Ewan hurriedly put a detachment of his sailors together and made for RNH Bighi.

Hazel found herself being pushed towards the old morgue, which was now used for storing damaged equipment and old beds; it had been derelict since 1942, following bomb damage from an air raid. It still showed the signs of serious damage, and no attempt had been made to repair it as it was already too small for use given the increased number of fatalities at the time. Once inside the old morgue, Hazel was confronted by another man, as tall as Kranz and dressed casually. He appeared to be of similar stature as Kranz; she guessed he was also SS. He was. Kranz ordered her and pushed her towards a large stone table; it was the mortuary examination table. 'Get her ready,' commanded Kranz.

'What are you going to do with her?' asked the other SS man.

'Kurt, she will pay for what she has done to me,' said Kranz, raising his gloved left hand that had been severely injured in a battle to rescue Hazel outside Tobruk in 1942.

'But this is madness. Forget it. The Tommies won't let up on you if you harm her. If nothing else, that's what we've learned, surely. We need to be away and quickly,' said Kurt.

Hazel understood enough German to realise that Kurt was worried and that he disliked Kranz.

'You will do as you are told!' Kranz was enraged.

'Very well. So, what do you want me to do?' Kurt asked reluctantly.

'Take her clothes off and put her on the mortuary table,' said Kranz. Looking at Hazel, he added, 'Befitting place for you, I think.'

Hazel shuddered as Kurt began to undress her. He had been used to doing tortuous things to Jews and others in the Balkans, but this was different. He was no longer at war, but nevertheless he obeyed Kranz.

In the dim light of the old morgue, Kurt could make out Hazel's slender and attractive body. He hesitated but then pushed her onto the mortuary slab. She felt the cold stonework of the slab sting, then invade her back and buttocks. She feared whatever Kranz was going to do to her. She only had seconds to wait when Kranz ordered Kurt to tie her wrists together and stretch her arms above her head. She struggled. Kranz quickly grabbed her legs and tied them down with some old coarse rope that bit into her. Kranz viewed her terrified face; his expression was sickeningly gleeful. He stepped back into the shadowy darkness of the room. Hazel caught a glance at Kurt. He was looking very worried and fearful.

'Herr Oberst, leave her. Let's get out of here. I think I heard footsteps outside!'

'Go if you wish. I will join you shortly,' said Kranz.

Kurt didn't need telling twice. He darted out of the room, almost tripping over some old bed ironwork.

Kranz stroked the muzzle of his Luger down Hazel's body and placed it inside her. 'How does it feel to be fucked by a Luger?' he said coldly. 'Scream out if you wish. It will be too late for anyone to rescue you.'

'You're sick, you lousy bastard,' said Hazel slowly but with fortitude.

'Stubborn to the last,' said Kranz, cocking his Luger.

He did not notice that Hazel had loosened her wrists from Kurt's bonds. It was something she had learned from Ewan that if tied up, strain your muscles so that when relaxed, your wrists may well free up. It worked. Before Kranz could reset his Luger inside her, she lunged herself up and smashed her fist into his face. He was momentarily stunned but soon straightened himself, waving his Luger pistol at her breasts.

This is it, she thought. *He is going to shoot me.*

Suddenly the rickety old door to the mortuary room burst open and a soldier thrust himself in. He stumbled to the floor. Kranz rounded on him and caught sight of another soldier following. Self-preservation took over Kranz; instinctively, he took flight. He charged out of the room through an opposite door, the one used by Kurt. He raced outside, aiming towards the main entrance, where he spotted two sailors holding Kurt. He raised his Luger towards them.

A shot rang out and Kranz was felled to the ground. An MP soldier and a sailor ran to his motionless body and turned him over, one of Ewan's detachment, pointing a Thompson sub-machine gun to his body. There was no need. Kranz was dead, shot through the heart—a single shot from a Lee–Enfield rifle. The marksman who had finished Kranz was Able Seaman David Gregg, who strolled over to the body of Kranz. Ewan ran onto the scene and eyed up the body.

'Well done, Gregg,' said Ewan. Gregg was under explicit orders from Ewan and Mark Williams to shoot any man not in uniform or anyone attempting to run away.

'Where's Hazel. Sister Jones?' said Ewan, fearing the worst.

'Here,' came a soft voice from the direction of the old morgue.

Ewan spun round to find Hazel being helped along by two MPs, her dress limply covering her. She held her dress in place while clutching her underwear. 'Thanks, lads,' she said, almost stumbling, her nervous energy ebbing away.

Ewan approached her and embraced her. 'He didn't hurt you, did he?'

'No. These lads came in the nick of time.'

Ewan was overjoyed, holding her tight to his body. He really thought he would never see her alive again.

Hazel looked down to the body of Kranz. 'Is he …?'

'Yes. Well and truly dun, miss,' said an MP corporal, looking up from his position kneeling down beside the body.

Mark Williams arrived on the scene. 'No mistaking it this time,' he said.

Ewan nodded.

Hazel passed Kurt, who now had been handcuffed. 'He was mad,' said Kurt. 'I hope I didn't hurt you.'

Ewan looked deeply at him, supressing his bitterness.

Hazel was expressionless. 'A spell in a prison might answer your question.'

Ewan and Hazel strolled to a waiting car. Ewan ordered the driver to take them home, to their married quarters.

CHAPTER 47

NEW AGE

AZEL AND EWAN settled into a daily routine with little or no excitement in their duties. The end of the war seemed to fade into history, except for the visible evidence of bomb damage, which was slowly being repaired and buildings renovated; it was, nevertheless, a constant reminder. They had moved out of the married quarters to rent an apartment, and then later they settled on buying a house in Bugibba Bay overlooking the sea.

Time seemed to drift by until November 1947, when Hazel returned to their home after visiting her medical doctor in the hospital. She was pregnant. How could she break the news to Ewan? They had discussed the issue of having a family; it was something they both wanted. But it had been several months since the discussion, and now the reality had arrived. She busied herself in the kitchen, preparing a dinner of grilled bream fish with roast potatoes and vegetables. The gilthead bream fish was one of Ewan's favourites. He had phoned earlier to confirm the time he would be home. Hazel raided their small store of wines and chose a local Maltese white to go with the bream. With everything ready in the kitchen, Hazel took the few minutes before Ewan was due to change into a casual loose-fitting dress. She tucked in her waist with a simple leather belt without tying it too tight, although there was no perceptible increase in the size of her lower abdomen just yet. She stood on the balcony of their lounge and looked out to sea. It was a relaxing view. She sipped at her glass of wine. The front door unlatched.

'I'm home,' Ewan called out as he deposited his briefcase on the hatstand in the hallway.

Hazel turned to face Ewan as he entered the lounge. *The moment of truth,* she thought. She pointed to the bottle of wine and the accompanying glass.

'Celebration?' asked Ewan.

'Sort of,' she replied, taking a step towards him. 'I've some news—great news, in fact, and long awaited.'

'OK,' he said slowly as he finished filling his wine glass. 'And?'

'Guess.'

'I haven't a clue. Give me a hint,' he said.

'What's the one thing we both have wanted for some time now?'

Ewan stood in deepening thought. He didn't raise his glass to drink.

'Still no idea?

'We need to increase the size of our crew,' she said softly.

Still having no idea, he thought more deeply and gazed at her slender figure, which was silhouetted against the evening sky through the balcony window. He could just about make out her alluring smile changing to a wide grin as she lowered her wine glass.

As if hit by a flash of lightning, his mind tumbled to the realisation that he was going to be a father. 'You're having a baby!'

'Er, I'm pregnant, and we're having a baby. You know, Ewan, you're such a wonderful husband and a great naval commander, but when it comes to real life, I do sometimes wonder,' Hazel said, giggling.

Ewan put his wine glass back down onto the table and almost jumped towards her.

'Steady on!' she said, Ewan taking the wine glass away from her. 'You'll spill my drink down my skirt.'

'That's no problem. We'll have the skirt off.'

'Hell, give a girl a chance! That can come after dinner,' she said.

He took hold of her and embraced her tightly at first and then relaxed his grip. 'Oh. Had better not get too excited. Must be careful,' he said.

'Not to worry about that for some months yet. Anyway, don't you want to know when our new addition will be due?'

'Yes. When?' he said excitedly.

'Third May. Same day as your dad's birthday.'

'Boy or girl?'

'Doesn't matter, does it?' she said, steering him towards the kitchen.

'Something smells good,' he said, picking up his glass of wine again.

They talked about almost everything to do with their new life. Ewan was so excited that he lost all control of his senses and opened another bottle of wine.

'I think that will be yours. I'll drink less from now on,' said Hazel.

Their dinner finished, they sat together on the balcony absorbing the cool evening air. Ewan clutched his glass of wine, sipping at it and occasionally topping it up. Hazel stuck to her one glass. For a moment Ewan's mind drifted back to the adventures he had had in the past five years or so. The harsh reality of the war set in, which was then countered by some of the more pleasurable moments, which led to a wry smile. Hazel caught his secret smile and turned squarely to face him. 'Something on your mind?' she asked softly.

'Oh, just a few memories creeping back,' he replied, turning to her.

'Want to share them?'

'Someone once said to me that reminiscing is good for the soul.'

'That's the good past and not the bad, isn't it?'

'Not sure. Sometimes I think of the lads whom I served with who are now gone.'

'That's war,' said Hazel, putting her hand out to Ewan.

Ewan extended his arm to her. 'They were some good lads. It's just that I sometimes wonder whether it was all worth it.'

'You've not talked like this for a long time. Can I help?'

'You already have. We're having our first child. Hopefully we've created a better world to bring someone into.'

Hazel squeezed his hand affectionately and turned her head slightly. 'First child, eh? So, you're planning on more?'

'You know, Hazel, my love, you are wonderful.'

'And so are you. What's your next adventure?'

Ewan took his glass of wine and downed the last vestiges. 'That's easy to answer, but it will be the most difficult. It will also be our adventure— me a father and you a mother.'

The chilled evening air of November invaded their view from the balcony. They withdrew to the lounge. Ewan switched on the radio. They listened to the BBC evening news. There was nothing of any importance, at least not for them, although for a fleeting moment they both picked up on the continuing tensions between East and West Germany, the Allies controlling the west and the Soviet Union controlling the east. Berlin seemed to be a mounting problem, although this was to be a year away. For the moment, Ewan and Hazel embraced each other, looking forward to their new family life. Ewan looked past Hazel's shoulder; she followed his gaze to the horizon.

'The world's changing, and we're changing with it,' said Ewan.

She kissed him on the cheek. 'The most important thing is that we are together; nothing will separate us.'

They hugged each other.

ABOUT THE AUTHOR

Malcolm is a scientist, specialising in explosives chemistry, CBRNe and emergency planning. He gained a Master of Philosophy (MPhil) degree in Explosives Chemistry from the City University, London. He is a Chartered Scientist (CSci), Chartered Chemist (CChem), Member of the Royal Society of Chemistry (MRSC), and a Fellow of the Emergency Planning Society (FEPS). He is a former UK Home Office Civil Defence Scientific Advisor (stood down in 1992). He has the unusual combination of working with explosives and radioactive substances that led him to work at the UK's Atomic Weapons Establishment (AWE) Aldermaston. He has worked as a Local Government Emergency Planning Officer and has undertook the preparation of special emergency plans, such as Chernobyl, Ukraine.

Although experienced in writing reports and plans, he has ventured into the world of writing fiction, mainly based on life-time experiences, characters encountered, places visited, and set against suitably fictionalised real scenarios. He has written technical articles for professional journals and lectured at the UK Cabinet Office's Emergency Planning College (EPC), Easingwold, and at international conferences, such as the International Disaster and Emergency Resilience (IDER) conference, where he was a committee member (2005-2012).

Lightning Source UK Ltd.
Milton Keynes UK
UKHW010658210221
378983UK00009B/277